FAKE MONEY, BLUE SMOKE

FAKE MONEY, BLUE SMOKE

A THRILLER

JOSH HAVEN

THE MYSTERIOUS PRESS
NEW YORK

FAKE MONEY, BLUE SMOKE

Mysterious Press
An Imprint of Penzler Publishers
58 Warren Street
New York, N.Y. 10007

First Mysterious Press edition

Interior design by Maria Fernandez

Library of Congress Control Number: 2022906680

Cloth ISBN: 978-1-61316-363-4
eBook ISBN: 978-1-61316-353-5

10 9 8 7 6 5 4 3 2 1

Printed in the United States of America
Distributed by W. W. Norton & Company

For my grandparents

FAKE MONEY, BLUE SMOKE

1

Matt Kubelsky was surprised to receive a phone call from an ex-girlfriend offering to pick him up from prison. She called him a week before his release; he'd been in prison almost five years and they hadn't talked in almost twenty.

"I saw your name in the newspaper," she said. "I know your parents are dead and I didn't know if anyone would be there to pick you up. I thought maybe I could offer you a couch to crash on for a while, if you needed it. And anyway, there's something I want to talk to you about."

They'd broken up in spring 2002 because he'd cheated on her. He'd begged her to forgive him, said the other girl didn't mean anything to him, which was true, and that it had only happened once, which wasn't true. He said he was young and stupid, which was true. He was a high school senior in Decatur, Georgia, and she was a freshman at Georgia Tech. She was a transplant from New

England and she'd wanted to spread her wings a little in college. She had regretted going for the first guy she met. And she hadn't known he was still in high school when they'd started dating. They'd met at a college bar.

He was the one who cheated and he was the one who ended up with a broken heart. He'd dropped out of high school and joined the army. He'd spent fifteen years in in the army, been promoted all the way to platoon sergeant, and then was convicted of murdering an unarmed prisoner. He was sentenced to twenty-five years at Leavenworth. His lawyer had raised objections to the prosecution's handling of evidence and requested a mistrial. The judge refused but reduced the sentence to eight years and granted a request for transfer to a medium-security civilian prison. In the end, Matt had been paroled after five years and two months at the Ray Brook Federal Correctional Institution in upstate New York.

In Ray Brook's parking lot, he spotted Kelly Haggerty through the glass of her windshield. She looked the same as she had in Georgia: light brown hair that was nearly blond, a pointed, somewhat large nose and high cheekbones, and a cigarette in her mouth.

❖

Kelly saw Matt before he saw her; she'd watched as he waited for the chain-link gate behind him to close, the chain-link gate in front of him to open, and then continued to watch as he'd looked around the parking lot for her dark green Honda.

When he climbed into her car, she saw he had a swastika tattooed on his neck. That was new.

"Hi Kelly," he said, and pushed a blue plastic duffel of personal items through the gap in the front seats. "Thanks for picking me up."

"No problem. It's good to see you."

"Can I have one of those?" He pointed to the cigarette she was clutching in her teeth (flattening the filter).

"Yes," she said. "In the cup holder."

Matt pulled a pack of Camels out of one of the cup holders and a Bic lighter out of the other.

"Turkish Silver?"

"They're ultra-lights," said Kelly. "I'm trying to quit."

"Why not smoke the electric ones," he asked, lighting and inhaling.

"They're bad for the environment," said Kelly. Matt shrugged.

"Before we talk about whatever you want to talk about," he said, "I need you to drive me into town." He was watching the security booth at the entrance to the parking lot and tapping his fingers nervously. The guard waved them past, no problem. Matt seemed to relax a little after that.

"Where in town?" Kelly pulled up at the stop sign at the end of Ray Brook's leafy access road. It was early autumn.

Matt pulled a slip of paper out of his breast pocket. His shirt was plaid flannel. She wondered where he'd gotten it, coming straight to prison from the army. Maybe he'd had it with him in Iraq.

"Here," he said, holding the paper so she could read the address.

"I don't know where that is," she said. "I can put it into my phone."

"I think it's in a shopping plaza just after where 73 and 9 meet. Do you know where that is?"

"I guess," said Kelly. They were already on 73, she was pretty sure, and heading south toward Route 9 and I-87.

"Thanks," he said, and opened the window. "It should be close." He exhaled a small cloud of smoke and watched it get sucked out of the car. "So what's up? What did you want to see me for?"

"I, uh, well I mean I wanted to see how you were doing. They talked about you on the news the other night, how you were getting out of prison and how a lot of people said you were innocent and that you might have been pardoned if you hadn't been paroled."

"Yeah, I heard that too," said Matt. "There it is. Pull over here."

Kelly pulled the car into a small plaza and into an empty spot.

"I'll probably be like twenty, thirty minutes."

Matt climbed out and Kelly watched him walk into a tattoo parlor. She finished her cigarette, then walked across the street to a fast food place and bought a cup of coffee and two burgers. She put the foil-wrapped burgers on the hood of the car, in the sun, where they'd stay warm, then got back into the driver's seat, drank her coffee, and waited.

After a little more than an hour, Matt came out of the tattoo parlor and walked back to the car. The swastika on his neck was covered by white gauze and masking tape. From a distance, it looked like a giant blister.

When he was in earshot, she put down her window and pointed to the burgers. "I got those for you." He picked them up and climbed into the car.

"Thanks."

"I got you two," she said, "'cause they were out of fries."

"Out of fries?" He shook his head. "That's fucking bizarre." He took a bite of one of them. "That's really good. That's delicious."

Kelly wondered if she should ask about Matt's neck. For a few seconds she watched him eat, then decided it wasn't the right time, turned the key in the ignition, and pulled back onto Route 9, heading south.

"It's about four hours to my place in Queens." She looked over at him. He yawned. "You could nap if you want."

"I appreciate you letting me crash there," said Matt. "You don't want to talk?" He was starting on the second burger.

"It can wait. And anyway, I want to show you something at the same time."

Matt shrugged again. "Sounds good," he said, reclining the seat. "Lap of luxury here."

"You want to listen to some music?" Kelly put up the windows and pulled onto the highway.

"Yes," said Matt. "Weezer."

"I don't have any Weezer," said Kelly.

Matt said, "Put on whatever you want, then," and fell asleep.

2

"So," said Kelly. "I have a business proposition for you."

Kelly had pulled off the highway at a Best Buy near Albany and bought Matt two CDs Weezer had released while he was in prison. She would have played them, but Matt didn't wake up till they were in Queens. In fact, she'd been a little insulted by that. He doesn't see her for twenty years, spends five years in an all-male prison, and five minutes after their reunion he falls asleep? To be fair to him, though, she figured he probably hadn't felt safe anywhere in at least five years. Maybe longer. Maybe since before he'd joined the army. Anyway, he'd thanked her for the CDs and slipped them into his duffel, saying he'd come back down to her car later to listen to them. The CD player he'd had with him in prison had died during the Obama administration. She said he could listen to them on her laptop and led him up to her apartment—a loft—with his duffel and her pack of cigarettes.

"Mind if I smoke up here?" he asked her, waiting in the doorway as she felt for her light switch. It was nighttime and the only light was coming from a traffic signal outside. The whole place was slightly red, then slightly green, and then Kelly flicked the ceiling lamps on.

"Only on the fire escape, please," she said. "This stuff is a little sensitive."

To Matt, Kelly's setup wasn't especially impressive. There were three plastic dinner tables arranged in a U, with a half dozen boxy, black plastic machines on them, and some arts and crafts–looking stuff mixed in. There was a desk in the U's middle, with a two-monitor computer surrounded by stacks of files. The bed and kitchen, and a couch and a door to the bathroom, were at the far end of the room, which was about ten yards long and five wide. There was a little art on the walls, museum posters, that kind of thing. Wooden floor, white walls, wooden slat ceiling.

"What are those? Printers?" He looked past the black plastic machines, looking for the window that led to the fire escape.

"Yes," said Kelly. "Really, really good ones." She saw him playing, unconsciously, with the pack of Camels in his right hand. "Let me turn on a fan and you can smoke if you stand by the window. Just try to breath toward Brooklyn, okay?"

"Which way's Brooklyn?"

"Out the window," she said, bringing over a fan and a chair to stand it on. Matt sat down on the windowsill and lit a cigarette. He inhaled deeply, leaned back, and scratched the underside of his chin. He exhaled out the window and asked Kelly what the business proposition was. She was kneeling down in front of her desk and unlocking one of the drawers. She pulled out a paper box, the sort of box you get donuts in, and walked it over to him.

"Can you keep a secret?" asked Kelly.

"Yes," said Matt.

"Sorry, did that sound insulting?"

Matt shook his head.

She handed him the box. "Open that. Don't let the fan blow anything away."

He held the cigarette with his lips and pulled up the cardboard lid. Inside were rubber-banded bundles of money. Multicolored. Not dollars, not euros.

"Is that Gandhi?" he said, sticking a finger among the bundles, counting how many were in the box.

"Yeah," said Kelly. "They're rupees. That's ten thousand dollars American, in Indian rupees."

"How much is that in rupees?"

"About seven hundred fifty thousand." The bundles were different denominations: purple 100-rupee notes, orange 200s, dollar-bill-colored 500s, purple 2,000s. They were all slightly different sizes.

"Why five hundred and two thousand but no one thousand?"

"They don't make one thousands anymore. They got canceled as legal tender. Too much counterfeiting."

Matt closed the box again, and took the cigarette out of his mouth. It burned his fingers and he threw it out the window.

"So what's the secret?" He handed the box back to Kelly.

"I'm a counterfeiter."

Matt lit another cigarette and didn't say anything. He just looked at her.

"I was studying computer science at Georgia Tech, remember? But by my junior year I couldn't cut it anymore and I didn't like it anymore. I ended up majoring in fine arts."

She waited for Matt to make a joke about getting a fine arts degree from a top-notch tech school but he didn't say anything so she went on.

"Anyway, I wanted to be a museum curator but I couldn't find work. It's a tough field to break into."

"Yeah, I bet," said Matt, knocking some ash into the fan's current, watching it float away toward Brooklyn.

"So anyway, I bounced around for a while, took some office work, taught art and science at a parochial school in Crown Heights. Tried to get back into computer science, get back up to speed on coding and all that. And then I had this idea . . ."

"Why rupees?" said Matt. "Could I have some water or something?"

"Sure," said Kelly, walking toward her kitchen nook. "I've got some local beer, too, if you'd like, and Diet Coke."

"Have you got milk?"

"Yeah," said Kelly, getting a glass from a cabinet.

"I'd like some milk."

"I chose rupees," she said, pulling a half-gallon carton out of her fridge, "for four reasons. First, because dollars are out—too many people in New York check for fakes. Second, rupees have weak security features, it's a third-world currency. Third, it's the most popular third-world currency, except Mexican pesos, and no one uses pesos in New York."

"Mexico isn't a third-world country, is it?"

"Whatever," said Kelly. "That's not the point."

"Is India?"

"India is *the* third-world country. I mean, it invented the phrase to describe itself, meaning it was part of the third world, outside the worlds of Soviet and Western influence. During the cold war."

"I thought it meant poor," said Matt, knocking some more ash out the window.

"Well, yeah, I mean, that's how I was using it. Relatively speaking. The fourth reason is that there's a lot of Indian tourism to New York, so currency changers are used to it. But also they're not as used to it as euros, pounds, yen, or renminbi."

"What're renminbi?"

"China's currency."

"I thought they used yuan."

"They're called yuan, too, but that's the official name. Renminbi. Means 'the people's currency.'"

"I guess a lot changed while I was in prison."

Kelly felt awkward. She tried to hide it by reaching into Matt's breast pocket and pulling a cigarette out of her pack.

"Anyway, I actually started with dollars. I had them perfect, actually. I was printing twenties on bleached singles so they felt right, but only a couple weeks in a guy at a bodega ran one of the bills under a UV light to check the security strip, but singles don't have security strips. I saw him figure it out, though he didn't say anything, so I ran. Rode the subway all over the city to make sure I wasn't being followed. I was kind of paranoid. Anyway, it took forever to change fake dollars for real money. That was when I had the rupee idea. I can change a hundred thousand fake rupees for fourteen hundred real dollars at JFK and no one bats an eye. Then I drive over to LaGuardia and do the same thing. Or I drive into

Times Square or Newark. There are like fifty currency-changing spots I've got mapped out around the city and New Jersey. I wear hats and sunglasses and I change my hair color every now and then and change outfit styles, just in case they get me on camera, but I haven't had any problems yet, touch wood. I just make sure I don't go to the same place too often."

"That's your natural hair color, isn't it?"

"Yeah, well, I haven't done it in a while. Now I'm working on something bigger. That's what I wanted to ask for your help with."

Matt threw another butt out the window. "Okay," he said. "Ask."

"Do you wanna have sex first? I figure you haven't, in a while."

Matt wiped away a milk mustache. "Yeah," he said. "If you're offering."

"You didn't catch anything in prison, did you?"

Matt shook his head.

"Anyway," said Kelly, "I have condoms."

3

Afterward, Matt rolled off Kelly and began to feel around on the floor.

"What are you looking for?"

"My shirt," he said, pulling it out from under the bed.

"You don't have to get dressed," said Kelly.

"I'm not," said Matt. "I want a cigarette."

"Hold on, let me bring the fan over." She climbed over Matt and he opened the window next to her bed.

"So what's the favor?" he asked, as the little gray plastic fan started to spin.

"Did you know that all fans in South Korea have shut-off timers on them?" Kelly sat back down on the bed, by Matt's feet, with her legs folded under her. "Apparently, basically all Koreans believe a fan fanning air over you all night can kill you. It's called 'fan death.' There are government health warnings and everything. Some Koreans won't even use the AC in their cars."

"No, I didn't know that." He lit his Camel ultra-light. "You want one?"

"Yeah," she said. He handed her the one he'd just lit and lit another. She took a long drag on it, and he watched her slide closer to the window to blow the blue smoke out of her apartment. She looked good, very much the way he remembered her, even though she was exactly twice as old as she was when he'd last seen her naked. Her breasts drooped a little more, maybe, and maybe there was just a hint of loose skin between her shoulders and elbows, but that was it. She was fit, the way she'd been in college. He'd always thought she looked like the lead in a girls' soccer movie. He wondered how much longer she had to spend at the gym these days to maintain that. Or maybe all it took was the walking between currency kiosks.

"What's the favor?"

"Well, it's two favors, actually. A big one and a bigger one."

"Okay," he said. He waited for her to go on. "You want me to guess what they are?"

"No," she said, and smiled, a little nervously. "Do you speak Arabic? It said on the news you were social with the locals. In Iraq."

"Yes," said Matt. "I speak Arabic."

"I need to go to Qatar," said Kelly. "And I'd like you to go with me."

"Why?"

"I'm doing important business there and I don't speak the language. Plus I think it's hard for a woman by herself there, and I was kind of hoping that you could sort of be my bodyguard. The business isn't strictly legal, or with very nice people. I don't want to end up like Liam Neeson's daughter, you know?"

Matt's face was blank. Maybe he didn't know.

"There was this movie, maybe it came out while you were in prison? Some guy kidnaps Liam Neeson's daughter and tries to sell her as a sex slave, to some sheikh or something."

"It came out while I was in Iraq."

Kelly nodded. "Right, yeah. I didn't remember the year."

Matt scratched his throat, and then his neck, around the gauze that was taped over the swastika. Kelly was surprised it hadn't come off while they'd been banging around. She'd actually forgotten about it completely. What was under there now? She hoped prison hadn't fucked him up. Or war, or PTSD, or anything. He'd always been kind of reckless and contrary. She didn't remember him being solemn, all quiet, the way he was now.

"Is that the big favor or the bigger favor?" He noticed her staring at his neck. She looked up, saw that he saw, and blushed.

"Um, that's the big favor. The bigger favor is—and I'm assuming you made some contacts in Ray Brook, and I apologize totally if I'm being a shithead asking you—I wondered if you could hire some armed robbers for me."

"Armed robbers?"

"Yes."

He stared at her for a minute. Then he peeled off the gauze bandage and crumpled it up.

"Where's your garbage can?" She pointed toward the U of tables. Where the swastika had been there was now a black square. It was bleeding slightly, the way fresh tattoos do.

"I have some antiseptic stuff in the bathroom, if you want."

"Thanks," he said, dumping the bandage in the trash and walking over to the kitchen sink to wash his neck and hands. "I was in a prison gang. No way around it."

"You know you can get tattoos removed."

"I know," said Matt. "But it takes weeks and I didn't want to wait. I'll have it done to this thing when I get the chance."

"I understand," said Kelly. She hoped that wasn't offensive. She didn't think it was polite anymore to tell people you understand things they've been through that you obviously don't.

"I was in a prison gang called the Fourteen-Eighty-Eights."

"What happened in fourteen-eighty-eight?"

"That's not what it means. The fourteen is for 'fourteen words,' a neo-Nazi slogan. 'We must secure the existence of our people and a future for white children.' The eighty-eight is for 'heil Hitler.' 'H' is the eighth letter of the alphabet."

"That's, uh, catchy."

"You pretty much had to have a group and that was the only one I qualified for. Apparently, I can't pass for Italian."

"It's none of my business."

"I don't want you to think I was actually a Nazi, though. Sometimes you go along to get along, you know?"

Kelly nodded. For a second, she felt like crying. Matt walked into the bathroom and she heard the sound of her medicine cabinet opening.

"It's Neosporin," she called to him. "Bottom shelf."

"Thanks."

He came out of the bathroom a minute or two later with a thin white film over the black square.

"Anyway," he said, "yes, I do know some armed robbers. What do you need them for?"

4

"Do you spend a lot of time in museums?" Kelly had put on an oversized T-shirt with the Georgia Tech logo on it. Matt was looking through her refrigerator.

"Is that a joke?" He pulled out a white carton of Chinese takeout. "What is this?"

"Chinese food."

"No shit, Kelly," he opened up the top. "What's in it?"

"What does it look like?"

"Meat and sauce and broccoli."

"I think it's sesame chicken." Matt began to open drawers, looking for a fork.

"I meant, you went to museums in Atlanta, before the army and everything?"

"You want to rob an art museum?"

"No. But did you?"

"There are no art museums in Atlanta. There's a Coca-Cola museum. I went there once, it was pretty dull."

"Well, there are a couple art museums but it doesn't really matter. You can warm that up if you want. Just pull off the metal handle thing." Matt was digging into the Chinese cold.

He shook his head. "Cold's fine." Then, before Kelly started talking again, "In between when you stopped answering my letters and when you saw me on the news, did you think about me at all?"

"Yes."

"A lot?"

"Yes."

"We were only together for, what, eight months? Nine months?"

"You made a big impression. And then after you started writing me, we were pen pals for . . . I don't know. A decade?"

"Uh-huh." Matt stuck a forkful of soggy fried meat into his mouth. "Okay, tell me about the art stuff."

"Okay, so, pretty much, there's no, like, Monet museum or Leonardo museum. Most painters' artworks are spread out all over the world. Mostly in Europe, some in the U.S. and Japan, and the rest are in private collections. Like, some of the greatest art in the world is literally hanging in people's living rooms. Or sitting in safety deposit boxes. So when museums want to put on a show of a specific painter—say, Gustav Klimt—they write to museums and private Klimt collectors all over the world and try to arrange to borrow stuff."

"Okay. This isn't chicken, by the way."

"What is it?"

Matt shrugged.

"I got beef stuff and pork stuff too. Help yourself. I mean, eat it all. I've been eating too much grease anyway." Matt clearly hadn't; he was extremely fit. He'd been spindly when she'd seen him last. Now he was muscly and hairy and still naked. A few scars on him, a few more jailhouse tattoos, and a few professional ones that looked army related.

"So. You want to rob a safety deposit box? Or a mansion?"

"No, neither. That's all super-security stuff."

"Okay, wait though." His head was back in the refrigerator. "What does this have to do with counterfeiting?"

He couldn't see her roll her eyes. She had her whole story worked out. But fine.

"Okay, so the thing about counterfeiting is that it's hard to convert the fake money into real money. I can clear a few thousand a week, the way I'm doing it, so it's a pretty good living, but it's not retirement money or anything. And there's always the risk of getting caught. You get twenty years for counterfeiting."

"Yeah. It's no fun." He emerged from the fridge with another box of Chinese. He popped it open. "This one's noodles and whitish meat."

"Pork lo mein. That's going to taste like shit if you don't warm it up, though. Cold noodles are like cardboard."

He began to eat it. "No, it's good." Kelly shrugged.

"Anyway, so what I want to do," she continued, taking a sip from the glass of milk Matt had left on her bedside table. "What I want is to do a really big cash deal, convert a lot of fake bills to real equity, all at one time. I wanted to buy something really, really valuable with a huge bundle of fakes, and then resell it for a huge bundle of reals. See?"

Matt nodded, and Kelly added, "And I'm going to cut you in, of course."

Matt nodded again. "Throw me the cigarettes."

"Come stand by the fan. But the cash deal has got to be with people who can't go to the police and turn me in, right? So, I thought, I'll buy something stolen. But then I realized that didn't make any sense. What am I going to do, put an ad on Craigslist? 'Stolen goods wanted'? So I had a much better idea. Instead of paying fake money for something stolen, why not pay fake money to have someone steal something. I can work out in advance the optimal thing to steal, something I can find a buyer for, and get a buyer lined up. Which I've done."

"So you want me to set you up with people you're going to rip off."

"Yeah. I mean, I don't know if there's some sort of ex-prisoners' code or something, but I figured there must be people in there you didn't like. Though again, if I'm putting you in an awk-ward position . . . I mean, the idea is for them not to know who I am, and for you to have plausible deniability. Like, you're just the go-between middleman. For when-slash-if they figure out the bills are fake. Or I thought maybe you'd just want to take your share of the money and disappear. Start fresh some-where new. But either way . . . I mean I'm not trying to pressure you. Would, um, ripping off someone from your prison be a problem for you?"

Matt chewed and swallowed a mouthful of noodles.

"Nope. It wouldn't." He forked out another tangle of lo mein. "I'm going to need a prepaid cell phone," he said, with his mouth full. "Not a smart one. Like an old flip phone."

"Sure," said Kelly. "Yeah, definitely. No problem."

Matt pointed at the carton of lo mein with his fork. "You were right, I should have microwaved this," he said, and took another mouthful. "This is awful."

Kelly laughed.

5

Kelly had more details she'd wanted to go into, but Matt had interrupted her and asked if he could take a bath. He'd seen the big white tub with the iron lion's feet in her bathroom and it was calling to him, he said. She said sure, of course. He'd taken the fan with him so he could soak and smoke. She'd put on a pair of gym shorts and gone over to her desk to do some work.

She was *not taking advantage of Matt*, she reminded herself. She was telling him it was risky. And she was going to make sure, or try to make sure, his parole didn't get violated. They would fly to Qatar on a private jet, so no customs. She'd discovered, only slightly to her surprise, that in this respect (like every other respect) the super-rich are absurdly pampered. When a private jet lands—not just in banana republics but even in the United States—someone comes on board, stamps your passport, and that's it. (Unless you've done something stupid, like donate to the wrong political party.) So that wouldn't be a problem. Actually, the only risk he was taking was, maybe, meeting with a known criminal. But probably he'd only have to do that once. Or actually, twice, since she'd want him to drop the money off too. She didn't want any of the *real* bad guys—armed robber types—to ever see her. She supposed they might want to come after him when they figured out the bills were fake. But that was why she was being up front with him. She hadn't *had* to tell him the bills were counterfeit. She could have just asked him to be her liaison and money drop-off guy. But she'd been up front with him. He'd know the risks going in. And he could take care of himself, clearly. He'd murdered someone. Apparently. And probably killed a bunch of other people. He'd been at war in Iraq and Afghanistan for a combined ten years. And then handled prison. He could take care of himself.

The truth was, she *had* thought of him after she'd stopped answering his letters. Not *a lot*, but some. She'd even thought of getting back in touch with him once or twice, though she'd never gone through with it. When your love life is going bad, you tend to circle back to the people who loved you. And he'd definitely loved her.

And that was why it was important to remind herself that *she wasn't using him.* He would make up his own mind.

She was impatient to get on with the planning. Matt was still in the tub. Kelly's eyes wandered around her counterfeiting equipment. The big printer for printing sheets of bills, the slicer for cutting them, which always made her think of preschool art class and glue-stick collages. Her scanners, whose software she'd written herself because the software they came with automatically put big black Xs over any images of currency the machine scanned. The

3-D printer she'd tried to print polymer security strips with. It hadn't worked. She'd tried a few 3-D printed guns, too, for fun, before she started to worry it might attract government attention. She sighed deeply. In the end, the only real use she'd gotten out of it was printing comedy dildos, in increasingly absurd dimensions and shapes, stretching her artistic muscles a little. A few days ago, she'd used the paper slicer to dice them and thrown them away, to avoid offending Matt. She sighed again. Well, she could replace everything in the home office she'd have in her villa on some Greek island. Touch wood.

◆

Matt had no illusions about what was going on with Kelly. He doubted she'd thought about him at all, except maybe as a story to tell at parties. But he'd thought about her. He'd been seventeen when he met her, and had never been in love before. He'd never been in love since. And he wasn't in love now. Least of all with Kelly. But he wanted her to need him. He wanted her to treasure her relationship with him the way he'd coveted her for years in the army and in prison until he finally gave up on her. He wanted her to want him and use him and he was going to use her too. It would work out fine for both of them. He wasn't a criminal. He certainly didn't see himself that way. What he was, was bitter. Deeply goddamned bitter. If doing a little something for little Kelly would help him close the book on a few things—well, if rich people didn't want their art stolen, they shouldn't send guys off to war and then thank them by destroying their lives.

The cigarettes were starting to make him feel a little sick. He took the one he was smoking out of his mouth and dipped the tip in his bath water. The *hiss* of it going out was satisfying. He used his big toe to pull out the plug and let the water around him drain away. Then, stretching as he stood up, he took a quick shower. Because baths don't really get you clean.

He walked out of the bathroom five minutes later, wrapped in a fuzzy pink towel.

"Where are my clothes?" The pile on the floor by the bed was gone.

"I'm washing them," said Kelly, swiveling in her desk chair and pointing to a washer-dryer disguised as a kitchen appliance. "Do you have a change in your bag? Or you can just wait. They'll be done soon. You were in there for a while."

"If that's your washer," said Matt, pointing over his shoulder at a big white washer-dryer pair hooked up in the bathroom, "what's that?"

"That's where I bleach and crisp the fake money."

"Huh," said Matt, nodding. "Okay, what is it you want to steal?" He sat back down on the bed.

"Okay," said Kelly. "So I'm actually dispersing my big chunks of fake money in two parts. The first is going to an art insurance guy in Manhattan. In exchange for a briefcase of money, he's giving me the details of an art loan his company's insuring. For a Klimt show at the MoMA."

"The hmm?"

"The Museum of Modern Art. In Manhattan, a few blocks south of the park. Central Park."

"Noted," said Matt, adjusting his towel.

"A Gustav Klimt show," said Kelly. "Klimt's the guy who painted that famous sort of abstract, geometric portrait of the woman in gold?"

"Yeah, I saw the movie," said Matt. "We had movie nights. I don't know how Helen Mirren stays so hot. I mean, I'd marry her now. We might not have as long together as I'd like, but I'd make do."

"She's married."

"To who?"

"Taylor Hackford."

"Who's that?"

"A director. He made *An Officer and a Gentleman*."

"Never seen it."

"Anyway," said Kelly, "the woman in that painting, Adele Bloch-Bauer? Helen Mirren's aunt?"

"Maybe he'll die first. Men tend to die first. Then I can swoop in."

"Klimt actually painted Adele Bloch-Bauer twice. The second painting is a little less famous—though, in my humble expert opinion, it's actually even more beautiful. I saw it once, at a show at the Neue Galerie where the *Woman in Gold* lives. *Adele II* is in a private collection. Oprah sold it to a mystery buyer a few years ago. Guess for how much."

Matt shook his head. "Tell me."

"A hundred and fifty million dollars."

"You want to steal something that's worth a hundred and fifty million dollars? That's fucking insane. I want no part of it."

"No," said Kelly, "I agree, that would be stupid. No, for this show, though, they're also getting ink and pencil studies Klimt did for the two Adele portraits. They belong to the great-grandchildren of a friend of Klimt's. They live in California now, in safety deposit boxes. The drawings, I mean. It's a shame. They're rarely shown and they've never been on the market, but the insurance company is valuing them at twelve million dollars. More—a lot more—than your average Klimt sketches, but the Adele paintings have gotten so famous over the last few decades that Adele sketches have been bumped way up in valuation. Special collector's items."

"How many are there? The ones you want to steal."

"Six."

"Is that twelve million each?"

"No. Total."

"You say that like twelve million isn't still a gigantic amount of money. I'm pretty sure for twelve million dollars they're going to have security that won't be fucking around."

"No, yeah, of course they will. But I'll have all the details from the insurance guy."

"So what do you have in mind?" Matt was moving himself out of a damp spot he'd made on the bed. "An armored car holdup, like in *Heat*? Or do you want to hijack the plane they fly to New York on."

"I figure I'd leave that to the experts," said Kelly, a little acidly. "But I'd imagined a car stickup. Either on the way to the airport out there or coming to MoMA from wherever it lands here."

"And all you want me to do is what? Make the deal and hand over the insurance company plans?"

"And drop off the money to pay for it all."

"The counterfeit money."

"Right. And also chauffeur me around Qatar. That's part of it. Separate part."

"Yeah. I'm looking forward to that, actually."

"Look forward to all of it. It's going to be fun."

"The guy in Qatar's agreed to buy the things?" asked Matt, adjusting his towel.

"Yes."

"Then why are we going, again?"

"He won't agree to a price till he sees the insurance photos and estimates. Which I'm getting tomorrow. And for obvious reasons I can't email them."

"How much are you expecting to get?"

"Maybe ten million. Maybe eight."

"And what do I get?"

"Ten percent?"

Matt sucked his teeth and took a minute to think.

6

Kelly's black plastic suitcase was sitting under her table. It was one of those four-wheel models that you don't have to drag, just roll, and she was rolling it back and forth between her feet. Two and a half million dollars, U.S., from the Kelly Haggerty mint. Twenty-five thousand fake hundreds; her best work ever. They had all the microprinting, the watermarks, the iridescent color-shifting ink that she'd mixed herself using artists' ink and aftermarket "chameleon" car paint. There were security strips baked into the image that looked real when they were back lit. They wouldn't glow in black light. That was the only flaw in the whole thing. Other than that, she reckoned they were the best fakes this side of North Korea. Sometimes she almost regretted getting out of the business.

She was in Port Jefferson, Long Island. This was the insurance guy's idea; spy movie stuff. He was spending the day in

Connecticut, allegedly, hiking, and he'd have toll receipts to prove it. But he was actually taking the Port Jeff ferry round-trip from Bridgeport, so he could meet with Kelly in secret. Kelly thought it was a little melodramatic, but if he wanted to waste his time that was his own business.

She was waiting in a small restaurant called the Beach Comber with a view of the harbor and the ferry dock and, in the background, giant hills of coal and the power plant the coal was headed for. She figured it powered a good hunk of the North Shore. Kelly wondered when Long Island waterfront real estate would finally become so expensive that they'd tear down the power plant and sell the land to a developer. What would the island folk do for power then? They didn't want wind farms ruining their beach views and they were all frightened of nuclear.

The big white ferry was moored and unloading a hundred or so cars along with a few dozen walk-on passengers. Among them Kelly spotted the insurance man, wearing sunglasses and a Mets hat with his jeans and T-shirt. They weren't really necessary; he was already featureless and unnoticeable. Medium height, medium weight, brown hair and eyes. Oval face and a regular shaped nose. She watched him walk across the ferry parking lot, across the street, and through the Comber's front door. A minute later he emerged on the deck where Kelly was sitting.

"Hey," he said, as a waitress put down a menu, and then to the waitress, "Thanks."

"Hey," said Kelly. "Do you want to use code names?"

"No," said the insurance man, taking a tightly folded packet of paper out of his right front pocket. "This is it. The final travel plans, times, schedules, security. Photos. Or, actually, photos of the photos. It's all in there." He tapped his foot on the suitcase. "Is this the money?"

Kelly was flipping through the pages, looking bemused. "Did you type this on a typewriter?"

"Yes," said the insurance man. "I didn't want a computer record and I didn't want it in my handwriting."

"Okay," said Kelly. "But I'm confused. You said it was coming by plane."

"Now it's coming on Amtrak," said the insurance man. "Our policy director tried to up the price after the 737 Max crashes so the owners said they'd send it on the train and asked for a discount. Which they got. I'm pretty sure the director won't be getting a bonus this year."

"Maybe you'll get his job."

"Maybe," said the insurance man. "So . . . ?"

"Yes, that's your money. You want to take it into the bathroom and count it?"

"Yes," said the insurance man. "But I don't see how I can without attracting attention."

"Just tell the waitress that you're bringing the suitcase 'cause you need to change your underwear. You had a little accident."

"Very funny."

"It's all in there," said Kelly. "If there's any missing, you have my number. I'm not trying to cheat you."

"Okay," said the insurance man. "I trust you."

"Good, thanks," said Kelly. "Remember that if you put it in the bank, use a safety deposit box. Don't start to put the bills into circulation for at least a year."

"Why?" said the insurance man, looking nervous. "Was this money stolen?"

"Yes," said Kelly. "But I took out the dye packs. Just wait till the heat is off to start spending it." Kelly had rehearsed her lies in the bathroom that morning while she flossed.

"This wasn't what we agreed to," said the insurance man, using his forearm to wipe a single bead of sweat off the tip of his nose.

"Well, it's not *not* what we agreed to. Where do you think two and a half million dollars in cash comes from? You've heard of the IRS, right?"

"Fuck you, Stacy." For this deal, she'd used the pseudonym Stacy Maranzano.

"Well, fuck you too. If you don't want it, leave it here. And if any of the details you're giving me are wrong, you're going to have an accident. *Capisce?*"

The insurance man nodded sulkily and said nothing. Kelly finished a cup of coffee and stood up.

"Shouldn't we sit for a while, so if someone's watching it doesn't look like a . . . you know, a handoff?"

"No one's watching," said Kelly. "Stop being so fucking paranoid." She put a twenty (a real one) under the sugar shaker and walked off the deck, toward the Port Jeff train station.

7

When Matt's lawyer had arranged for his transfer from Leavenworth to a civilian, medium-security prison, he'd thought it was some kind of divine blessing. Leavenworth was absurdly regimented, a maximum-security prison (Nidal Hasan was there at the time; probably was still) with military discipline thrown in on top. A medium-security prison would mean dorms instead of cells, maybe a chance to work outdoors in a vegetable garden or something, get some fresh air. Something less than constant twenty-four-hour-a-day supervision. Access to the internet? God he had hoped so.

"Federal Correctional Institution: Ray Brook," in North Elba, New York, sounded like a lucky pull. It had started life as the Olympic Village for Lake Placid in 1980. Do you believe in miracles? etc. It had a pilot program for inmates to do coursework, by mail, from a local community college. He'd been excited.

When he arrived, what he'd found was a wet, dripping, falling-apart place blanketed in comical quantities of razor wire. The prison guards didn't pay much attention to the prisoners, who were given considerable leeway to police themselves. On his fifth night Matt was raped. There was some sort of gang and race thing happening that he'd been made party to. A few days after, the 1488s raped and murdered an unrelated, newly arrived black prisoner to even the score. The only way to survive another round was for Matt to accept the '88s' admissions offer. The swastika tattoo had been mandatory. Even if it hadn't been, Matt still would have gotten one. It was protection. He felt he'd sold his soul . . . for the first few weeks. His grandfather had been the bombardier of a B-17 during the Second World War, and he'd liked to look at the Nazis and think about how many his grandpappy had killed. But you can get used to almost anything.

"Why's your pride covered up?" asked a 1488 who'd gotten out two years before Matt. He was pointing to the black square on Matt's neck and lighting a cigarette, sitting across from Matt in a greasy-spoon diner that Matt had suggested as a spot for them to meet and do business.

"You can't smoke that in here," said a waitress refilling the Nazi's coffee cup. "But there's tables outside."

"Thank you, ma'am," said the Nazi, and to Matt, "Get a cup and let's sit outside."

"I got the cover-up for work," said Matt, as the Nazi pulled an umbrella out of a wooden table's umbrella hole and laid it on the ground.

"It's too nice out here for shade," said the Nazi. "You found work already?"

"Yeah, in a manner of speaking," said Matt, pulling a cigarette from the Nazi's outstretched pack. "That's what I want to talk to you about."

The Nazi cocked his head slightly. "I thought I was here to sell you something."

"Yeah," said Matt. "That too. I've got the money, but I've got some more money for you, too, if you're interested."

"Okay, shoot," said the Nazi, lighting Matt's cigarette with a Zippo that was hand-engraved with two SS lightning bolts.

"You ran some of the funding programs? After the Order knocked off Alan Berg." Alan Berg was a Jewish anti–white supremacy radio host who'd been murdered in 1984.

"No, I didn't run them—I was still pretty young then. But I was involved and did a lot of the planning. And when I joined the Fourteen Eighty-Eights, I was running some of that stuff on the outside and then on the inside." After murdering Berg and committing some petty, terroristical arson, some white nationalist groups had realized that crime could be profitable and started robbing banks and armored cars. It was how they paid for their big forest compounds and camo clothing and Wagner albums.

"And that's what they got you for?"

The Nazi looked wistful. "Yeah. We had a new guy on the crew, someone's nephew. I tell you, fucking nepotism is ruining neo-Nazism in this country." He smiled and took a drag on his cigarette. "We had this new young guy on the crew and he forgot to check for dye packs before we rolled out of the bank. The thing, the dye pack, in a wad of twenties, went off just like it was supposed to, thirty seconds after we tripped the proximity timer carrying it out of the bank." The Nazi shook his head and chuckled. "It went off right in his fucking face. He remembered between the bank and the car and had his sack open looking for it. I guess he's lucky it didn't blow his damn ears off. What it did do—he was wearing a ski mask, understand—it inked big red circles around his eyes and big red lips around his lips. He looked like the fucking Joker. Which was just hilarious, in a way—you should see his mug shots—but the damn thing inked the side of our car. Bright red. Nothing we could do about that. Nephew's dead now. I didn't kill him or anything like that but can't say I was too sad to hear about it."

The Nazi shrugged. "Though, I mean, it was my fault, really. I was in charge. I should've checked it before we stepped out of the lobby." He shook his head and smiled again, looked off into the distance for a moment. Probably thinking about the ten or so years he could've spent not being in prison.

But that's life. The waitress came out and refilled their coffee cups.

"Could I have a donut or something, sweetheart? Nothing frosted."

"Sure," said the waitress, who was about sixteen and wearing a 1950s-style waitress outfit. They were in the Poconos, and a ways off the beaten path. Matt wondered if the foam-green dress and white apron were originals. They were a bit tattered and matched the deep-stained linoleum and flatware. Maybe it was just an original pattern.

Once the waitress was inside and safely out of earshot the Nazi resumed.

"Why d'you ask?"

"You did armored cars?"

"Yep. Banks and Brinks."

Matt nodded. "Interested in some work?"

The waitress returned with a plain donut on a dinner plate.

"I don't speak for the Eighty-Eights," said the Nazi, looking flattered. He was in his late fifties but fit, despite a paunch. Shaved head. His own swastika tattoo was half-covered by a stiff denim collar. Matt wondered if the waitress had noticed it.

"I'm not looking to hire the group, just you. This has got to be a small-circle sort of thing."

"How small?"

"You and the minimum number of guys you need to do the job. But you make the plans. I'm just the middleman."

The Nazi dipped his donut and ruminated.

"Who for?" His mouth was full.

"Huh?"

"Who are you a middleman for?"

"The *Louv*-ra."

The Nazi smiled and raised an eyebrow. Then he shrugged.

"Okay then. What do you want robbed?"

Matt pulled out the packet Kelly had given him. She'd retyped it and cut the detail down to the bare-bone essentials. Bullet points plus photos, plus details of a rendezvous to exchange the drawings for her money.

The Nazi looked them over, carefully. He scratched his jaw, picking occasionally at the stubble.

"The Louvre," he said, examining the photos. "Funny. I'd need some money in advance."

"You get eighty K now, for expenses, and two million when the job's done." Kelly had given Matt a hundred thousand in real money—most of her savings—to bait the hook. Matt was keeping twenty for himself, for his own expenses.

"One million now and one on delivery."

Matt shook his head. "Everything on delivery. I got strict instructions. It's not about the money, but the secrecy. My employer doesn't want anyone skipping town with the plans and a million bucks in his pocket and then shooting off his mouth. Not my words."

The Nazi flipped his Zippo open and closed. He was thinking.

"I'll need three guys and some equipment. Eighty's not enough."

"Get a credit card."

The Nazi struck the Zippo and used it to burn an orange-brown leaf that had fallen on the table. Fall in the Poconos is beautiful.

"Okay," said the Nazi. "It's a deal." He stuck out his hand, and Matt shook it, noticing the letters H-E-I-L tattooed on the Nazi's knuckles.

"Good," said Matt, taking another cigarette from the Nazi's pack and lighting it off the embers of the leaf. "And, of course, I won't tell you your business, but if you're going to use tweakers make sure they can keep secrets."

"I'm not going to use tweakers," said the Nazi. "I'm going to use cowboys."

8

Matt paid for the coffee and donut and then walked the
Nazi across the crunchy gravel parking lot to Kelly's car.
He reached under the passenger seat and pulled out a manila
envelope with eighty thousand dollars in it. He held it open for
the Nazi to inspect—the Nazi nodded—and Matt handed the
envelope over.

Of the twenty K Matt had decided to keep, fifteen was in the
glove compartment and five was stuffed in his wallet. Now he followed the Nazi over to an orange Ford Bronco. The Nazi opened
the passenger door and pulled out a cheap plastic backpack. This
was the business they'd discussed on the phone when Matt had
asked the Nazi to meet him. The stuff the Nazi was there to sell
him. The Nazi held the bag open for Matt's inspection. Inside,
padded by old T-shirts, were three pistols. Two of them looked

like old police revolvers—Smith & Wessons and stainless steel. The third was a black semiautomatic.

"What is that? A 226?"

"No, a 220. West German, with a nice old zipper mag. The mag release is on the bottom of the grip. It takes a little getting used to."

"Nine or forty-five?"

"Forty-five."

"And the other two?"

"One's a .38 Special and the wooden grip is .357 Mag, but they'll both fire .38s. There're three boxes in there, though, fifty rounds of each."

"Anything tying any of these to each other?" Matt was rezipping the bag.

"No," said the Nazi. Matt took out his wallet and pulled out the rubber-banded five thousand dollars, which he handed over. The Nazi added it to the manila envelope.

He and Matt shook hands again.

"I guess I'll see you in about a month," said the Nazi.

"Yeah," said Matt. "I hope it all works out."

"I b'lieve it will," said the Nazi. "And I b'lieve you'll have that two million dollars with you when we meet."

"Yeah," said Matt. "It'll be in a couple gym bags, I guess. Won't fit in envelopes."

"No, I don't think it would," said the Nazi. "I don't know exactly what's going on with you and the group and that cover-up job on your neck. I b'lieve I don't have to tell you that if you screw me I'll cut your balls off."

"You don't," said Matt. "But hey—right back at you."

The Nazi laughed. Matt smiled slightly.

"Okay, good, it's good to understand each other," said the Nazi. "I was planning to ask you if you needed help adjusting to being outside again. But you seem to be getting on fine."

"So far, anyway. Seems that way."

"Course I would like to know who you're working for but I'll mind my business. I thought maybe you'd try to get work killing some more Arabs. Since you've got a certain amount of expertise in that area."

"I'll see you next month," said Matt, closing his trunk.

"Didn't mean to offend you," said the Nazi.

"I'm not offended," said Matt. "But I've got a ways to go. I'll see you."

"Yeah," said the Nazi. "See you."

Matt got into Kelly's car and turned onto route something-or-other—two lanes and no traffic. In his rearview mirror he saw the Nazi toss the cash envelope into the orange Bronco and climb in after it.

◆

Matt didn't have a smartphone and he hadn't wanted to print out directions, which might have attracted Kelly's attention. Who knew how closely she watched her magical printers? Matt wanted no paper trail, so he'd memorized the route from the diner to a public library in Stroudsburg, PA. He'd chosen Stroudsburg at random—just a small town on his way back to New York, away from the highway but not too far. It was a cute little place. A sign in "Downtown Stroudsburg" claimed a population of 5,505, though the autumn leaf tourists might have bumped that up to around 5,550.

Matt parked in the lot behind the library, walked to the front, and nodded to a friendly librarian at the circulation desk. He followed some laminated 8.5-by-11 signs pointing him to a small computer room, which he was glad to find empty. He sat down at a ten-year-old Dell and logged on to Google. There were some addresses he needed to look up.

The first two belonged to two of the three men who'd raped him, who'd been out of prison now for one and two years, respectively. The third of the three was dead already—killed in his early forties by, Matt was sorry to say, complications from diabetes. Rumor from the medical wing said he'd gone peacefully in a sugar coma, though that may have been tongue in cheek; no one knew for sure. The other two had been released at the end of decade-plus Ray Brook residencies. There's no parole for nonmilitary federal crimes but one of the two had got a year off his sentence for good behavior. That was Darrel Clinton, who, after Matt had crossed off a lot of obviously different Darrels, seemed to be in North Carolina, near Winston-Salem. Living with a niece, whose daughter had a Facebook page and was excited that her Uncle Darrel was helping her build a terrarium. There was no photo of him but there was a decent family resemblance in both the niece and the grand-niece.

The next name on Matt's list was Reuben Harry, who had his own Facebook page. He was in Florida—St. Petersburg—working in a food truck and taking selfies on the beach.

Matt wrote down the name of the food truck (the "Gator Trough") and some of the places it parked, and then the name of Darrel Clinton's niece and the name and number of the public school her daughter went to. Maybe he'd call and tell them he was a parent looking for a phone number for another parent—and could they possibly email him a new copy of the names and addresses of the parents in his son's grade? It's tough being a single dad. He hoped the school was big enough that this wouldn't raise any eyebrows.

If that didn't work, he could just go to the school and follow the kid home. But he didn't want to involve her if he didn't have to.

The third address Matt needed was for Captain Kirby Monroe, who'd led the investigation into Matt's having shot an Iraqi civilian. Matt's platoon had been sent to arrest an Iraqi man who'd thrown an eight-year-old girl in front of a Humvee. The platoon searched the man's property and found an ISIS bomb-making manual and plastic explosives hidden in a cesspit. The man denied knowing anything about them and denied being the man who'd killed the girl.

Less than three weeks later, the man was ordered released for lack of evidence. Matt's squad was sent to deliver him back to his house. At his house, Matt's lieutenant had taken the man aside, into the kitchen, and turned on the tap. He told the man he'd drown him in the sink if he didn't say where he'd gotten the explosives. Matt asked the man if he knew what waterboarding was. The man grabbed a knife—a bread knife, off a counter—and stabbed the lieutenant with it. Matt shot the man dead.

The platoon guarded the house until an army forensic team arrived under the command of Captain Monroe, who'd been appointed as the investigating officer. The knife had never been entered into evidence, and Captain Monroe had stated in his report to the Article 32 hearing—the grand jury before the court-martial—that there was no physical evidence at the sight of the shooting of an attempted homicide by the victim. Matt believed this was retaliation for the refusal of any member of the platoon to testify to the drowning and waterboarding threats, despite several having remarked on them during preliminary interviews, which hadn't been recorded.

Whatever Monroe's reason was, the prosecution had persuaded the court-martial that the lieutenant's knife wound was self-inflicted, after the fact, as a cover story. Maybe that was what Monroe really believed. Matt doubted it but it wasn't impossible. There had been a spike in this kind of war-crimes prosecution lately. The same way that soldiers were pissed that terrorists were being released for lack of evidence, army prosecutors were pissed that soldiers were getting off scot-free for murdering civilians they believed to be terrorists. Getting away with it because their buddies, their comrades-in-arms, wouldn't testify against them. The army lawyers had started seeing themselves as the good guys in a Mafia legal thriller, fighting against a Cosa Nostra code of silence. So some of the army lawyers had started massaging the evidence a little. A few years down the line, this would lead to some heads rolling, some cases being thrown out, and half a dozen presidential pardons. But all that would be hindsight.

Matt had been convicted of premeditated murder and sentenced to twenty-five years. His lieutenant—who was twenty-four years old, to Matt's thirty-one—had been convicted of conspiracy to commit murder, making a false statement, and conduct unbecoming an officer and was sentenced to fifteen years. Two hours after his sentence was handed down, the lieutenant hanged himself.

Captain Monroe lived in Greenwich, Connecticut.

9

Kelly did not think of herself as a lucky person.

The Arab world was rapidly becoming one of the world centers of fine arts—the Louvre had opened a branch in Abu Dhabi, and the British Museum and Guggenheim were on their way. The UAE and Saudi Arabia were building the works of the world's great architects as fast as the great architects could design them. NYU and the Sorbonne had both opened Arabian branches, and other universities were sure to follow. The Arabian Peninsula hosted two *Grand Prix de Formule Un,* which were much more about style and couture than cars. A Qatari had made the most expensive art purchase in history by buying Cézanne's *Card Players* for a third of a billion dollars.

That record had stood for only five years. The thing that had really given Kelly the idea of seeking a petro-money buyer for the Klimts was a Saudi buying *Salvator Mundi*—the rarest of rare in the art world, a Leonardo; there were only twenty in existence and never, ever on sale—for half a billion dollars . . . and then keeping it on his yacht. To Kelly, it looked like West Asia was a wild west art market, a sort of fine arts gold rush, and she figured that finding a buyer for some hot Klimts wouldn't be too difficult, even for a neophyte. She looked up lists of donors to the new Louvre and Guggenheim, found a few who had homes in Paris and London, and, during the Christie's season, she bumped into as many of them as she could, stalking them around parties, using her breasts to start conversations, segueing into talk of the art market. After a little chitchat, she'd casually bring up some private collectors she knew who were interested in selling without having to give an auction house twenty-five percent.

Eventually she'd settled on a charming, gregarious, unabashedly eccentric man in his late fifties named Simon Abbas. She would have described him to a girlfriend as a silver fox, though he was silver only at the temples. He'd invited her to a private party to watch the race at Monte Carlo from his pied-à-terre above the hairpin. The apartment had six Chagalls and a Pissarro in it, which Simon pointed out as the core of his beloved "Jewish art collection." Kelly wondered if he was showing off his open mind or if he thought she was Jewish. After a while she got him alone in a corner and "asked for a friend" about his interest in the Klimts.

He was interested and they'd made a handshake deal, pending further details from the insurers. He promised a private jet to bring her to his home in Doha, where her documents could be evaluated by some people he trusted. A few harmless texts and emails were exchanged—thank-yous for good times at parties, etc. And that was what got her in trouble.

Because it turned out that Simon—actually Salman—Abbas was wanted by the DEA in regard to some money coming his way from Ciudad del Este in Paraguay. Money the DEA believed belonged to Hezbollah, which was generating enormous amounts of cash trafficking cocaine. The DEA believed Abbas was laundering it for them so it could be used to buy weapons for Hezbollah fighters in Syria.

Which is why the DEA was reading his emails. Which is how it heard about Kelly and why it obtained a search warrant for her apartment. Which is why, when Kelly got back to her apartment, from Monaco, she found a DEA agent named Levi Quintero and his entourage waiting for her.

This was about two months before she called Matt Kubelsky in prison.

She asked what was going on. Quintero produced identification and asked Kelly if she knew who William Buckley was.

"The politics guy?"

"No, a different William Buckley. A CIA agent in Lebanon. That doesn't ring a bell?"

"I don't understand what's going on."

Quintero rolled Kelly's desk chair over and motioned for her to sit. He grabbed a second chair, putting the fan sitting on it on the ground, and sat down facing Kelly, with four or five feet between them.

"Bill Buckley was chief of the CIA's station in Lebanon. In 1983, Hezbollah drove a van with two thousand pounds of explosives in it up to our embassy in Beirut. Beirut's the capital of Lebanon."

"I know," said Kelly.

"You know about the embassy bombing?"

Kelly shook her head "no."

"You heard of Hezbollah?"

Kelly shook her head again.

"Oh no?"

Head shake.

"They're a terrorist group. The bomb in the van killed sixty-three people, Americans and Lebanese and some other people who just happened to be there at the wrong time. A hundred and twenty more were injured. Afterward, Hezbollah bragged that it had killed, among others, CIA agent Bill Buckley. When it found out it hadn't, it got embarrassed and decided to kidnap him.

"He spent a year and a half in a space the size of a filing cabinet, hooded, with his wrists and ankles bound. The only time they took him out of his cell was to torture him. Three video cassettes of Bill were sent to American embassies in Europe, a few months between each one. I've seen them. You can see that Bill's body has been wrecked. Parts of him are . . . very damaged. He's screaming and gibbering and rocking around, looking terrified but not totally awake. His eyes are rolling around in his head. He had track marks on his arms and legs. He'd been injected with things. For a year and a half they did that to him—Hezbollah. He didn't kill himself and they didn't execute him. He died of a heart attack, probably. What was left of him was found dumped on the side of the road."

Kelly wrapped her arms tightly around her shoulders. She was shivering. She was so confused.

"I want to make sure you *really* understand what kind of people you're dealing with."

Kelly shook her head. "I don't understand what you're doing here or why you're telling me this."

"Simon—Salman—Abbas launders money for Hezbollah. You and Salman Abbas have become buddies. I search your apartment and find a counterfeiting operation par excellence. Small, yes, but very good. High-quality stuff. Now, you tell me what conclusions you would draw."

Levi Quintero stood up and began to pull evidence bags out of a large plastic milk crate. The bags had rubber-banded bundles of bills in them.

"Rupees."

He pulled out another bag. "Rubles."

And another. "Euros."

Another. "Pounds."

Another. "Dollars."

Another. "Canadian dollars."

Another. "Australian dollars."

Another. "I don't know what these are."

"Kroner," said Kelly. "Swedish."

"Okay," said Quintero. "Pesos."

Another. "I think these are yen."

"Won."

"Whatever," said Quintero. "Point is, you've got a worldwide operation here."

"They were just test runs, I never tried to spend most of those."

"Uh-huh," said Quintero. "Between 1982 and 1984, Hezbollah conducted thirty-six suicide attacks targeting American, NATO, and Israeli targets, killing a total of six-hundred fifty-nine people. In 1985, they hijacked TWA flight 847. From 1982 to 1992, Hezbollah took a hundred and four hostages—among them twenty-five Americans, sixteen Frenchmen, twelve Englishmen, seven

Swiss, seven Germans, and one Irishman. Of those, eight died from starvation and torture."

"Please stop," said Kelly.

"In 1992, they bombed the Israeli embassy in Argentina, killing twenty-nine. In 1994, they bombed a Jewish community center in Argentina, killing eighty-five. Also in 1994, they blew up AC flight 94 from Panama, killing everyone aboard. In '96, they set off a bomb at an American barracks in Saudi Arabia, killing nineteen American servicemen. In 2005, they assassinated the former prime minister of Lebanon. They fought in the Balkan wars in the 1990s, and in the 2000s they trained insurgents to kill thousands of American soldiers in Iraq and Afghanistan. In 2012, they blew up a bus in Bulgaria, killing six. Right now, they're working for Iran and murdering Syrians, Kurds, Druze, Lebanese, Turks, Iraqis, and Americans in Iraq and Syria."

"I didn't know any of this," said Kelly, shaking her head. "I mean, I had no idea Simon had anything to do with any of this. I barely know him."

"Except that you were in his apartment in Paris, his apartment in Monaco, and have plans to see him again in Qatar, and appear—based on your own texts—to have attended at least three art auctions with him."

"I just thought he was an art collector."

"And I think I'm going to arrest you and charge you with material assistance to an enemy of the United States, a crime that carries the death penalty."

Kelly didn't say anything. She looked scared.

"You may be wondering what this has to do with the DEA." Quintero sat down again, across from Kelly, and scratched his cheek. He had rings under his eyes; he looked like he hadn't slept. "Terrorism is expensive work, and though Iran pays for a lot of it, Hezbollah decided they needed other sources of income. In the late 1990s, when they were murdering people in South America, they noticed that most of the people murdering people in South America were also getting rich selling drugs. They liked the idea. We estimate they're turning a profit of more than a billion dollars a year smuggling cocaine, tens of thousands of tons of it, and most of it ends up in the United States. Basically, Americans are buying drugs with money that ends up buying guns for Hezbollah to use to kill American soldiers. Among others."

Quintero leaned forward and rubbed his eyes.

"So," he said, now looking at Kelly, who was looking at the floor, "what have you got to say for yourself?"

"Only that I didn't know any of that and had nothing to do with any of it and would never have anything to do with any of it."

"Mhmm."

"I'll take a lie detector or whatever you want."

"You're just a counterfeiter?"

"Yes. Just for personal use."

"Why did you care that Abbas is an art collector?"

"I'm a fine arts major."

Quintero just looked at her.

"I wanted to sell him something."

"What."

"Drawings. Very valuable ones."

"That you made?"

Kelly shook her head.

"That you purchased with counterfeit money."

"Yes."

Quintero shook his head. "Who'd be suckered into that?"

Kelly shrugged. She was still looking at the floor.

"They're stolen, aren't they."

After a moment, Kelly nodded.

"Where are they?"

"I don't know exactly. A . . . colleague is holding on to them. Till we rendezvous. I can't contact him. Phone tracking. You know." She hoped Quintero was too exhausted to tell, or care, that she was lying. Quintero sighed.

"Okay. I don't really give a shit about fine arts theft but I'm going to start out by saying, right at the beginning, that you're going to have to return those to their rightful owner when this is all over."

"When what is all over?" Now Kelly was looking at him again.

"We want Abbas. We want him to name names of the narco terrorists he's changing money for."

"You can't arrest him?"

"We have no extradition treaty with Qatar, even if they would arrest him for us, which they won't. We've tried to get him in France but the French won't arrest him because, A, we won't provide our sources, and B, because France only recognizes the *military* wing of Hezbollah as a terrorist organization, but claims that since Hezbollah members sit in the Lebanese parliament it has a legitimate political wing, and C, because France will not extradite someone for a capital crime to a country that employs capital punishment."

"Ah."

"Yeah. Fuck France. And we've had the same problem with every other European country he's got apartments in. None of the fuckers execute people anymore." Quintero rubbed his cheeks and yawned. "Wish he'd visit Japan. They've got fantastic art collections and, since they're civilized people, like us, they don't give a shit about killing bad guys." He yawned again. "I've always wanted to go to Japan. And China. I'd like to see that Terracotta Army. Every one of those statues has a unique face . . .

"Anyway, we want Abbas and we want you to help us get him."

"In exchange for not arresting me."

"That's right."

"For anything."

"I don't give a shit about counterfeiting either, as long as you stop doing it. There'll probably be some kind of parole thing to keep an eye on you for a while after it's all over. It'll be like a plea agreement. You can have a lawyer look at it for you. We're drawing it up now."

"I'll be free and clear on all the stuff, crimes, from the counterfeiting *and* the art theft, 'cause I'm using it to help you?"

"If we get him. If not, you're on your own and we turn the case over to the FBI."

Kelly nodded. She could still go ahead with her plans. She'd have to find someone else to do some of the dirty work and heavy lifting, though, in case they started watching her.

10

The Nazi's orange Bronco was in pretty good shape and it took him only three days' driving to get from the Poconos to Bozeman, Montana. Not counting the day he'd spent at home in Miles City.

From Bozeman he'd turned south, off the highway, onto rural and rural-er roads, until a dirt track led him to the Fotheringay Ranch. Fotheringay is one of those weird names that is pronounced nothing at all like it's spelled. *Funjee* is how you say it. Calling it Funjee Ranch used to be a way of showing you were a local, a real Montanan. These days, though, there weren't enough people who knew the ranch for it to make any difference. The born-and-bred locals mostly left to find work and were gradually being replaced by California tech people who worked remotely and wanted quiet and scenery and low taxes.

The Nazi buttoned his collar to obscure the swastika. He'd already wrapped tape bandages around the "heil" on his knuckles and taped over the SS logos on his lighter and wristwatch. The Fotheringays were the type who stocked a ten-year supply of food in their cellars, and enough guns and ammo to fight off an invasion from Canada, but they'd be as likely to kill a Nazi as talk to one. They didn't mind the tweakers and meth makers or weed growers. Those were just folks trying to make a living, but white nationalists were a horse of a different color. Sometimes the Nazi wished he'd known that Montanans, generally speaking, loathed all that skinhead shit before he'd gotten involved. In his high school, being a Nazi had been like being a goth or joining the AV club. Depended on who your friends were. The Nazi sucked his teeth. But fuck that, no regrets. He'd enjoyed his life and he'd enjoyed prison and he liked the people he rolled with. But the Fotheringays wouldn't, so for a few weeks he'd keep it in the closet. No one on a ranch would notice taped-up fingers.

He was kicking up a cloud of dust as he turned through the Fotheringays' front gate and drove up toward the house. There was a man on a horse way off to his right with a flock of sheep around him. He turned toward the Nazi's Bronco and cantered over. The Nazi pulled up in front of the house, next to a couple pickups and a VW Beetle that someone had turned into an off-roader—raised suspension and giant, chunky tires—and climbed out.

The man on the horse was Joel Fotheringay. He was a cowboy. Actually, these days, a sheepboy. The new ethanol laws had increased the demand for corn enormously, which had increased the price enormously, and feeding cows didn't pay for small ranches anymore. The Fotheringays were making a run at sheep, but word was sheep weren't paying too well either. Lamb prices were down. Too many farmers had made the same switch. Wool sales barely covered the cost of sheering, which was done strictly to keep the sheep from roasting. (Ha ha.) The Nazi knew the ranch had quietly been put on the market. In fact, he'd seen it on a real estate website, so he figured Joel and his brothers would probably welcome a business opportunity. Folks need to make a living.

The Nazi waved to Joel. He'd known the Fotheringay boys for years, since, as teenagers, they'd picked up extra money working shifts in his brother's drugstore. He'd had to fire them for selling too much Sudafed. He knew at least one of the brothers—Frank or Caleb, he couldn't remember which—had done a stretch at Crossroads Correctional for smuggling. He'd been caught driving a truck filled with drums of duty-free Canadian maple syrup. Maple goddamn syrup. Hot syrup, so to speak. The Nazi shook his head and smiled at the memory.

"Joel," he called out. "How's life been treating you."

"Mr. Wharton," said Joel Fotheringay. "What brings you out here?"

"Well, I got a job offer for you," said the Nazi. "If you and the boys can take some time off from grazing pregnant sheep. And I got gifts for you."

The Nazi pulled a plastic bag out of the Bronco and removed a T-shirt, which he tossed to Joel, who was still on his horse. The horse backed away from the T-shirt's trajectory but Joel caught it anyway.

He held it up in front of him. It said "Fuck Ewe" on it. Joel laughed.

"Thank you, Mr. Wharton. Very thoughtful. What's the offer?"

Two more riders had appeared at the crest of the sheep-covered hill. The Nazi looked at them.

"That Frank and Caleb?"

Joel looked over his shoulder at them. "Yeah. We had to let all our guys go, knew there wouldn't be enough to pay them with out of this herd. Once they lamb we'll graze them down around Hellroaring and then drive them up to Bozeman. After that, we'll be looking for work. So I hope you can wait."

"I can't, but I could give you a little capital to get some of your Mexicans back."

"They're Peruvian. I don't think Mexicans do sheep."

"Whatever," said the Nazi. "Lemme ask you, how d'you boys feel about Jesse James?"

◆

It was a subject they picked up again a few hours later, after the Nazi had helped the Fotheringay boys put the ewes in for the night. They were seated around a fire pit behind the ranch house, drinking a handle of cheap whiskey that the Nazi'd brought with him.

"Well, I mean," said Frank Fotheringay, slurring a bit, "they were the model, weren't they? I mean, we were always going to be cowboys 'cause it was the family business. But they were the guys who made us *want* to be cowboys. Jesse James. Butch and Sundance. Bill Miner. Billy the Kid. Curly Bill. Buffalo Bill. Wild Bill. A lot of Bills."

"Bill Doolin," offered Joel.

"Yeah, Doolin-Dalton."

"Not lawmen?" asked the Nazi.

"Nah. We played cowboys and Indians not cowboys and peace officers."

"Doc Holliday was cool," said Caleb Fotheringay, the youngest of the three brothers, who were all in their early to mid twenties.

"Yeah, Doc Holliday was cool," said Frank. "'Cause he fuckin' killed Johnny Ringo."

"And I like Rooster Cogburn," said Caleb.

"Rooster Cogburn's not real," said Frank.

"Well, Doc Holliday wasn't a doctor," said Caleb.

"I think he was a dentist," said Joel, yawning.

"Whatever," said Caleb, filling his cheek with chewing tobacco.

"How do you drink without swallowing that stuff?" asked the Nazi.

"Sometimes you swallow it," said Caleb. "It's like Russian roulette." They all laughed.

"You know, when the James Gang robbed trains, he'd check the men to see if they had calloused hands," said the Nazi, "'cause he didn't want to steal from working-class guys. Just rich folk."

"Amen to that," said Frank.

"Fucking Robin Hood," said Caleb, who nodded in agreement and spit out a shot of brown liquid. "A good man."

Joel took another sip of whiskey. "So. Mr. Wharton," he said.

"Bob," said the Nazi.

"Bob. You've been cagey since you got here. What's the job offer?"

"I wanna know if you cowboys wanna do some real cowboy shit. Save your ranch. Robin Hood a few people."

Joel looked at him. Narrowed his eyes a little. Not angry, more caught off guard. Frank was the first to speak.

"Amen to that."

Caleb spit out some more tobacco juice and Bob Wharton smiled.

11

Kelly and Matt were lying next to each other in Kelly's bed. They were naked and sweaty and, Kelly having turned on the fan, both smoking. Kelly was thinking that all the cruel hardships Matt had been put through, all the heroism of fighting overseas followed by the disgusting injustice of prison, had made him really attractive. He was so self-possessed now, so confident. Matt was thinking Kelly probably still thought he was stupid and unworldly next to her and was using sex to make sure he didn't back out of their arrangement. He exhaled a puff of smoke and she ran a finger over a long scar on his leg.

He looked over at her.

"It's sexy," she said.

"Yeah," said Matt. "I cut myself on a fucking screw or something climbing out of an upside-down Humvee. The ISIS types figured out that Americans love dogs—so much that we don't like driving over dead ones, which is evidently something some people aren't so touchy about. I don't know why exactly but there are dead dogs everywhere there. I guess a lot of their owners died in the war. Anyways, they started putting dead dogs out knowing we'd drive around them, and then leaving roadside bombs in the places they knew we'd drive to get around them. So then the people in charge told us to start driving over the dogs. So they started putting the bombs in the dogs. So every time we saw a dead dog in the road we'd have to shoot at it just in case there was a bomb inside. It wasn't fun."

She took her hand off the scar and placed it flat on the inside of his thigh, rubbed it up and down. Trying to be comforting, not titillating.

"Anyway, a dog bomb blew a Humvee I was in off the road and I cut myself climbing out of it."

Kelly put her head on Matt's chest. She didn't know what to say.

"I'm going to head down to Georgia for a couple days," said Matt, tucking a bit of sweaty hair behind Kelly's ear. "Say hello to some people."

Kelly got up on one elbow. "But I need you here. We're going to Qatar on Friday. *Friday.*"

"I've still got most of the week," said Matt. "I'll be back by then. I'm flying down in a few hours, catching the first plane down in the morning. I'll spend the day and the next day in Atlanta, then fly back on Thursday. I'll be here in plenty of time."

Kelly didn't look convinced. Matt smacked the inside of her thigh, sort of the way you'd punch a friend in the shoulder.

"Don't worry. I'll be back on Thursday. In and out." He rolled over her and walked toward the bathroom.

"Do you need some money for the ticket and stuff?" she called after him.

"No thanks, I'm good."

She heard him turn on the shower and flopped her head down on the pillow, annoyed.

◆

A few hours later, a little before three in the morning, Matt left for Newark Airport in a cab. At the airport, he rented a car and drove seventeen hours south to Tampa, Florida. Of course, he would rather have taken a plane, but he was only about eighty percent certain the TSA wouldn't find the two guns he was carrying, and it wasn't worth the risk.

Driving over the bridge to St. Petersburg, he began to map in his mind a route around the parking spots of the Gator Trough food truck. He decided he'd drive south around the little bay—not Tampa Bay; Boca Ciega—and then north along the beaches. If he didn't find the truck out there, he'd sleep in the car (he needed some sleep) and find a public library in the morning, see what Twitter said. But he wanted to avoid doing that if he could. The fewer people who saw him the better.

His first stop was southward to the tip of the barrier islands, Pass-a-Grille and St. Pete Beach. He cruised up and down for a little while with the windows open, enjoying the salt breeze that he hadn't smelled in so long he'd almost forgotten what it smelled like. God it was nice. He didn't see the Gator Trough anywhere, but he did see a few other food trucks and he hadn't eaten since somewhere around Savannah. He bought himself a Cuban sandwich from a truck called Bay of Porks and walked down to the water to eat it, plopping himself on the white sand, plopping a can of Coke into the sand next to him, and peeling open the sandwich foil. Some steam wafted out, moistening his eyes.

He took a bite. There was salami in it, along with the usual pig and cheese. The guy at the truck had explained that that's what made Cubans special around the bay. Did so few people smoke these days that "Cubans" meant sandwiches and not cigars? Strange world. Though Matt had never smoked a Cuban and meant never to smoke one till Cuba was free. Fuck Castro and his Caribbean Taliban.

Matt ate half the sandwich, closed the foil over the rest, popped the Coke, and lit a cigarette. The sun was just setting over the water, and it was absurdly beautiful. Farther up the beach some people were fighting off a seagull that was trying to raid an evening picnic. It flew away toward Matt, looking, Matt thought, dispirited. Matt pulled a slice of salami out of the sandwich, waved it around a little, and threw it toward the seagull. The seagull landed, picked it up, tried to figure out how to carry the floppy meat disc in its beak, then took off and flew inland. Looking, Matt thought, pleased and thankful. Would it kill people to be nicer to animals? He shook his head and looked back out at the sunset.

Goddamn it was nice. And the sand was warm but not hot, and the breeze was warm but not hot, and not too humid. He could just sit here all evening and then sleep the night here. This looked like a safe enough little tourist town. But he had a schedule.

He sighed, wolfed down the rest of his sandwich, and stood up, brushing some crumbs off his shirt and—wishing the crabs and the creeping things bon appétit—walked back toward his car. He checked to make sure the .38 Special and the .357 were still hidden under the seat among the Toyota Corolla's seat-runner struts and headed north, up along Long Key, past a Chick-fil-A (his mouth watered a little; how he'd missed the South!), past a place called Punta Vista, and up to Upham Beach Park. A lot of activity but no Gator Trough. There seemed to be a lot of traffic back and forth through the parking lot to the motels behind the beach. A lot of cars coming in and out. Some light tailgating and something that was either a bar mitzvah or a quinceañera. As he drove past it looking for a parking spot, a few of the happy, dancing Jews and/or Cubans waved and shouted for him to come join them, that there was plenty of food and booze. He smiled and shook his head, shouted "Thanks, though," and drove to the far end of the lot. He found a space, turned off the Corolla, cracked the windows so the salt breeze could drift in, and quickly fell asleep.

◆

He slept till around noon the next day, longer than he'd meant to. He might have slept even longer if a cop hadn't started tapping on the window.

"You all right, sir?"

It took Matt a moment to remember where he was—looking around, seeing the beach signs and the beach grass and hearing some reggaeton playing somewhere nearby.

"Yeah, officer, I'm fine. I didn't think I was good to drive so I figured I'd wait it out. Must have fallen asleep."

"Okay, no problem, but this isn't a campsite, so sleep somewhere else tonight. After Labor Day and before winter the motels aren't too expensive."

"Thanks, officer. It was a spur of the moment vacation thing. I'm not living out of my car."

"Well, I agree the car's a little clean for a homestead. Just don't let me find you parked here again tonight."

"No, sir."

"Have a good day."

"Thanks."

Matt did a loop through the parking lot and turned left onto the road, continuing his route north, crossing the bridge from Long Key to Treasure Island, the next of the barrier islands that run along the edge of the peninsula that hems in Tampa Bay. He figured he'd finish last night's beach circuit now and get the lunch traffic. He could try to find a library sometime before the dinner rush if he had to.

He drove slowly past Sunset Beach on Treasure Island's southern tip. The only food truck, if it counted as a food truck, and Matt supposed it did, was a Mister Softee. Next up was St. Petersburg Municipal Beach, which was so densely packed with food trucks that Matt had to pull over and survey them on foot. No luck, though he did grab a breakfast ice cream cone from a second Mister Softee.

Back on the road north, Matt crossed over to Sand Key and Madeira Beach. No food trucks; too many real restaurants around. Then Redington Beach. No food trucks. Indian Shores, Indian Rocks Beach, Belleair Shore, Belleair Beach—a few trucks but no Gator Trough. Matt was getting annoyed. There were two beach islands left—Clearwater and Paradise Key, which connected the string back to the mainland, over the Clearwater Causeway. On his rest-station map, they were small and Matt was starting to lose hope. The traffic around the causeway was gridlocked. Car horns were blaring. Matt turned up the volume on Weezer's *Blue Album* and then shut the stereo off as he spotted the Gator Trough food truck pushing its way through an intersection. The driver's middle finger was out the window in response to shouts and honking. It almost took off Matt's wing mirror as it turned south toward the big tourist beaches that Matt had just searched.

Matt waited until the truck was out of his sight line, hidden by the hump of the bridge he'd just crossed from Sand Key, then stuck his own middle finger out and did an aggressive U-turn. He ignored the honks and sped up slowly, keeping the Gator Trough six or seven car lengths ahead.

The truck spent half an hour wending its way south through the late-afternoon traffic. Matt followed it all the way back to the St. Pete Municipal Beach on Treasure Island. It pulled into the food truck area, end on, among half a dozen competitors. Matt pulled into a parking spot fifty yards away and watched it until he was sure it was open for business and not going anywhere. Then he pulled out of the lot and drove south again to Sunset Beach, where he parked the car in the shade of some boat trailers, by a slipway on the bay side of the island. He retrieved the .38 Special Smith & Wesson police revolver from under his seat and tucked it into the back of his waistband. He crossed the narrow island on foot and walked north along the gulf-side beach, back up to St. Pete Municipal, where he bought a soda and a bag of chips from the shower-house vending machine. He sat down at a picnic table with the water to his left and the parking lot ahead of him, to the right.

He'd bought the chips so people wouldn't give any thought to his sitting at the picnic table. Having a spot at a right angle to the water let him keep his eye on the Gator Trough, waiting for a glimpse of Reuben Harry.

About once an hour, or maybe once every forty-five minutes, someone would come out of the truck for a smoke or to walk to the shower house and its public bathroom. It seemed to be a two-man operation, with the occasional breaks alternating between the two. Neither of them was Harry.

The sun was setting. Matt wasn't especially hungry but he couldn't keep sitting at the picnic table without a good reason without starting to attract attention. He should have brought a book or something. But he hadn't, so he got up and went to the nearest food truck, Tampenadas, and got a burrito. When he got back to his picnic table it was occupied by a family of six so he walked a little way along the beach and planted himself on a sandy berm among some tall wavy beach grass and resumed his watch, now with the food trucks on his left and the sunset on his right.

He had a few bites of the burrito. It was fine; not great, just fine. And he wasn't hungry so he wrapped it back up in its wax paper and planted it in the sand like a can of soda, leaned back on his haunches, and tried to look casual.

An hour later, it was dark and Matt's pack of Winstons was dwindling. There were still plenty of people on the beach but the center of activity had moved to the parking lot, where a block party seemed to have sprung up—an overflow, maybe, from one of the nearby motels. Someone had strung up pastel and white Christmas lights, plugged into one of the food truck's generators. People were dancing to Latin music. Bum . . . bum-*bum*-bum. Bum . . . bum-*bum*-bum. There was laughing and an occasional shriek of delight as a girl got pinched or tickled by her boyfriend. It looked like a good time. Matt had another couple bites of his burrito.

About half an hour after that, the back of the Gator Trough opened and one of the two guys working it climbed out. Matt couldn't hear what he was saying but he was mad about something. He gestured a few times to his wrist, where a wristwatch would have been if he'd been wearing one, then threw up his hands, shouted something to the guy still inside the truck, and stalked away toward the parking lot.

A second later the second guy climbed out of the truck, dialing his phone. He stopped dialing and slipped it into his pocket. He threw up his hands in a kind of "where the hell have you been?" gesture, and a man jogged around to the back of the food truck and climbed in. Matt couldn't see the man's face but he was the right height to be Reuben Harry and had the right build. Matt put out his cigarette. He didn't want the orange cherry to keep him from disappearing into the dark.

Another hour passed. The beach was empty except for a couple of teenagers who had made a little nest for themselves right down by the water and were probably boning, though it was too dark to be sure. The back door of the Gator Trough opened again and the late arriver climbed out. He walked pretty much straight toward Matt, unzipping his fly. Matt put his hand on the revolver. He couldn't kill Harry here. If it was Harry. The noise and music from the party would probably drown out the sound of the shot, but a

.38 Special is a powerful round and the bullet might pass through Harry's body and hit someone dancing in the parking lot.

Matt could sneak around behind him, maybe. He could be pretty much silent walking on sand.

The man who might be Harry stopped. He was going to take a piss.

The other guy in the truck shouted to him. Matt couldn't quite hear the words, but the gist was "don't do that there, use the goddamn bathroom."

The latecomer put his dick away, waved dismissively at the truck, and walked down the beach toward the shower house. Matt scattered the remainder of his burrito—the seagulls would take care of it now or in the morning. He patted his pocket, feeling the cigarette butts and counting them to make sure they were all there. He patted another pocket to make sure the pebbles he'd collected hadn't rolled out. Then he got up and walked toward the shower house, arriving about thirty seconds after the guy he hoped was Reuben Harry.

Matt walked into the men's room. The man was at the urinal, emptying out and humming to himself. He looked like Harry. Sounded like him too. Matt walked past the urinals and began to check the stalls to make sure there was no one in any of them.

There were three stalls, all empty. Matt stepped into the first and left the door open. The man at the urinal finished, zipped up, and turned toward the door.

"You going to wash your hands?" said Matt. The man turned around.

"You going to mind your own fucking business?" Yeah, it was definitely Reuben Harry. Matt pulled out the revolver. Harry's eyes widened, though he didn't really look scared. Matt waved him closer.

"Come over here." Harry put his hands up.

"Come over here," Matt repeated, stepping out of the toilet stall and gesturing for Harry to walk into it. "Sit down."

"You want my wallet? Can't buy your own meth with your own money?"

"Sit down on the toilet," Matt said, backing up a few feet to keep Harry out of arm's length. Harry did what he was told.

"Why you want me on this?" asked Reuben, sitting down on the lidless toilet. "You got a piss fetish? You going to give me a golden shower?"

"I don't want to get any of your blood on my shoes when I walk out of here."

Now Harry looked scared.

"Take my wallet man. I didn't mean to insult you. Take my wallet and I'll throw in a free dinner, okay?"

"Do you recognize me?" asked Matt.

"No," said Harry. "Should I?"

"Eh. It doesn't really matter." Matt shot him through the face. Harry's skull and brain puffed out the back of his head. Matt's ears rang from the shot. It made him a little dizzy. The sound was bouncing around the tiled room. He opened the revolver's cylinder, and shook the five unused .38s and one spent casing into his hand, and tucked them into the pocket with the cigarette butts. He wiped the revolver down with his T-shirt, made sure there were no fingerprints in case he had to dump it fast, and walked casually out of the men's room.

It was dark outside, with no light between the orange bulb over the shower-house door and the glow of the food trucks a hundred yards away. Matt walked straight down the beach, into the water, and swam away from shore. After about twenty yards he rolled over onto his back, to look back at the beach and make sure no one had seen him. He couldn't see anyone on the beach and there didn't seem to be any commotion other than the festivities at the parking lot party. Matt floated for a minute, watching. It was peaceful, and the water was beautifully warm. In a few minutes, the guy in the Gator Trough would start to look for his friend. Matt swam farther out, then turned south toward Sunset Beach.

He was a good fifty, sixty yards from shore now, swimming parallel to the beachfront. When he guessed he was about halfway back to his car, he dumped the revolver, let it float down to the seabed beneath him. He took the unused bullets out of his pocket, wiped them on his shirt, one at a time, and tossed them into the sea. He took a few pebbles and stuffed them into the spent casing to weigh it down, wiped it off, and tossed it away too.

The current was with him and it only took about forty minutes to swim back to the beach nearest his car. No one was on it. He walked out of the water, shook himself off a little, wrung out his T-shirt, and walked back to the rented Toyota.

He climbed in and drove north toward Route 699, which would take him back to the mainland. As he rose up onto the humped bridge, a little fishing boat was passing under him, coming home for the night. He looked over his shoulder, back toward the St. Petersburg Municipal Beach parking lot. It was hidden by hotels, but the hotels were blinking red and blue and purple as police lights closed the roads.

Matt passed a couple police cars and an ambulance as he headed into St. Pete proper, then onto I-275 and across the bay into Tampa.

It was almost midnight. He'd hoped to make a stop in North Carolina on his way back—a visit to Darrel Clinton—but that would have to wait. I-275 turned north, and turned into I-75, and around two in the morning into I-95. Ninety-five would take him all the way home, as soon as he'd pulled over for some gas and coffee.

12

The Nazi Bob Wharton flew one-way to Los Angeles, took a cab to Union Station, and booked a roomette on Amtrak's Southwest Chief, which would pass through Arizona, New Mexico, Colorado, Kansas, Missouri, and Illinois on its way to Chicago. This was the route the Klimt drawings were going to take. Once they got to Chicago, they and their minders would switch to the Lake Shore Limited to New York. That was the plan filed with the insurance company, anyway. Wharton's plan had them getting off the train somewhere before Kansas. He wasn't sure exactly where yet. That's why he was riding the train.

For his roomette, Wharton had been picturing something along the lines of Eva Marie Saint's digs in *North by Northwest*. That had been aboard the 20th Century Limited, to Chicago, whose tradition Amtrak claimed to be carrying on. His roomette was, uh, much less nice. It had not been inspired by the 20th

Century Limited. It appeared to have been based on the economy bathrooms in a jetliner. It was about that size—smaller than the solitary cells at Ray Brook, actually—with a toilet beside a lounge seat, which folded flat into a single bed. He'd sort of been expecting the toilet to have its own room. The style of the plastic and metal fixtures really did make it look like it had been ripped from a Boeing. So did the switches and the little signs telling you what not to flush and where not to stand. So did the fold-down tray table.

On the other hand, the lounger was very comfortable. There was wood veneer here and there, which was nice. The floor was carpeted; being in prison had given Wharton a soft spot for carpets. And—the only important thing—the room gave him the privacy he needed. On the tray table, he laid a yellow legal pad, a pen, a pencil, and a super-accurate GPS tracker-odometer-speedometer he'd spent three thousand dollars on. Then he pulled out a big, floppy, highly detailed map of the western United States onto which he'd traced the Southwest Chief's route. He laid a finger on the starting point, just as the big diesel electric Viewliner train started to growl and roll forward toward the first of thirty-one station stops.

Wharton pulled out a thermos of coffee and sat back to enjoy the ride, which started out obnoxiously slow. Almost slow enough to test Wharton's unflappable, sociopathicly cool temperament. It took two more stops and about two hours just to get clear of Los Angeles. But, once they were clear, there were only two more population centers between Wharton and Kansas City: Flagstaff and Albuquerque. The ideal spot would be after Albuquerque, when the train turned north and cut through Colorado's southeast quarter. But Wharton would keep track of every usable spot on the route, just in case they weren't quite as common as he hoped.

What he needed was a place, clear of any towns, where the train came up to a curve, on more or less level ground. The train—he looked again at the speedometer—seemed to run mostly around eighty miles an hour. Approaching a curve, it had to slow down. How much it had to slow down depended on how sharp the curve was. What he needed was a curve sharp enough to get the train down under thirty miles an hour for at least two minutes.

He poured another cup of coffee, took out his aged iPod, and put on the Eagles album *Desperado*, starting with "Doolin-Dalton."

13

Somewhere in southern Virginia, Matt had to pull over and get a few hours' sleep. By the time he'd returned the car in Newark and got an Uber back to Kelly's apartment, it was around three a.m. again, and Kelly was about ready to pull her hair out. They had to leave for Islip Airport before seven. Simon's jet was meeting them there at ten. Matt pointed out that private planes don't leave without their passengers. Kelly didn't want to hear it. She told him to shower and shave and get ready. He shaved and took a bath, falling asleep in the tub.

Her banging on the door woke him up.

"*What the fuck is going on in there?*"

Matt yawned and pulled his eyes open.

"Sorry, sorry. I drifted off. Don't worry. Plenty of time."

"Jesus fucking Christ, Matt, would you please—"

"You can just open the door and come in," he said. "It's not locked."

Kelly opened the door and stood in the doorway. "Jesus fucking Christ, Matt, would you please take this a little more seriously. This is my life here, you know? This is my life we're talking about."

Matt climbed out of the tub and spread his arms.

"I'm clean. I'm shaved. Give me a toothbrush and I'm good to go."

"There's one in the cabinet over the sink."

"That's your toothbrush."

"Yeah."

"You don't have a spare?"

"What have you been using since you got here?"

"I bought a toothbrush the first morning."

"Where is it?"

"I threw it out, it smelled mildewy."

"So use mine."

"That's . . . yech. That's gross."

"What the fuck is wrong with you."

"Is this the dark ages? Sharing a toothbrush?"

"Three days ago your tongue was inside me. Inside my body. You know what else goes on down there?"

"That's fucking gross, Kelly."

"And you don't want to use my toothbrush? *Grow the fuck up. Brush your teeth before I stab you with a makeup pencil. And then get the fuck out here.*" She slammed the door, and shouted through it, "*Hurry the fuck up!*"

Matt laughed. After all these years she was still crazily high strung. It was kind of a turn-on. He wondered how she'd react to his taking a couple minutes to rub one out. He shook his head and squeezed some toothpaste from the middle of the tube.

◈

Five minutes later, after a careful flossing, Matt emerged and Kelly had calmed down a little. What was he in such a good mood about? He hadn't been playful with her once, not since the moment she'd met him at Ray Brook. He'd been either quiet or testy the whole time. Maybe he was just excited for the private plane deluxe vacation thing. He seemed like a different guy today. She liked it. But not when she was in a rush. He could be happy once they were on the plane.

"Here," she said, as he moved to turn on the fan. "No, no cigarettes right now." She picked up a suit bag and tossed it to him. "I bought that for you yesterday."

He caught the bag and looked at it.

"This is a 'suit' kind of trip?"

"Matt, are you kidding me? Come on." She pressed her fingers into her temples and exhaled. "Yes, it is. I was going to take you to get one tailored but you disappeared to Georgia. Did you have a good time by the way? I was too stressed to ask when you came in, sorry. Rude."

"Yeah, I had a good time. And don't worry about it." He unzipped the bag and pulled out the black suit inside.

"Black for Qatar? I hope this guy's got AC. And umbrellas."

"Oh shit," said Kelly. "Was that stupid?"

"No, no," said Matt. "It's fine, I'm just kidding." Was he comforting her? So he still had a little empathy banging around in there, then, thought Kelly. The thought made her want to smile.

"Tom Ford," read Matt, holding the brand label. "Is that fancy?"

"Very," said Kelly. "But this is a fancy situation."

"Then I will fancy myself up," said Matt.

"Thank you."

"I will put my fancy foot forward." Who was this person? Kelly asked herself, and smiled.

"Just put on the suit," said Kelly. "Okay? Tick tock."

"For sure," said Matt, pulling out one of two white dress shirts that were hung with the jacket and starting to slip it on.

Kelly watched him dress until she realized she probably shouldn't and went to sit at her desk.

"By the way," she said, trying to sound casual. "Do you have a gun?"

She knew that he did. She'd given him a drawer in her dresser that locked, to keep his things in, and given him what she said was the only key. When he left, she went through his stuff. She'd found a gun barrel inside the empty shell of an electric razor and, after considerable searching, she'd found most of the rest of it submerged in a bottle of shampoo.

Matt looked at Kelly for a few long seconds. "Yeah, I have a gun." He looked down at the shirt and continued to button. "Why do you ask?"

"Well, since you're going to be sort of a bodyguard, I just thought it would be good. Help you play the part." At first she'd been scared to have it in her house, then relieved he'd have it to bring along, and then later, as she fell asleep, a little aroused thinking about it hiding in her bureau. The next day when she'd bought him the suit, she'd visited a high-end pop-up costume shop; it was only a month till Halloween.

"I thought maybe you'd want this? I hope it fits." She tossed him a heavy-plastic shopping bag. He reached into it and pulled out a shoulder holster. Kelly had a bit of a James Bond fetish. She was willing to bet Matt had one too. She hadn't known too many men who didn't.

"Are we going to be going through security anywhere? Customs?"

Kelly shook her head. "Our host tells me he's got an arrangement with the customs people. They don't search his plane, and a few times a year he lets them confiscate some cash and Rolexes."

Matt nodded. He was in the white shirt, black pants, and bare feet. He slipped on the shoulder holster, which was like one he'd worn in Iraq, but elastic instead of leather, and actually a little less uncomfortable. In Iraq he'd worn one because the new all-encompassing flak vests had made wearing a regular holster inconvenient—and because, like smoking, shoulder holsters are cool. He turned and looked at himself in the full-length mirror on Kelly's bathroom door. He looked good.

Kelly thought so, anyway. "I got you some shoes also. Hold on. And socks." She dug through a pile of stuff on her couch and pulled out three shoe boxes and a cardboard sock envelope. Matt was opening his locked dresser drawer and removing the various pieces of the Sig Sauer automatic from their hiding spots. Kelly laid out the shoe boxes on her bed while Matt rinsed the shampoo out of his slide and zipper mag. She watched him reassemble the gun, absentmindedly picking lint off the lining of the Tom Ford jacket as she did.

"Shouldn't you get ready?" asked Matt, looking at her looking absentmindedly at him.

She shook her head. "I don't like to suit up for a long flight any sooner than I absolutely have to. That way I don't get frumpled."

"Frumpled?"

"It's a word," said Kelly. "It means what it sounds like."

"So why am I suiting up then? We've still got at least a couple hours."

"I needed to make sure the suit fit. I've got two others from Nordstrom as backups. I had to guess your measurements. Obviously."

"Fair enough," said Matt, putting the gun in his holster and giving Kelly a small thrill. He wasn't James Bond handsome—his chin was a little too weak and his nose was a little too big—but it was close enough. He wasn't *un*handsome, she supposed. He looked a little like Nick Foles, that backup quarterback guy who'd come out of nowhere to take the Eagles to the Super Bowl.

Now he was putting on socks and the correct size of shoe. Black oxfords. He stood up and put on the jacket. It wasn't quite a perfect fit, but it was a good fit and he looked good in it. *Focus, woman.*

Matt, meanwhile, felt that he looked good and also a little stupid. Like he was Kelly's dress-up doll. The purse holder of the smart and successful lady on the red carpet whose husband obviously isn't good enough to be there with her. But having the gun helped. He patted it under the jacket.

Kelly smiled at him. "Chic as hell."

"Thanks," he said. "Thanks for the suit. Is it a rental?"

"No," she said, frowning.

"Good. I won't worry about deodorant then." He winked at her and she smiled again.

"Okay," she said, climbing off the bed. "Now me."

◆

Matt packed a small carry-on that Kelly furnished and then napped out the rest of Kelly's travel prep. When she woke him up to go, smoothing out the new creases in his shirt and hurrying him toward the door, he had to remind himself that he'd concluded, absolutely, that he was not in love with her anymore—not since he finally gave up writing her letters, which she'd never answered. But, goddamn it, she looked gorgeous. She was thirty-six and more beautiful than she'd been at eighteen. Maybe all the art-world stuff had rubbed off on her. She was just so . . . cool. It drove him crazy how cool she looked. Her hair was pulled tight in a ponytail that started at the crown of her head and went up a little before draping down. She was wearing a ladies' suit in a darkish red color. Matt didn't know the word. Brighter red moleskin-ey heels that zipped up on the side and covered her whole foot, like little boots. Pale bluish green shirt. Yellow-rimmed circular sunglasses. The thought popped into his head that, really, she looked like a sexy box of crayons.

She handed him the jacket she'd made him remove before lying down and brushed him off. He put the pistol in the shoulder holster. He didn't have a spare magazine but he had the box of .45s in his carry-on, if he needed them, though he couldn't imagine he would. He'd actually been to Qatar once before, in 2011, when he was in the army, when a few weeks of R&R had happened to coincide with the Pan Arab Games. He and a few of his squadmates had caught a commercial flight from Baghdad to Doha and lived it up for a few days. The games were great. They'd mainly gone out for the sports you don't get on TV: squash, wrestling, fencing, archery, judo, tae kwon do, karate. Boxing, too, and they'd even watched some chess.

Matt liked Arabs. He hadn't really had any opinion about them one way or another until he'd joined the army. When he'd been in basic training, he'd assumed he'd hate them because they'd hate him. But an interesting thing had happened when he'd started going out on patrols in Baghdad. Everywhere he went, people would offer him drinks to cool off. Bottles of Coke or water from their shops, or freshly brewed mint tea, hibiscus tea, cinnamon tea. Arabs make wonderful tea, and wonderful coffee. People would invite passing soldiers to weddings—not so much because they wanted the soldiers there, but because it was courteous and hospitable, and hospitality seemed to be the essence of good manners in Iraq. And Matt, as a good southern boy, had the utmost respect for good manners. Arab hospitality had been the rule in Qatar too. Every sporting event seemed to end with an invitation to someone's house or someone's restaurant, for daqoos and hisso spiced stuff and lots of seafood and lamb and rice. No booze, but that didn't stop people from dancing. Matt was glad to be going back.

"Where are we going to stop for gas?" asked Matt, as they closed in on the airport. MacArthur Airport, formerly Islip, roughly dead center of Long Island, for small commercial planes and big and small private ones.

"What do you mean?" said Kelly. They were in a cab. Cabs generally provide their own gas.

"Where is the plane going to refuel? It's like seven thousand miles to Qatar."

"It's nonstop." She was looking at a map on her phone. "Follow the signs to the private departure lot, please." That to the cabdriver.

"Bullshit," said Matt.

"No, really. It's a nonstop flight."

"A private jet?"

"There it is." She showed him a picture of the plane on her phone; Simon had emailed her a picture so she knew what she was looking for. "There it is," she added to the cabdriver, pointing to the service road that carried people up to their jets.

And there it was, waiting for them, with some kind of hostess at the bottom of some stairs rolled up to its open door. It was a long, tubular two-engine jet, with swept wings and . . . fourteen windows, not counting the cockpit. Matt figured it was about a hundred feet long.

Kelly paid the cabdriver and then counted out two hundred dollars in twenties and handed them to Matt.

"So you don't get embarrassed by me having to pay for everything." Matt's face reddened and he stuck the money in his pocket. Kelly was already climbing out. "Is it real?" he asked to her backside.

Kelly's head spun around and she gave him a death glare. "Yes."

The cabbie took their bags out of the trunk and Matt carried both of them over to the plane. They had wheels, but Matt carried them anyway. The hostess at the foot of the stairs was wearing a white-and-black stewardess ensemble.

"Welcome, welcome," she said, in a wonderfully cosmopolitan English-Arabic accent. "Ms. Somerset? Mr. Fisher?"

"Yes," said Kelly, remembering that she'd forgotten to tell Matt what his alias was. She hoped he'd just roll with it. "Thank you. I hope we haven't kept you waiting."

"Not at all, Ms. Somerset. We are at your disposal as soon as you are ready to depart."

"We're ready," said Kelly, walking up the stairs.

"What kind of plane is this?" said Matt, who was following Kelly, to the hostess, who was following him.

"This is a Bombardier seventy-five hundred, sir. May I take your bags?"

"No thanks, I've got them. What's the range? If you don't mind me asking."

"Not at all, Mr. Fisher. The range is seven thousand, seven hundred nautical miles, at a cruising speed of point-nine-two-five Mach."

"Jesus Christ, this thing must have cost a mint," said Matt, and then, "Sorry. Excuse me."

"Not at all, sir." Matt followed Kelly into the plane. Directly across from the entrance door were two full-size ovens.

"This thing has a kitchen?"

"Yes, sir," said the hostess.

"Hey," said Kelly, to Matt, quietly. "Chill."

Matt nodded.

"May I show you around?" asked the hostess.

"Please do," said Kelly.

The hostess squeezed around Matt, and then Kelly, and walked toward the back of the plane. The cabin was large enough for Matt to stand up straight. Just. Kelly, in her heels and vertical ponytail, had to stoop.

"This is the main space, the conference area and the dining area." It was about twenty-five, thirty feet long with a scattering of plush white recliners and coffee tables.

"Beyond, we enter the lounge suite"—a sofa on the right and a big-screen TV on the left. "The couch is a bed as well, which, if you like, I can make up for you any time you choose. And then the bedroom suite."

She stepped through another doorway: a full-size bed on the right, a dresser on the left, and another big TV at the foot of the bed. At the far end was another doorway.

"That is your en suite."

"Hmm?" said Matt.

"Bathroom," said Kelly.

"And there is another at the front of the plane, in the crew suite," said the hostess. "May I bring you something to drink?"

"Thanks," said Kelly. "White wine?" The hostess nodded.

"Milk?" said Matt.

"Certainly, sir. Ma'am. I will be back momentarily."

Matt opened the door to the bathroom. "Holy shit, there's a shower in here."

"Oh, yeah?" Kelly plopped down onto the bed.

"You don't look impressed," said Matt closing the bathroom door and looking out the bedroom windows.

"I'm anxious."

"Don't be," said Matt. "It's going to go fine."

"Yeah, well, I wish I had some way of knowing that. You saying it doesn't really help that much. You don't know."

"True," said Matt. "I don't."

"Your drinks, Ms. Somerset, Mr. Fisher," said the hostess, returning with the wine and milk on a small silver tray. "And the pilot wonders if you're ready to depart."

"We are," said Kelly.

"Very good, ma'am. Traffic is light so we should be off the ground in between five and fifteen minutes. Our scheduled flight time is ten hours. We will be passing over New Brunswick and Newfoundland, Ireland, Great Britain, the Netherlands, Germany, the Czech Republic, Slovakia, Hungary, Romania, Turkey, and Iraq."

"Is that safe," said Kelly, absently. She still had her sunglasses on and sounded more tired than curious.

"Yes, ma'am, it is."

The hostess seemed to be waiting for Kelly's permission to continue. Kelly nodded to her.

"Depending on whether you wish to stay on American East Coast time until you land, or wish to switch to Qatari time now, or anything in between, we are prepared to serve breakfast, lunch, or dinner at any time. For dinner, we ask only for an hour's notice."

"Why don't you just bring us breakfast every time we cross into a new time zone?" said Matt. It was supposed to be a joke. No one seemed to get it.

"We'll let you know about the meals," said Kelly. "Do you mind if we hole up back here for a while?"

"Not at all, Ms. Somerset. Would you like me to unpack your bags for you?"

"No thanks," said Matt.

"Then I will close the door between the lounge and the conference area on my way out," said the hostess, backing out of the bedroom.

Matt took a sip of his milk.

When the lounge door was shut, Kelly shut the bedroom door, too, and Matt said, "Do you think, when we land, I should give her a tip?"

Kelly sighed and replopped onto the bed.

"Your name is James Fisher, by the way."

"Jim Fisher? Jimmy?"

"Whatever you want," said Kelly, then with a note of apprehension, "You don't think they're listening to us, do you?"

"I don't see why they would be."

"Yeah," said Kelly. "Yeah, I suppose you're right."

"You look like a sexy box of crayons."

"I'm not in the mood, Matt."

"I'm not hitting on you. It's just been on my mind since we left."

"I didn't sleep last night. I think I'm going to take a nap," She was about two-thirds done with her white wine.

"Yeah, me neither. Or, I mean, me too. You want me to use the couch?"

"No, you can stay here." She took off her jacket. "Could you hang that up?"

"Is there a closet?"

"I think it's behind the TV." Matt pulled on the TV. The panel behind it opened up.

"Hey," he said. "How 'bout that. How'd you know that was there?"

"Just a guess," said Kelly. Matt hung up her jacket, then his own jacket, the holster, and his not-too-wrinkled white shirt. Kelly was lying pencil straight on the bed, looking at the arched ceiling.

A voice came over a PA system. "This, uhhhh, is your pilot, Captain Anholt." He was doing the airline pilot voice, but with a Dutch accent. "We'll, uhhhh, be taking off, uhhhhh, in about two minutes. Please take a seat and buckle up."

"Why do they all talk like that?" said Matt, climbing onto the bed between Kelly and the windows.

"'Cause it's how Chuck Yeager talked. It just became a thing."

"Really?"

"Really."

"How'd you know that?"

"I don't know. Someone told me." She rolled over on her left side. "You can spoon me, but don't poke me with anything."

"Yes, ma'am," said Matt, looking down at Kelly's feet.

"You wanna take off your shoes?" He had kicked his own onto the floor.

"No, I'm okay," said Kelly, shimmying back into him and then reaching for the light switch above the headboard. The lights went off. The cabin was lit brightly by the windows.

"You want me to close the drapes?"

"Uh-huh," said Kelly. Matt looked around for the right button. A minute later, the room was dark except for the emergency exit light.

14

There was an old, disused airstrip about an hour northeast of the Fotheringay Ranch, in a high valley that was sort of triangular. Surrounded on all three sides by mountain peaks, grassy, green, and peaceful, with one dirt access road that connected it, eventually, to the town of Emigrant, Montana—population 300, more or less. The airstrip was built for crop dusters, who didn't use it anymore. Sometime in the 1980s, the landing strip had been lengthened so it could serve as an emergency landing spot for planes coming into Bozeman Yellowstone International, though none had ever used it. Forest-fire planes dropped in once in a while but not in the fall. All told, the place probably didn't see more than half a dozen planes a year.

But the long landing strip made it a good place for Bob Wharton and the Fotheringay boys to practice.

Amtrak security isn't too substantial, certainly nothing like airports. After all, you can't hijack a train and crash it into a building. Even so, it hadn't taken Wharton long to work out that all the stations had security cameras, that buying a ticket required a government-issued ID, and that conductors checked IDs along with tickets on a random pattern. So if you wanted to get on and off and be certain that no one knew who you were, you'd have to do it between stations.

When the Southwest Chief made its stops—always for at least ten or fifteen minutes—people got on and people got off. A few of the people getting off had reached their destinations but mostly they were people who needed a smoke. There were always a few dozen smokers wandering the platform, sharing lighters, and chatting. The chatting seemed to intensify at the late-night stops. For some reason, smoking at two a.m. makes everyone friends, even people who'd ignored each other during the day. Wharton figured there must be something foxhole-ish about fixing your nicotine in the middle of the night in the middle of nowhere.

Anyway, even with the chatters, it wasn't hard to slip away from the crowd to the dark side of the train and take some measurements of the big diesel electric engine at its front. Luckily, the Southwest Chief still used Dash 8 trains, which had catwalks on either side, unlike the more streamlined Genesis trains they were using east of Chicago, where the tunnels were narrower. Wharton measured the catwalks' length and width: how high off the ground they were; the height of the railing and where the balusters were; the length and width and height of the access ladders and stairs. He was even able to get close enough to check if the doors to the engineer's cab had locks or latches. There were locks, small cylinder locks. He climbed down from the engine and walked up the track a ways, then into the bushes, where he took a piss, and walked back onto the platform zipping his fly in case anyone wondered where he'd been.

When he'd gotten back to Montana he'd bought an old bus—an old school bus, actually, yellow and everything. The Fotheringay boys got to work welding a steel-tube duplicate of the Dash 8 catwalk along the bus's left side. They had to shorten it front to back a little, relative to the real thing, just because the bus was about fifteen feet shorter than the train engine. But the important dimensions were all correct. It took about a week to get it on and strong enough for their purposes, and then they started practicing.

Of course, when they did this for real, they'd be working at night at about thirty miles an hour. But they started off in the daytime, going around ten. Wharton was at the wheel. He'd back the bus up as far as it would go, onto one of the big yellow Xs painted on either end of the runway to show it wasn't maintained anymore. And then he'd drive as steadily as he could to the other end, watching in the wing mirrors as the Fotheringays rode up and alongside. Right now, Wharton was driving because they needed a driver. Of course, when they did it for real, he'd have to be with them to gather up the string of horses and lead them away from the train. He was too old to jump.

Though they wouldn't actually be jumping. Right now, they were just getting the horses used to being next to something big and fast-moving. And when they actually jumped, they'd be grabbing the rail and pulling themselves up so they still wouldn't actually be jumping. But Wharton was still too old.

They spent all day, until the horses were tired out, gradually increasing the speed, gently urging the horses closer and closer, rewarding them with sugar and apples as their work improved. One horse just wouldn't do it, so they swapped him out for one of the spares they'd brought along. By the time the sun was setting, they were close enough for the boys to reach out and touch the catwalk. But by then the horses were knackered and, anyway, unprepared for night work. They called it a day and slept in the bus. They each took a two-hour shift keeping the horses safe from wolves and bears.

The next morning, Caleb decided he'd be the first to try the horse-to-catwalk transfer. Joel drove the bus, so Wharton could watch from the outside. He kept it at a steady five miles an hour, which was lucky. Caleb's hands slipped as he tried to pull himself aboard and, if the bus had been going any faster, it would've run him over before he'd had time to snap to his senses and roll out of the way.

He tried again, with gloves (he hadn't wanted to use the gloves, so he'd be able to use his gun if he had to). Joel was driving again, keeping it at five; Caleb grabbed on to the rear access stairs' railing and pulled up, off his horse, and onto the steps. He climbed them, and then, half-crouched, he walked forward along the bus and up the stairs to the imaginary engineer's cab and mimed kicking its door open. Frank shouted and cheered and Wharton whistled with two fingers in his mouth. Caleb's horse was confused. After half a minute of following the bus, twisting its head up at Caleb, it peeled off and circled back to where the other horses were waiting with Wharton and Frank.

Frank went next, with gloves, and this time Wharton rode alongside him, leading his horse away after he'd climbed off.

By the end of the day all three Fotheringay boys had made the transfer and they'd sped it up to ten mph.

15

There was a gentle but persistent knocking on the door to the sleeping cabin. "Ms. Somerset? Mr. Fisher?"

It took Kelly a moment to remember where she was. Beside her, Matt was softly snoring.

"Ms. Somerset? Mr. Fisher?"

"Yes?" said Kelly.

From the other side of the closed door: "We will shortly enter our landing pattern and should be on the ground in forty-five minutes to an hour. Could I perhaps get you some breakfast?"

Kelly poked Matt. "Yes," said Kelly. "Breakfast would be lovely, thank you. We'll come out and eat it in the main cabin."

Matt yawned and rubbed his eyes.

"Would you like to see a menu of what we have?" asked the hostess.

"Eggs and bacon?" asked Kelly.

"No bacon, Ms. Somerset, I'm afraid."

"Oh," said Kelly. "Right. Well, scrambled eggs, then."

"Very good, Ms. Somerset."

"You got cereal?" said Matt, who had hit the switch to raise the shades. It was dark outside.

"Yes, Mr. Fisher. Hot or cold?"

"Cold, thanks."

"Very good, sir."

"What time is it, local?" asked Matt

The hostess's voice was a little farther away now. "Ten minutes to eleven in the evening, Mr. Fisher."

"Thanks," said Matt. He looked at Kelly, who was still lying down. "I'm going to take a quick shower."

"We're landing. Why don't you shower at the guy's house? It'll be palatial."

"'Cause I have the feeling that this'll probably be the only chance I ever have to shower on an airplane."

"We're going back on the same plane, you know."

Matt was massaging a knot out of his shoulder. "Okay. Well, I hadn't thought of that."

"Put your shirt on and come have some breakfast."

"Very good, *Ms.* Somerset," said Matt. "By the way, what's your first name?"

"Kelly."

"I mean your fake first name."

"It's Kelly Somerset. I thought it'd be too confusing to use a fake one."

"Why did I get a fake one then?"

"Because no one's going to call you by your first name. They're much too polite for that. But me and Simon are already on a first-name basis."

"Okay," said Matt, picking up his shoes. "If you say so."

◆

Kelly had two eggs and Matt had three or four hundred Cheerios and then they were on the ground in Qatar, which is about the size and shape of Puerto Rico but rotated ninety degrees, and it's a peninsula instead of an island. They were at Hamad International Airport, which is just east of Doha, right in the middle of Qatar's east coast. The flight crew bid them farewell at the cockpit door and the hostess led them out of the plane, down the stairs, and into a waiting Bentley.

The Bentley's chauffeur took their bags and loaded them into the trunk, which he closed with a button press and a quiet hydraulic hiss. The chauffeur was wearing a black-and-white uniform that seemed to match the air hostess's outfit. Matt wondered if it was Simon Abbas's livery, like a stable owner had for his jockeys. Or maybe the clothing's cut and color were what all servants of the superrich wore. Matt shrugged inwardly.

"Ms. Somerset, Mr. Fisher," said the chauffeur, once Kelly and Matt had climbed into the backseat and he'd closed the Bentley's big, thick, totally soundproof doors. "It is my pleasure to drive you this evening. Mr. Abbas asked me to show you a small number of Doha's artistic landmarks, which he believed would edify Ms. Somerset, if you were not too tired from the flight."

Kelly looked at Matt. Matt shrugged.

"Yes, thanks," said Kelly. "We'd appreciate that."

"Very good, Ms. Somerset." The chauffeur put the car in drive and rolled it two hundred yards forward to a side entrance of the main terminal. "This is Terminal 1. Inside there is one of Qatar's many civic art works, *Lamp Bear*, by Urs Fischer. A relation of yours, perhaps, Mr. Fischer?"

"I saw *Lamp Bear* when it was at the Seagram building in Manhattan, so we'll skip it, if you don't mind."

"Of course, Ms. Somerset," said the chauffeur, pulling the Bentley away from the curb and back into the late-evening trickle of traffic, mostly cabs and limos collecting people from the arrivals annex.

"What's *Lamp Bear*?" said Matt, to Kelly. Kelly answered in a low voice.

"It's a three-story-tall bronze teddy bear painted yellow with a lamp on its head."

"Well, that sounds . . . kinda interesting."

"It's hideous. I hate Urs Fischer. You are *not* related to him." Matt chuckled.

The Bentley merged onto a highway, then sped past a desert neighborhood on the outskirts of Doha, backlit by the city center close behind it. From the look of it, the airport was only five or six miles from downtown. Nondescript concrete apartment blocks separated by sandy alleys gave way to luxury apartment buildings surrounded by lush, green parks. Everything was lit up by rather chic streetlights—"These lamps were designed by the prominent Barcelona architect Beth Galí. There are one thousand of them," said the chauffeur, unprompted.

"Beth Galí," said Matt. "Sounds Israeli."

"No," said the chauffeur. "She is from Barcelona. On our left now we are approaching the National Museum of Qatar, designed by Jean Nouvel."

"Wow," said Kelly, earnestly. It was a giant, sprawling structure that seemed to be made up of a hundred flat discs that intersected one another at random angles. "It's wonderful. Beautiful."

"Thank you, Ms. Somerset."

"It looks like a giant busboy tripped and dropped a tray full of giant dinner plates," said Matt. Kelly ignored him. So did the chauffeur.

"Now, on the right, this is the Museum of Islamic Art, designed by I. M. Pei."

"I love Pei," said Kelly. "This is beautiful." The museum was all hard angles and looked something like a sand-colored stone stack of giant packages from a day of shopping on Fifth Avenue. Big clothing boxes on the bottom, smaller shoe boxes giving way to a Tiffany ring box—a cube—at the very top. "I love it," said Kelly.

"Who's I Am Pei? Is he related to the Black-Eyed Peas guy?" Kelly shook her head. Matt was getting tiresome.

"Here we will pull up in Dafna Park," said the chauffeur. "Which will give you a view of the skyscraper district."

It was a park of rolling, grassy hills along Qatar's crescent-shaped waterfront. To the east was the Persian Gulf. To the west was an immense line of immense skyscrapers in exotic shapes. Modernist, undulating shapes like giant hand-blown glass vases, others sharp and jagged, like cave crystals. One was . . . well, it was a little suggestive in its shape. A giant, slightly bulging cylinder with a rounded top. Being lit up in an orangey flesh tone didn't help. Many of the buildings were lit up by millions of LED bulbs. The orange tower was flanked by two in blue and one in purple. On the other side was a smaller, squatter building lit up in green and another in yellow. The chauffeur ran through their names—the Aspire Tower, Palm Towers 1 and 2, the World Trade Center of Doha, the Al Faisal Tower, the Doha Tower (that was the big phallus). Kelly was thoroughly impressed. She took ten minutes to admire the architecture and breathe the clean air blowing in from the sea—it was warm, hot actually—a breeze in the high eighties, but after a day of endlessly recycled airplane air it was deeply refreshing. Matt smoked a cigarette and offered one to the chauffeur, who politely declined.

When they got back in the car, Kelly opened her window; the fresh air seemed to take the edge off her nerves. Matt opened his window to stop the helicopter-chopping sound of a single open window in a fast-moving car. The Bentley was back on the highway, moving west through the city center; Kelly had told the chauffeur she didn't want to keep Mr. Abbas waiting any longer. The chic skyscrapers gradually gave way to shorter, unremarkable office buildings, and then to monotonous cement apartment blocks like the ones near the airport. The city gave way to desert and then to an upscale suburb of walled compounds dotting a sandy Arabian hillscape.

"This is Al Rayyan neighborhood," said the chauffeur, "where Mr. Abbas's residence is located." They'd driven twenty minutes west from the sea and the skyscrapers. "And now we are here at the residence." The Bentley turned off a perfectly paved, perfectly smooth suburban street, up a short driveway, and through a tasteful and traditionally Arab peaked gate in a twenty-foot limestone wall.

Inside the gate, everything was green and lush: golf-course-quality lawns studded with palm trees and waist-high flowering shrubs, and a geometric network of narrow canals—about kayak-width, in the sort of elegant, recursive pattern that the Muslim world does so well. The sort you find on the floors and walls of mosques lined with white marble. Kelly was willing to bet that, besides irrigating everything, they had koi in them. She would check when she had the chance.

The Bentley seemed at first to be driving across the lawn. It took Kelly a moment to realize it was a grass-covered driveway of little concrete cubes. The Bentley drove toward a wide, two-story mansion. There was a two-story entrance door made of what appeared to be ebony in the white limestone facade, the same shape as the entrance gate. It opened in the middle and was opened wide. A man was standing in it—black and gray hair, tanned and clean-shaven, in a fashionable blue suit, with his arms opened wide.

"That's Simon," said Kelly. "Simon Abbas."

"And I'm Jim Fisher."

Kelly ignored him and climbed out of the car.

"Simon!" she said.

"Welcome!" said Simon at the same time. They both laughed. "It's good to see you," he said, stepping toward the car. Two servants had appeared from nowhere—in black-and-white livery—and were taking Matt's and Kelly's bags out of the trunk and into the house.

He and Kelly hugged, kissed each other on each cheek, and he said, "Come in, come in," then, turning to Matt: "You must be Mr. Fisher. Friend and security?" He stuck out his hand and Matt shook it.

"Yup, James T. Fisher. T for Tiberius. Please call me Jim." Kelly glared at him; Simon laughed.

"Well, Jim T. Fisher, you're very welcome. Please come in." He took Kelly by the arm and walked her into his house. Matt followed.

"Simon," said Kelly, "thank you so much for having your chauffeur tour us around, it was wonderful! I had no idea you lived in such a beautiful city."

"Well, we're very fortunate that our royal family loves art. And that its traditional one-upmanship battle with the Emiratis has led to a sort of arms race in architecture." Simon's foyer was all white limestone and marble and beautiful oriental rugs. "I don't want to tire you out. We'll talk business tomorrow," said Simon, "but the real question is, do you want to go straight to your rooms and rest or would you like a quick look at my collection first?"

"Oh," said Kelly, "definitely the collection."

"Good!" said Simon. "I was hoping you'd say that. Come along." Still holding Kelly's arm, he led them out the back of the foyer into a hallway and then into a large octagonal room.

"The windows on the back wall are Tiffany," said Simon. They were stained glass, in green and turquoise and yellow. "The chandelier"—which was all glass and looked like a confused coral growth, in coral red—"is a Chihuly. The statue under it"—a freestanding blue and green mobile—"is a Calder."

Matt nodded his head. He recognized the name Tiffany, though he didn't know they made windows. Kelly was looking at the navy blue walls. A Rothko, a Pollock, two de Koonings, two Hans Hofmanns. A Jasper Johns.

"Is that a Singer Sargent?" she asked.

"Yes!" said Simon. "My dear, you have such a wonderful eye. Can you do the others?"

"Well," she said, "the abstracts are easy. And the Picasso." It was a little Picasso, and an ugly one. "But I think . . . Manet? Degas, Renoir. The drawing . . ." She stepped forward and squinted at a sketch of a woman masturbating. Matt was looking at it too, appalled. "Schiele?"

"Yes!" said Simon. "Yes, yes, yes, and yes. Your score is perfect. But the last few, they are hard."

"Dufy," said Kelly.

"Yes!"

"Kees van Dongen," said Kelly.

Simon clapped his hands together; his face was pure excitement. "Yes!"

Kelly looked at the last painting, having started clockwise from the left of the door they came in by. She sucked her teeth and shook her head.

"Aha," said Simon. "You're stumped?"

"Derain?" said Kelly.

"Aw," said Simon. "Vlaminck. Close though. And very good. Very impressive. You have really a wonderful eye."

"I have just been on a ten-hour flight, you know," she said, smiling.

"Come, come," said Simon. "No sour grapes. And you notice, there's still some space on my walls, ey?" He smiled and looked at his watch. "My friends, I must be on a business call shortly, and then to bed. Stay and look for a while and, when you're tired, you'll be shown to your rooms. Ask for anything you need. I'll see you at breakfast. And I'll show you the rest of my collection afterward.

Some of the best work is scattered elsewhere around the house. Mr. Fisher, you were a soldier?"

Kelly tightened up. How did he know that? Maybe because he was her bodyguard. Who but ex-soldiers and ex-cops become bodyguards?

"I was, yes," said Matt.

"Yes, I thought so," said Simon. "You carry yourself like a soldier. You will enjoy my antiquity collection, I think. Soldiers love loot, ey? I'm excited to show it to you. Now, adieu!" He clapped his hands again, rubbed them together, and then left the room by the door they'd come in through.

"Are these good?" said Matt, waving around at the art.

"Yeah, yeah," said Kelly, looking at one of the de Koonings. "Outside of New York, Boston, Chicago, LA, Philly, and Washington, this would probably be the best collection in any city in the United States."

"Better than the place in Atlanta?"

"Well, the place in Atlanta has some Renaissance stuff, and Baroque stuff, which is a lot rarer, and technically more valuable. But this is very good. Let's say this would be the best permanent collection of any museum in Scandinavia."

"They don't have good museums in Scandinavia?"

"Not really."

"Why not?"

"No one knows."

Matt shrugged. "I know we just slept for eight hours but I honestly can't keep my eyes open. Are you planning to browse long?"

"No, not long. I'm tired too." She was looking at the other de Kooning now.

"What's the big glass thing? The chandelier."

"It's a Chihuly. He's a glass artist."

Matt nodded and looked at it seriously for about a minute.

"I'm not going to lie to you, Kelly," he said, with his arms crossed. "I kind of want to throw something at it."

Kelly looked over her shoulder at him. "Why?"

"I do not know."

Kelly smiled and shook her head.

"I guess it makes me think of a big glass piñata," said Matt.

"I get that," said Kelly. "But please don't."

"Is Chihuly a big deal?"

"Yeah, for a living artist, definitely."

"He's alive?"

"I think so."

"Huh," said Matt. He was still looking at the big glass coral thing.

"What, don't you like it?"

"I do like it," said Matt. "I like it a lot. It's the first art that's ever given me an emotional reaction."

"What emotion?" asked Kelly, looking at him like she'd look at a puppy.

"That I kind of want to throw something at it."

Kelly laughed.

"No," said Matt, "but I do like it. It's kind of beautiful, isn't it?"

"Yes," she said. Matt looked at it for another minute or so.

"Okay," he said. "I'm going to bed."

"Okay," said Kelly. "I'll see you in the morning."

Matt walked toward the door Abbas had exited through, where a servant was now standing. The servant bowed at the waist. Matt wasn't used to being waited on and instinctively bowed back.

"Wait," said Kelly, with a final look around the gallery. "I'll come with you."

The servant showed them to a grand, ultra-modern (but with Arab-style influences) staircase to the second floor, a gradual 360-degree loop with no railings. Kelly thought it was beautiful; Matt liked that is had no railings, though he wasn't quite sure *why* he liked that it had no railings. Maybe because people are getting soft and railings discourage natural selection. Anyway, the servant showed them to a guest suite, with a master bedroom for Kelly and a servant's bedroom for Matt. Their bags had been unpacked, their clothes pressed and put into bureaus and closets. The decor was butterfly-themed: chromolithographs of butterflies and a central cage with some iridescent blue ones flying around in it. There was also a wet bar, which—to Matt's surprise—had alcohol in it.

"You want a drink?" he asked Kelly once the butler had departed. Kelly was looking at his bedroom.

"This is a little dingy," she said. "Simon must not think much of his guests' employees."

Matt poured himself a glass of spiced rum and followed Kelly into his room.

"Oh, it's not bad. It's like a hotel room. A nice hotel room." It was a little small but done in the same style as the rest of the suite, with a Juliet balcony and a bathroom.

"It's smaller than the bedroom on the airplane."

"This is awful," said Matt, tasting the rum. "Why did I choose rum?"

"You can stay in my room if you want," said Kelly.

"Thanks," said Matt. Was she still trying to butter him up so he'd do what she wanted? He was already here, wasn't he?

Kelly walked across the suite to the master bedroom. Her heart was beating out of her chest; she hoped her voice hadn't cracked while she'd been talking to Simon. The things the DEA agent had told her about Hezbollah had scared the living daylights out of her. The weekly check-ins with him kept her frightened. She was a good liar but she wasn't used to lying to people who had a reason to be suspicious. And who might kill her if they found out the truth.

She was glad Matt was with her. She wanted to ask him to make sure he kept his gun handy but she also didn't want him to suspect she hadn't been totally forthright with him, that there was a second layer of deception going on. She sighed deeply.

"What's wrong?" asked Matt, who'd followed her into her room.

"I'm tired," said Kelly. "And stressed. Do you think your guys are going to be able to pull this off? I'm fucked if we don't get those Klimt drawings."

"I think they'll be fine," said Matt, who was undressing and walking into Kelly's giant en suite, all marble with a big marble tub that he began to fill. "We'll hear about it soon enough. One way or another I'm sure it'll be in the papers."

16

The next morning, Kelly and Matt went down to breakfast together. Simon had already eaten but was waiting for them, reading through a stack of newspapers and sipping thick coffee.

"Good morning, good morning," said Simon, looking up and setting down his coffee cup. "What do you want for breakfast? Tell him." He pointed over his shoulder to a white-aproned servant, who was standing at the far end of the giant-umbrella-shaded courtyard where Simon apparently breakfasted.

"No bacon, I suppose," said Kelly, smiling and taking a seat by Simon at the big oval breakfast table.

"I'm afraid not," said Simon, smiling back. "There is turkey bacon, if you like, though I can't vouch for its similarity to the real thing."

"Just eggs, then," said Kelly, to the breakfast servant. "Over easy. And coffee."

"Coffee for me too," said Matt, taking a seat opposite Kelly. "And cold cereal."

"What brand of cereal would you like, Mr. Fisher?" said the servant.

"Anything's fine," said Matt. "Surprise me."

"They can make grits if you like," said Simon. "I gather from your accent that you're a southerner? Myself, I love grits. I had some this morning in your honor, actually."

"Then grits. Thanks," said Matt, to the servant, and nodded his thanks to Simon.

"I hope we haven't kept you," said Kelly. "Our internal clocks are a little off."

"No, no, not at all," said Simon. "I always get up early. I don't answer the Adhan myself but it has set my own internal clock. And I don't like to set a bad example for my employees."

Kelly nodded. She wasn't one hundred percent sure what Simon meant but felt it would be rude to ask.

"How is it you happen to like grits?" said Matt. "If you don't mind me asking."

"Not at all," said Simon. "I studied for a year at George Washington University. I lived over the river in Arlington, in a hotel where they were a staple."

Matt nodded. A waiter was pouring coffee—for him first, then Kelly.

"Anything interesting in the paper?" asked Kelly, taking a sip. "Wonderful coffee, by the way."

"Yes, actually. A lost Cimabue has turned up in some French woman's kitchen, near Amiens. *Christ Mocked*. She didn't know what it was. Now it's going to be auctioned off. I'll be bidding on it, though I may not be able to keep up with the Emiratis." He shrugged. "It's always better to buy direct from the seller, ey?" He smiled.

"Would you like to look at my documents now?" said Kelly.

"No, no," said Simon. "Eat your breakfast first. Look, here come your eggs."

"What's a Cimabue?" said Matt, spooning up some grits. They were a little too fine and mushy for his taste, but not bad. Needed salt.

"Cimabue was the first master of the early Renaissance," said Simon. "Not really to my taste, but thirteenth-century art doesn't come on the market very often."

Matt nodded thoughtfully. He'd never understood collectors collecting things they didn't really want, though they all seemed to do it.

Kelly was fingering the folded Klimt insurance stuff in her pocket.

◆

When they finished their grits and eggs, Simon led them into a sort of sitting room where he let his guests admire another slice of his collection—antiquities of all sorts from all over the world. Small Mesopotamian statues; terra-cotta pots with faded Greek figures painted on them; carved, yellowed elephant tusks; a jade Buddha; some yellow and blue china; something that looked Incan; and several dozen Roman coins. Simon was explaining to Kelly that one of the coins had been minted to pay Brutus's army during the civil war that followed Caesar's stabbing and had been stamped with a contemporary portrait of him. Matt was looking at a skull in a gold and glass box with a pair of swords crossed under it. It looked like a Jolly Roger.

"And who's that?" said Matt, cutting off the discussion of Brutus's profile, pointing to the skull.

"It is *said* to be the skull of John Fisher. Saint John Fisher—no relation, I hope!—who was decapitated by Henry the Eighth during his, uh, quarrel with the Catholic Church. I have my doubts, frankly, because the head was taken from a pike in London and thrown into the Thames. Allegedly it was recovered afterward. Who knows, five hundred years ago, how many skulls were down there?"

"You have a Catholic relic in Qatar?" Matt wasn't Catholic but he was captivated by the display. "Is that legal?"

"Oh yes," said Simon. "*Having* it is legal, anyway." He winked at Kelly. "There are churches in Doha, you know. Dozens, I believe. You know that, oh, four out of five residents of Qatar are foreign workers—from southern Asia, mostly—and many of them are Christians. So yes, many churches. Don't mention my head, please, or my house may become a destination for pilgrims."

"No synagogues?" said Kelly. An attempt at being wry.

"Ah, actually, there is rumored to be one, for Jewish tourists and diplomats, that lives in a hotel conference room in one of the big hotels. I don't know if it's true or not. But maybe. Do you like the swords?" Simon was carefully lifting one of the crossed swords off its display pegs. It looked Japanese.

"Yes, very much," said Matt. "They're beautiful."

"This one," said Simon, "belonged to a *kaishakunin*, the man whose job it was to cut off the head of a man who'd committed seppuku. To spare everyone having to watch the disemboweled man writhing around, ey?"

He held it out to Matt, who took it gingerly, admiring the gentle thread design on the hilt.

"Can I slide it out?"

"Please do," said Simon. "It's not so old, from the early nineteenth century. The other one is even newer, though I think even more interesting."

It was a scimitar. Simon lifted it off the wall and held it out for Matt, who, after admiring the Japanese sword for a moment and sliding it back into its sheath, handed it to Kelly, who held it in front of her like a tube of toxic waste.

"It's not really much of an antiquity—it was being used up until the 1990s, for executions by our neighbors down south in the House of Saud. It took off the heads of some of the men responsible for the Haram Mosque crisis in 1979. This is my decapitation corner, ey? I didn't plan it that way but I already had the *kaishaku* sword and the Saint John, so when a friend offered to sell it to me, I thought, why not?"

It was a simple design but extremely elegant, long, with a gentle curve, a beautifully shined and sharpened blade, and a hilt made out of fine silver wire woven into a dense, complex repeating pattern.

"It's beautiful," said Matt, who couldn't take his eyes off it. He held it straight out in front of him and looked down its edge. "Beautiful. May I?" Matt lifted the sword in a backswing.

"Certainly," said Simon, smiling to see his toy being appreciated.

Matt sliced it back and forth through the air.

"You can kill that throw pillow, if you like," said Simon, pointing toward an innocent white cushion on a white sofa.

Matt, grinning like an idiot, stepped toward the sofa, stabbed into the pillow, and flicked it into the air. As it came down again Matt swung at it. The pillow sliced cleanly in half; Matt quickly swung backhand and quartered it. Gouts of cotton puffed out and spilled onto the floor.

"You must be a fine tennis player," said Simon.

"Never tried," said Matt. He held the sword out at arm's length again. "But thank you. This is just beautiful."

Matt knew what he was doing. He didn't feel guilty about it. He felt he was advancing the cause of justice.

"You must have it then!" said Simon, with a smile that showed no regret, just noblesse oblige. It's an old Arab tradition of hospitality to give as a gift anything a guest appears to covet. Making it, of course, very bad manners to linger on your desire for someone else's stuff.

"Oh no," said Matt, halfheartedly. "I couldn't."

"But you can," said Simon. "I insist. A weapon belongs with a soldier. It shouldn't just languish on a wall, ey? Maybe you can use it to protect Miss Somerset here."

17

The stout-hearted horses had been loaded into a long trailer without much difficulty and driven south, on back roads, to a place called Bobblers Knob, Colorado. It's at the edge of the Rockies, just north of New Mexico, just east of Las Animas Perdidas en el Purgatorio River. That is, "The River of the Lost Souls in Purgatory," which, thought Wharton, was an awfully fancy name for what was, at best, a mediocre river.

Bobblers Knob is a very remote and, per Google, a very unpopular riding trail. It wasn't as close to their destination as Wharton wanted but, to him, the loneliness made it the best choice. From Bobblers Knob, they'd ride southeast toward the Raton Mesa, across the Raton Plateau, down into the Raton Basin—under Route 25, at night—and up toward Raton Pass. Here, tucked up and away from the highway, and away from any town or any people, Amtrak's Southwest Chief began a long, slow, right-handed turn through a sandy, sagebrushy field in a high mountain dale, toward the Raton Tunnel, which would take it across the border into Colorado.

That was where they were going to jump it.

Pulling the trailer as far as he could off Bobblers Knob's gravel parking lot into the surrounding trees, Bob Wharton was aware that Joel Fotheringay hadn't said anything in hours. The only sounds he made were yes-and-no grunts. Wharton watched him gently lead the horses, one by one, out of the trailer. It was wide enough that they could turn and walk out forward, instead of backing down a ramp, which horses hate. Joel had misgivings. He'd had them from the beginning but he'd been swept along by the enthusiasm of his brothers, and by some special eldest-brother, man-of-the-house sense of responsibility not only to make sure they didn't get into any trouble without him but to make sure the Fotheringay Ranch survived to be passed on through another generation.

But he wasn't happy. He'd asked Wharton to give him and his brothers some privacy to talk it over. Wharton had watched from the hood of his Bronco while the three brothers sat around the campfire, arguing, two against one. Joel had lost. But he wasn't happy. He was going to do it. But he wasn't happy. Wharton wasn't worried about Joel losing his nerve, otherwise he'd never have taken it this far. No, but he was worried about Joel feeling some last-second burst of guilt, something that might make his conscience overflow the dam that was holding it back.

But he wasn't *that* worried because Wharton figured he could handle that the same way he handled regular last-minute indecision.

For the time being, they were saddling up, late in the evening, for about three, three and a half hours of nighttime trail riding. They'd make camp at the other end and wait tomorrow out, taking it easy, being lazy, keeping their heads down. Then, about ten o'clock that night, Amtrak's Southwest Chief, and six Klimt drawings, and their insurance security men, would roll up the hill toward the tunnel. By then, the Fotheringay gang would be ready and raring to go.

◆

A few dozen cars buzzed overhead as the four riders passed under Route 25, an hour or so after sunset. Wharton was certain none of the drivers could possibly have seen them. The horses had been a little skittish to begin with but they'd settled down well, and the trail—even where they blazed it themselves—wasn't too difficult: hard-packed and dry dirt and sand, a smattering of brush, which the horses nibbled at. Wharton was in the lead with his fancy GPS. Joel was bringing up the rear, keeping a lookout over his shoulder. The star covering overhead was magnificent, though not magnificent enough to attract the attention of Montanans used to that sort of thing.

A little before midnight they made camp in a dip in the uplands surrounding the mountain valley where the train tracks curved. Wharton made sure the campfire was out of sight of the tracks, ensuring there wouldn't be someone on a freight train or something who happened to see it and get curious about who it belonged to. A slim chance but it cost them nothing to be cautious. They fed the horses and watered them at a little stream that the Nazi had found on Google Earth, a rivulet that would eventually run into the Purgatory, then the Arkansas, then the Mississippi, and finally the Gulf of Mexico. That was what the Nazi was thinking about when he let his fly down and pissed into it: how many cities and people were downstream of him, would dangle their feet in his piss over the next few weeks. He smiled and shook off a few drops, while the Fotheringay boys got the horses tied up. He put his dick away and cleared a dusty patch of ground for a fire and then started walking in a slow circle, picking up tinder.

18

Simon was pleased and impressed by Kelly's Klimt insurance documents. He poured over them for about forty-five minutes, before handing them off to an executive secretary who'd materialized. Matt took an instant liking to the secretary because he was dressed in full traditional Arab garb—which billowed around him as he entered the room, headdress included—but had a strong Canadian accent. When he shook Matt's hand and Matt asked him about it, he said he'd just broken ground on a private curling rink and hoped to assemble a team of Qataris to try to qualify for the 2022 Olympics. Or possibly 2026. Matt suggested he might get some shuffleboard players from the giant yachts they'd flown over as they landed in Hamad. The secretary laughed and said it was a good idea and hoped Matt would come back and cheer them on. Matt said he certainly would and regretted he couldn't give the man his real name.

The secretary withdrew with the documents.

"He's going to make copies and my, eh, attorneys are going to look them over," said Simon.

The conversation turned back to art, and how much Simon both hated and admired someone named Damien Hirst, and something about someone falling into a hole in a museum in Portugal that had been painted with something called Vantablack, the blackest paint in the world, so black that you couldn't tell a hole was a hole, apparently, because it looked two-dimensional. The hole was an artwork by someone called Anish Kapoor, who owned Vantablack but wouldn't share it. Kelly and Simon agreed this was a shame, though Matt didn't see why the man should have to let his pigment be used in someone else's art any more than the Beatles should have to let their music be used in someone else's movie. On the other hand, he was holding Simon's sword on his lap, so noblesse oblige maybe wasn't all bad. He sat back a little in his seat and looked at the skull relic.

After about forty-five minutes more, the curler-secretary came back and handed Simon Kelly's papers and a folded note. He sort of bowed to Kelly and then to Matt, who stood up and shook his hand and wished him luck on the curling. The man winked and said he was going to get advice from the Jamaican bobsled team. Matt laughed. Simon waved the man away. Matt sat back down.

Simon was still reading the folded note. Then he stuck it in his breast pocket and said, "Nine hundred apiece, five-point-four total."

Kelly shook her head. "Two apiece, twelve total."

Simon said, "Well, we both know I'm not going to pay full price." He tapped his breast pocket. "I'm advised not to go higher than a million even."

Kelly half smiled and gestured to Simon's breast pocket. "Mind if I see your advice?"

Simon half smiled back. "One-point-one."

"One-point-seven-five."

"One-point-one-five."

"One-point-seven."

Matt couldn't believe they could be so . . . casual? Blasé?

"One-point-two is my absolute maximum."

"One-point-five is my absolute minimum."

"I'll tell you what," said Simon. "Let's say we agree to one-point-five, but you give me a volume discount, ey? So it works out to one-point-two-five. Seven-point-five total."

Kelly tapped her fingers. In fact, none of this really mattered . . . she wasn't going to get to keep the money. She looked over at Matt and wondered what he made of all this. He looked back at her with unreadable blankness. That seemed to be his standard expression these days.

"Fine," said Kelly. "One-point-two-five." She stood up and extended her hand. Simon stood up and shook it.

"Perfect!" said Simon. "Very good! Come let me show you where I'm going to hang them, and let's talk about delivery. I'm paying you COD, yes?"

"Sure," said Kelly, smiling. She was glad they were in a country where no one would be surprised to see her sweating. Levi Quintero had given her very specific instructions for the delivery and payment. If Simon didn't agree, she'd go to prison. If he got suspicious, she was sincerely convinced he might kill her, or sell her off as a sex slave or something, *Taken*-style. Sure, he *seemed* nice, but so did Goldfinger and Hans Gruber. She felt herself going a little pale. She'd come this far. She could do it. She could do it. She exhaled deeply, following Simon out of the room.

Simon looked over his shoulder and smiled. "It's a lot of money, ey?"

Kelly smiled and nodded. "Yep."

Matt followed, with the sword resting on his shoulder.

19

Wharton and the Fotheringays heard the westbound Southwest Chief rumble through the valley around midday. They kept out of sight and it passed unaware, just as a few freight trains had in the morning and a few more would in the afternoon.

Without anything in particular to do, and because Wharton had made them leave their phones in Montana, they'd spent most of the day lying on their sleeping rolls. Joel was reading a paperback, a thick one, called *The Name of the Wind*, which Wharton assumed was some sort of wistful Western. Frank was reading through a stack of newspapers that Wharton had picked up for him at a gas station in Kansas. It had been Wharton who'd bought them because he'd insisted on unhooking the trailer each time they had to fill up and leaving it somewhere up the road, with the Fotheringay boys watching it, so no one who saw his face would associate him with it, and no one would see their faces at all. Frank apparently loved local newspapers. A little voyeuristic, if you asked Wharton. But whatever. Caleb, who didn't like sitting still, had spent most of the morning preening the horses, then hiking around to get the lay of the land—not going too far; Wharton had told him not to go too far. As the sun started to set, he made a little campfire and made coffee and then, once the coffee kicked in, went off to find a ditch to shit in. Wharton told him he had to throw some horse shit in with his own, to make sure no one tried getting DNA out of it. He'd wandered around for about an hour, until he came back to say he'd found an old, grown-over latrine someone else had dug and stopped using. Probably a rancher who'd grazed cattle up here. Wharton asked if he'd tossed in some horse shit. Caleb said he had, got some hand sanitizer from Joel, and lay down to stare at the pink and orange clouds and roll cigarettes.

Wharton stood up and dusted himself off. Now *he* had to shit.

"Where's that hole?" he asked Caleb, who offered him a fresh-rolled cigarette. "No thanks, I've got my own." He patted his breast pocket.

"It's about a hundred yards that way, over the hill, over another little crest. Got a little stand of aspens around it. Must be good fertilizer. All the old shit."

"Mhmm. Thanks," said Wharton, heading off in the direction Caleb pointed. He found the hole without much difficulty. The shit smell was regrettably fresh. The Nazi was crouched over it when he heard footsteps rustle up behind him.

"Oh shit," said a man's voice. "Sorry, sorry. 'Scuse me." The Nazi pulled up his pants and turned around. "I was hiking Climax Canyon," said the man. He was in his late thirties, had on a wide-brimmed hat with a walking stick in one hand and a water bottle in the other. "And I got sorta off track somewhere."

"You been walking a long way. What is that, eight, ten miles downhill? You crossed a lot of private property getting here."

"Oh, shoot, did I? I thought I was still in the park. There're no signs or anything. I was just following Old Pass Road, till it kind of stopped."

"Yeah, this is all private grazing land," said the Nazi. "Though it's out of season, so I guess it won't really matter. You with anyone else? Anyone else in trouble?"

The hiker shook his head and took a sip of water.

The Nazi continued. "I got a satellite phone if you wanna call someone."

"Thanks, no, I don't need it. I'm just up from Albuquerque. Just a day hike. I figured eventually I'll hit 25 and follow it back to the park, you know?"

"Can I have that water bottle?" asked the Nazi. The man looked at him, uncomfortably.

"Umm . . . okay?" The man handed the Nazi the water bottle. "I don't have too much left though, and I need it to get back, I mean."

The Nazi unscrewed the bottle's top and poured the water onto the ground. It sloshed out in one big gulp.

"*Hey*, what the *fuck*."

The Nazi pulled a Springfield .45 pistol, a semiauto, out of the holster hidden by his baggy flannel overshirt. He stuck the gun's barrel into the water bottle and shot the hiker in the chest.

The bottle worked like a low-quality silencer, letting the air diffuse out of the barrel slower than it would normally. But the shot was still loud as hell, like a single smash from a jackhammer.

The Nazi didn't want to fire a second time unless he had too. He watched the hiker fall backward, awkwardly clutching at his walking stick to try and stay upright.

The Nazi walked over to him, watched the shock drift out of the hiker's eyes. Felt the man's pulse. He was dead. The Nazi emptied the man's pockets—a cell phone, which he smashed; keys, which he threw away; and a wallet and a granola bar, which he stuck into his own pockets. Then he dragged the body to the shit ditch and rolled it in, and threw the walking stick, the hat, and the ruined water bottle in after it.

◆

About a hundred yards away, Joel Fotheringay looked up from his book. That was a shot, he was pretty sure. He looked at his brothers.

"You hear that?" asked Frank. Joel and Caleb nodded. "A shot?"

"Yeah. Hold on." Joel put down his book and got to his feet. "Wait here." He'd taken his own gun—a Colt Python revolver—out of its holster because lying down with it was uncomfortable; it kept poking him in the side. He retrieved it from his riding bag, made sure it was loaded, and slipped it and the holster back into his waistband. "I'll be right back."

Caleb shrugged. Frank nodded.

Joel headed over the hill in the direction of the shot, in the direction Caleb had pointed Bob Wharton. He went up and over the top of the hill, down into a little dip and up over another crest, and saw Wharton walking toward him. Away from a stand of ash trees.

"That a shot?" said Joel.

"Yeah," said Wharton. "Prairie rattler. Whole nest of them in that shit hole your brother pointed me to. I'm surprised he didn't get his nuts bit off."

Joel nodded. He wasn't sure he believed that. Wharton had been pretty emphatic about not making too much noise.

"You get it?" he asked.

Wharton laughed. "I don't know. Scared the shit out of me. Not literally." He laughed again. "Shouldn't've done it, but there you are. Don't like snakes. Go on back to the camp. I'm just going to dump out here in the open and cover it with a horse pat, which should be fine."

Joel looked at him. Wharton was standing—a little pointedly, maybe?—between Joel and the ash trees.

"Get on now," said Wharton. "Unless you're trying to catch a peek at my dick when I drop my shorts." He unbuckled his belt. "Get on now."

Joel hesitated, then walked back toward the camp, unconsciously resting his hand on his gun as he went.

20

Back at the camp, Joel told his brothers what Wharton had said. Wharton had almost caught up to him, was jogging down the hill behind him as he did, so he didn't get a chance to say anything more, to say he thought maybe Wharton had just shot someone. It didn't matter; no point in getting his brothers involved. In a few minutes he'd head back over the hill to take a shit of his own and to see for himself. In the meantime, he finished his cold cup of coffee and watched as Bob Wharton started to brew a fresh pot.

The Fotheringay brothers didn't know it, but it was a special pot. An old baseball trick, actually—it used to be that every baseball clubhouse in the majors brewed two pots of coffee before a game, known as "Coaches' Coffee" and "Players' Coffee," or "Unleaded" and "Leaded." The leaded Players' Coffee was brewed with amphetamines, little speed pills called beans or greenies. Almost everyone used them; a hundred and sixty-two games a year take a heavy toll on the body; it's not easy to keep playing hard through August and September without something stronger than caffeine. It was funny, Wharton always thought, how much people bitched about steroids, when Players' Coffee hadn't been banned till a year or two before Obama was elected. Back when Wharton had been running stickups for the '88s, he'd been introduced to the idea of Players' Coffee, with a special Nazi twist: instead of amphetamines, they brewed with methamphetamines.

This was literally a special Nazi twist: the neo-Nazis had gotten the idea from the originals—a story Wharton had belly-laughed at when he'd first heard it. Amphetamines entered baseball after the Second World War, when players coming home brought their army-issued speed with them. The army gave them amphetamines to use in emergencies—seventy-two-hour battle kinds of emergencies. The Nazis had a similar idea, but instead of speed they gave their soldiers meth. Which got 'em real wide-awake and peppy, and real mean and fighty.

Like license plate manufacture, meth is an area in which ex-prisoners and Nazis tend to have connections. It was nighttime now, a little after nine. Wharton poured himself a cup of coffee, and then poured some powdered crystal into the pot and let it simmer. No sleight of hand was required; the boys were off getting the horses ready. It was almost game time.

"Come and have a drink of this, boys," said Wharton. "This is the strongest shit north of Java. Caffeine is our friend tonight."

"Speaking of shit," said Joel, tightening the final strap on his horse's saddle, "I'm going to head back over the hill and take a dump."

Wharton stuck a cup of his Players' Coffee into Joel's hand and shook his head. "No time. Do it here, over where the horses've been doing it. We won't look."

Joel was prepared to argue. He took a sip of coffee first, and started feeling a little tingly and strange. He took another sip. It was good coffee.

Wharton was handing out cups to Frank and Caleb, telling them to drink up, that they had to get going, offering refills. Two minutes later he was telling Frank and Caleb to stop singing and get onto their horses. It was time to head down to the tracks and get up to the line of scrimmage. Not to mix his sports.

Wharton kicked out the fire and did a quick check to make sure nothing had been left behind. Joel seemed to have forgotten about having to shit. He was looking at his coffee cup, empty after a refill. There was something . . . he couldn't quite put his finger on it.

"Come on," said Wharton. "Let's move."

"Eeeyah," said Caleb, spurring his horse forward. Frank followed. They knew where they were going; Wharton had laid it all out for them during the day. Down the hill, to the field, by the tracks, behind some cottonwood trees.

Wharton waited for Joel to follow his brothers. Instead, Joel was staring at him. Wharton started his own horse, walked over to Joel's, made a clicking sound, and hit the horse on its rump. It trotted off after Frank and Caleb, with Wharton bringing up the rear.

Joel felt . . . a little dizzy. Very alive. Very awake. It was the adrenaline pumping through him, he figured. The excitement, the ready-for-action jolt you get before doing something big. He was, uh, he was . . . he had been thinking about that gunshot, about what Wharton had really shot at. There was time for that later, though. Now was time for action. He spurred his horse a little faster and caught up with his brothers who were riding downhill at a light canter.

When they were all in place—all lined up and ready to go—Wharton drilled them a final time, on exactly what each one of them was going to do. They knew their stuff. They were ready. None of these boys was stupid. Reckless, but not stupid. Those were the two reasons he'd picked them.

But now Joel was staring at him again. He could feel Joel's eyes; they made the hair on the back of his neck stand up.

Suddenly the low rumble of a diesel electric broke through the nighttime silence and nature sounds. Joel and Wharton, and Frank and Caleb, snapped their heads toward the sound as they picked it up. Caleb was pulling his gloves tight. He tapped Frank on the shoulder, and Frank reached into his pocket for his own gloves.

Then they both tied bandanas over their mouths and noses. Red for Caleb, black for Frank.

Fifteen, maybe twenty seconds later, a headlight came into view. The single headlight on the nose of the Dash 8 engine swept across the walls of the valley as it started its slow turn toward the Raton Tunnel.

Joel looked back at Wharton, who was holding a stopwatch. Something in his head was starting to crystallize. He looked down at his hands. There was a tremor in them. But he didn't feel nervous. Not at all. He licked his lips, and then his teeth.

The train was overtaking their hiding spot.

"*Now*," said Wharton. Caleb spurred his horse into a fast gallop. Five seconds passed.

"*Now,*" said Wharton. Frank galloped off after his brother. Another five seconds. A long five seconds.

"*Now,*" said Wharton. Joel was staring at him.

"What was in that coffee, Bob?" Wharton looked at him. There was fire in his eyes. There was fire in both their eyes.

"*Get the fuck going,*" said Wharton.

"What was in that coffee, Bob?"

"*There's no time, you'll goddamn miss it.*"

"What was in that coffee, Bob?"

Wharton drew his Springfield .45. Joel drew his Python.

"I'll kill you," said Wharton, "if you don't go *and I mean fucking now.*"

"You kill someone else already today, Bob?" Joel had the pistol pointed at Wharton's face. He could feel himself sweating.

"You're hanging your brothers out to dry. You going to visit them in prison, *Joel?*"

Wharton was right. Joel knew that. It snapped something into place in his head. He hit his horse hard on the rump and galloped away after his brothers.

Wharton was sweating too. He spurred his horse and followed.

21

Caleb was first to reach the head of the train. Thirty miles an hour feels a hell of a lot faster on a galloping horse next to a hurtling train than it does in, say, a car. Even so, this all felt very familiar. The train was moving at just the speed the bus had. The handrails and steps and catwalk on the Dash 8 were just the same as the ones he'd been practicing on. He matched the train's speed, easing off his gallop just a bit, and stuck out his right hand.

His fingers slipped. The metal was slick; the engineer must've climbed on with greasy hands. He squeezed tighter, got a good grip, then twisted his body over and gripped the other railing with his other hand. He pulled himself forward, up the access stairs, and felt his horse ride out from under him. He was on board.

Five seconds later, Frank was grabbing on to the stair railings, pulling himself up. He slid off his horse, got his feet on the stairs—and suddenly his left hand slipped. The gusting wind of the train's slipstream blew him off his feet. For a naked second he fluttered beside the Dash 8 like a wind sock. Before his right hand could slip, Caleb grabbed him by the collar and hauled him aboard. Frank nodded "thanks" to him and began to walk back along the catwalk, toward the luggage car. Caleb looked over his shoulder for Joel. He didn't see him. Frank didn't see him either. They both knew he was there, though, and that he'd be fine. And they didn't have time to wait for him.

Caleb walked up the steps that led to the engineer's cab. In his pocket was a filed-down flat-head screwdriver he could use to force the latch if he needed to. He tried the cab door's handle. It was unlocked. Crouched low—the door had a window in it—Caleb gently pushed the door open with his left hand while he pulled out his gun with his right. A Ruger Redhawk revolver, double-action .357 with a wood grip. He pointed it at the back of the engineer's head and stood up. At the same time, the engineer was twisting around in his seat, startled by the wind sucking in through the open door.

He saw Caleb's gun first, then Caleb, and his eyes got wide.

"This is a stickup," said Caleb. "Just keep her steady, and keep your hands where I can see them and away from any radios, or alarm buttons, or PA systems. Understand me? Just do that and you're going to be fine."

The engineer didn't say anything. He looked like he might vomit.

"Nod if you understand me."

The engineer nodded. Caleb was almost disappointed. He'd rehearsed what he was going to say, and what he was going to do, if the engineer didn't do what he told him to. All the hairs on

Caleb's arms and neck were up; his heart was pounding and he really wanted to pistol whip the engineer in the mouth. But heck, the man was complying.

"Hit the Wi-Fi cutoff for the train. If I see your hands do anything besides that, I'm going to blow your brains out, okay?"

The engineer nodded, reached for the passenger car panel, and flipped off the Wi-Fi.

Caleb took out the little walkie-talkie Bob had given him and keyed it on. "Everything's good in the engine."

"J.'s not here yet," answered Frank.

They were all on the same channel, and after a moment there was an answer from Bob. "J. got held up just a bit, he's catching up. Go ahead without him, he'll catch up. Just go ahead." Bob's voice over the radio was breathless; he was still riding, leading the horses away. Caleb was confused about Joel but not worried. He felt a little shiver of excitement run up his spine. He tilted back his cowboy hat and leaned back against the engine breaker panel.

He gestured with his gun for the engineer to turn back around and face the tracks.

"Just keep her steady," Caleb repeated, "and everything's going to be fine."

Beneath his bandana his nose itched. He scratched it with the barrel of his gun.

◆

Frank was standing at the very rear of the Dash 8, ready to step over the buckling and through the front-end door of the baggage car. But he and Joel were supposed to go in together. He wasn't absolutely sure what to do now. Bob had said go ahead. And he was all juiced up to do just that—though his mouth was awfully dry. He wished he could have another cup of coffee. Where the fuck was Joel? Joel was too good a rider to have fucked up. There was an emergency light at the back of the Dash 8's catwalk; the glare made it hard to see too far into the night . . . where the fuck was he?

There he was. Riding up breakneck, full gallop. But now he was peeling away . . . veering to his left, away from the tracks and the train. What the fuck, what the fuck, Joel, where the fuck was he going? He and that big rusty-red horse of his were charging up the embankment, a real steep embankment. What the fuck.

Then he vanished and Frank was almost sucked off his feet as the train shot into the Raton Tunnel.

◆

About forty feet above him, Joel was still at a full gallop, charging across an overgrown, sagebrushed access road that crossed the Raton Pass above the tunnel, skirting the edge of the mountain that the tunnel tunneled through. He knew from Wharton's map that the road followed the tunnel's route pretty close. And it was a clear night with about two-thirds of a full moon, so he could see the road decently well. He had no idea what kind of shape the packed-dirt road surface was in. If his horse dropped a hoof into a hole, they were both going to die. But there was nothing to do about that now. He knew the tunnel was narrow and curved slightly to the west. He knew the train slowed down to about twenty-five somewhere in the middle, before it started speeding up again as the tunnel straightened. Joel could beat it to the other side.

Maybe. He put his head down and gave his horse Rusty another slap on the ass, bellowing *"yah, yah"* into his ears.

At the engine's rear coupling, Frank had no idea what was going on. His radio couldn't get a signal, and he couldn't wait any longer. He stepped over the engine coupling, onto the luggage car, and pushed the door open. Like the door to the driver's cab it was unlocked. Frank's shimmy screwdriver stayed in his pocket.

The car's interior was stuffed with bags, empty of people, and lit by a single red bulb at either end. Frank shook his head to think that luggage cars didn't come with big iron safes to blow the hinges off anymore; he would have liked to have had a long, narrow stick of dynamite in his pocket. These days passengers had to take care of their own valuables. And this was supposed to be a service economy. He shook his head again and pushed his way toward the car's rear, sweeping his eyes around for any bag that had a superficially valuable appearance. Maybe something brown and stamped with that stupid LV logo. But everything seemed to be plastic and on wheels. Under the red bulb at the far end, he looked over his shoulder to see if Joel had magically appeared. He hadn't, and Frank pushed out onto the car's rear platform. He was outside again. Outside and inside. They were still in the tunnel. He made sure the bandana on his face was tight, pulled his cowboy hat low over his eyes, pulled out his gun, and pushed open the door into the first passenger coach.

There were fifteen or twenty people in the economy seats, all facing him, most of them dozing. He reached for the light switch on the door frame behind him. The overhead fluorescents came on. People started to stir, started to see Frank, and started to get scared.

"Ladies and gentlemen, this is a robbery. If I see you reach for your phone, I'm going to kill you. If you get out of your seats, I'm going to kill you. If you make any sudden moves, I'm going to kill you. If you don't do what I tell you, I'm going to kill you. Now, if you're the closest person to someone who's sleeping, wake 'em up."

Everyone looked around; four people were still asleep and four others reached out and shook them awake. It didn't take them long to get scared too. Frank repeated his instructions—"Once more for the heavy sleepers and slow learners"—as he reached, with his left hand, into his jacket and pulled out two cloth bags.

This would have been easier with Joel behind him, holding a gun. But he'd make it work.

"Okay, ladies and gentlemen, this won't be difficult. You're going to put your hands up and keep your hands up until I get to your row. Then you're going to take out your cell phones and wallets and take off your jewelry. You're going to put your wallets and rings and so forth in the left bag and your cell phones in the right bag. From my point of view. So, wallets are right bag for you, cell phones left. I don't need your laptops or your iPads or your gold fillings. Just what you got on you. And everything's going to be okay. When I pass you, keep looking forward. If I look over my shoulder and see anyone looking at me or if I hear anyone moving around, I'm going to kill you."

With his revolver in his right hand and the two bags in his left, he began to make his way up the aisle. The shocked and sleepy passengers were very obedient. And Frank did his best to be polite, even though he felt his blood boiling, like he was itching for someone to make a move. He found himself barking at the men to go faster—get their rings and such off faster. He hadn't been planning to take wedding rings, but what the hell. At the same time, he was apologizing to the ladies and the old folks for scaring them.

The very last guy in the car, a man of about thirty-five, accidentally dropped his cell phone in the same bag with his wallet. Frank cracked him across the face with the barrel of his gun. He felt the man's teeth break. It felt good. He hit the man again. The man lost consciousness and slumped forward in his seat, and then over sideways and onto the floor.

"All right, ladies and gentlemen, that's all for now. Our man at the front of the train has turned off the Wi-Fi, but keep away from your laptops anyway. If I come back in here and see anyone on any kind of electronic device, that person's going to die. But feel free to go back to sleep."

Frank hit the light switch and stepped out of the rear of the car. There were two more coaches to go before he reached the dining car and the sleeper cars behind it.

22

A head of him, Joel heard the *whoosh* of the train coming out of the tunnel and then two sharp blasts from the train whistle. The walkie-talkies didn't work underground, so the whistle was Caleb's way of signaling that everything was still okay in the cab and there was no need to bail off the train before it got up to speed again.

But now it was speeding up again. Joel could hear it shooting out of the tunnel; the *whooshing* was getting louder. He was close. There was no time, no time, no time to ride down the embankment and try to grab hold of a stairway or a doorway or jump onto a car buckling. Ahead of him he could see the lights of the train now, the nighttime running lights. He was almost to the end of the service road, above the tunnel's exit, where it ramped down into Colorado. There was no time to think about it. No time. No time. He would miss it and his brothers would go to jail. He felt what he thought was adrenaline coursing through him, suffusing every inch of his body. He pulled Rusty's reins tight and the horse pulled up to a fast stop, skidding a little in the dirt but not losing his footing or balance. Good horse. He was a damned good horse.

Joel was swinging his foot over Rusty's head, jumping out of the saddle, running toward the edge of the road—right above the tunnel's mouth. He was only about ten feet above the train, which looked now like it was going pretty goddamn fast. Not that either of those calculations mattered anymore. Joel was running too hard to stop or change his mind. He couldn't go forty, thirty, twenty-five miles an hour, but he needed to get as much speed as he could for this to have any chance at all of working.

For the tiniest split second he thought it was strange that he wasn't scared. He felt bizarrely rational. His brothers needed help. They were on the train and he needed to be on the train. It was logical.

At a full sprint, he jumped—right over the center line of the train coming out of the tunnel. He watched the roof come up to meet him. He was in the air for less than a second.

When his feet hit, he tried to fall forward, find a hand grip. But as soon as his feet hit, they were swept out from under him and he started to roll, head over heels, back along the train. But not perfectly straight. Toward the edge. He grabbed for the safety rail he saw pirouetting through his vision and caught it with his left hand. It was a square tubing and the edges cut into his fingers as he latched on with the grip—the crazy-man, super-strength grip—of someone who knows positively that he'll die if he lets go.

His body tumbled, his hand slid down the tube, but he didn't let go. His legs flopped over his shoulders. His arm and shoulder wrenched terribly, but he didn't let go. Now he was dangling off the side of the train, being blown back and forth by the wind. But he didn't let go.

He was hanging outside the observation car, the last car on the train. The caboose. He was dimly aware of how close he'd come to missing the train completely and jumping onto nothing. He was more keenly aware of the people in the observation car looking at him.

He banged on the window, trying to signal them to open it and let him in. They all just looked scared.

He was still wearing a bandana on his face. A dark navy blue kerchief. And they must have heard him hit the roof. No wonder they looked scared.

But he couldn't hold on for much longer.

He waved for the people to back away. Some of them did.

Joel pulled out his Colt, pressed the muzzle to the window, closed his eyes, and pulled the trigger.

Bits of glass stabbed into his face. The windowpane his feet were pressed against suddenly exploded and disappeared, and—swinging on his numb left arm—he tumbled into the train, rolling like a crash-test dummy over an easy chair and into the center aisle. His left arm was still numb and his right arm was wet. He looked at his right hand. It was red and slick with blood. He'd cut himself on something, god knows what. There were plenty of options.

People all around were staring at him. All scared. Some of them looked as if they wanted to help him but were too afraid to try. He brought his left hand awkwardly to his face. The hand still worked and his face was still hidden behind the bandana. His hat was long gone.

He struggled to his feet. A man in his sixties—a bald black man with a short white beard—reached out to help but his wife reflexively pulled his arm back. Joel looked at him and smiled. Could the man see his smile through the bandana? Joel blinked his eyes; there was blood dripping into them off his eyelashes. He fingered a deep cut along his hairline and with the same finger wiped the blood off his forehead. Funny, it didn't hurt at all.

"Thank you," he said to the man who'd almost helped him. Joel staggered to the front of the car, leaned against the door, turned around to face everyone, and said, "Everyone take out your cell phones."

No one moved. They were all just staring at him. He lifted his gun hand and waved the Colt, slowly, from left to right.

"Everyone take out your cell phones."

No one moved.

Joel pointed the gun at the window directly to his right and pulled the trigger. The glass exploded. Someone screamed, and Joel shouted: *"Everyone take out your goddamn cell phones!"*

Now everyone moved, reaching into their pockets, searching around their purses and backpacks. He was glad the older man and his wife both got their phones out fast—with baby boomers, he wouldn't have been sure if they'd had phones at all, but if they'd said they didn't he'd have had to accuse them of lying, try to scare them, just to make sure. He was glad he didn't have to.

With his gun, he gestured to the two shot-out windows.

"Throw 'em away. The phones. All of 'em."

Slowly, the fifteen or so people in the observation car shuffled around each other, tossing their phones into the train's airstream, two or three at a time. Joel counted them off on his left-hand fingers and knuckles to make sure the number of thrown phones matched the number of scared passengers. They did, and he waved the gun in a downward arc. "Everyone sit down."

Everyone sat in the nearest seat. It was a little like musical chairs, thought Joel, and laughed—and one man surrounded by quickly filled-up easy chairs sat down on the floor.

Joel pointed the gun at him. He went white.

"You can get up and go to a couch. It's all right."

The man didn't move. He was probably too scared to move. Joel shrugged.

"I'm going to be back to check on you shortly. If I see anyone calling anyone, I'll kill you."

Joel knew the threat sounded halfhearted, but it would have to do—and he figured it probably would.

He put a finger up to his lips—a gesture to be silent—then slid open the door behind him and backed into the rearmost sleeper car.

23

"What the fuck," thought Frank. "Was that a gunshot?" It sounded like it had come from a few cars ahead of him, toward the rear of the train. Frank was in the dining car, which had been closed for the night and was empty. He'd robbed the three coach cars—"robbed," though Wharton had promised the people would get their stuff back. The idea was to drop the wallets once they, the robbers, realized there was something a lot more valuable on the train. Bob wanted to make it look, at least superficially, like they'd stumbled on the Klimts by accident. And Joel had insisted that they not actually steal from regular people, and Frank and Caleb had more or less agreed that he was right, that robbing trust-fund kids and regular people wasn't the same. So the only things the people Frank had just terrorized—he smiled to himself; his heart was still pounding—the only things they were really losing was some peace of mind and a few teeth. They ought to thank him. Peace of mind, teeth, and cell phones.

Frank leaned into a dining booth, opened a window, and shook out the bag of cell phones. Getting rid of the cell phones had been insisted on by Wharton and Joel had agreed.

But now Frank was wondering what he was going to do about the sleeper cars.

Fortunately, the Southwest Chief used single-decker Viewliner cars instead of the double-decker Superliners you got on the more popular routes; that was why they were going to be able to rob them with just two men. But wherever the fuck Joel was, Frank was not two men. He wasn't sure how he could rob the roomettes and watch his own back. There was no way that wouldn't cause a ruckus. Of course, he could head straight for the "family bedroom," the one big private room on the train, where the Klimts were being kept. It was in a train car by itself, along with the sleeper cars' showers and bathrooms. (What luxury, to travel in the bathroom car. Frank smiled.) Of course, that would lose a little of the subterfuge Wharton had wanted.

Frank sat on a table for a second and thought it over. There was a big plastic tray full of knives next to trays of spoons and forks and napkins. Cloth napkins and metal knives. What if he wedged the roomette doors shut with the knives . . . slide them into the door frame, sliding door can't slide anymore, now people can't come out of their roomettes and sneak up behind him. Then he could do them one by one.

But that would take a long time. Time was tight here. Frank's brain felt a little fuzzy. He felt jumpy and he didn't want to just sit around here trying to decide. Fuck the knives. No time. He'd skip the roomettes and go straight for the toilet car with the family bedroom and the big prize in it.

Oh, and what the fuck was that gunshot? Was it a gunshot? How could it have been? Was it his imagination? His brain did feel a little fuzzy . . . maybe just something falling over and breaking.

Well, he'd find out.

Frank raised his gun in front of him—then lowered it, wiped a little blood off the barrel onto a nice cloth napkin, and raised it again—and slid open the door into the first sleeping car.

He'd try to do this quietly.

Gun out in front of him, he walked down the corridor, which was dimly lit by emergency lights. There were roomette doors on both sides. He was pretty sure this was the cabin where the crew slept. He was surprised there wasn't some sort of night watchman on duty. Wharton had said there wasn't, that if you needed something you could ring for service like on an airplane. But Frank hadn't really believed him.

At the far end of the corridor, Frank reached for the door into the next sleeping car. As he did, the roomette door to his left slid open. Frank turned his head. A sleepy face belonging to a woman who probably had one of the rooms with no toilet in it looked back at him. The eyes went wide, looked from Frank's bandana'd face to his gun and back to his face again. Silently, she reclosed the door.

Frank heard the lock snap into place. He smiled and stepped into the next car.

Another dimly lit sleeper. But this time—when Frank was about halfway to the far end—the silence was broken by the sounds of scuffling, fighting, shouting from up ahead, farther down the train.

Frank was confused. He paused, listened, and then sprinted toward the noise.

24

As Joel backed out of the observation car, he shut and locked the communicating door and, hearing a door open behind him, turned to see a man stepping into the corridor. White button-down shirt, black slacks and shoes.

"What was that noise? Was that a gunshot? What's on your face? Is that a gun?" The corridor was dimly lit. When the man saw Joel's gun, he reached toward his waist. He was going for his own gun, pulling it out of a holster, going into a crouch. He was only a yard or so in front of Joel and, as he crouched down, Joel's knee-jerk reaction was to kick the man's gun hand. The gun in it—a little black Glock—went flying. But with his other hand the man grabbed the ankle of Joel's other foot and Joel went flying too. The man sprang forward, grabbed at Joel's gun hand with both of his, smashed it into the wall, once, twice, and then Joel's gun went flying. The two men were tangled up on the floor of the corridor, bouncing back and forth between the walls. The man got his hands to Joel's throat. Joel connected a sharp right hook to the man's jaw and then pried the hands off, twisted the man's shoulder down and around, and put him into a headlock.

"Let him go!" shouted another voice, farther up the car. Joel looked toward it. Another man in a white shirt and black pants. This one had on a matching black jacket and pointed a matching black gun at Joel.

At the same instant Joel saw the second security man, Frank tackled him from behind, mashed him into the floor, and started to choke him.

Joel's guy was still in a headlock. Was starting to kick and gurgle. In a second he'd be unconscious.

Frank was being a little more aggressive. He smashed the second guy's head into the floor. Once, twice. He was unconscious already. Frank stood up, panted for breath, and stepped over the unconscious man, stamping down on his head as he did.

Joel's guy was still kicking and gurgling. Frank walked up to him and his brother, still tangled on the floor, and crashed his pistol butt down onto the security man's head. The kicking and gurgling stopped. Frank crouched down and looked at the unconscious man's face.

"Think he's dead?" asked Frank, scratching his left eyebrow.

Joel pushed two fingers into the man's neck and found a pulse.

"He's alive." Joel was panting for breath too. "How about yours?"

Frank looked over his shoulder at the facedown, not-moving body. "I don't know."

Frank walked back to him. The man's head was gently lolling back and forth, as the train's gentle rocking sloshed it and the pool of blood around it from side to side.

Frank searched for a pulse.

"Yeah, he's alive. I think the blood's just his nose."

"Well, roll him over so he doesn't drown in it."

"It's going to get soaked up by the carpet, don't worry. Anyway, it's bad to have a nose bleed lying on your back."

"Yeah, okay. Okay." Joel took a deep breath and climbed to his feet, letting the unconscious body sprawled across him slide to the floor. "Let's do this."

The brothers walked over to the Amtrak family bedroom's door. It was open. There were supposed to be two security guards in it and a curator. The security guards appeared to have been dealt with. The curator was in her bed, with her knees pulled up to her chest.

She looked at the Fotheringay brothers and pressed a light switch at her elbow.

"Are you going to assault me?"

Joel looked at Frank with a bewildered expression. Frank shrugged. They looked back to the curator.

"*No.*" Joel's tone made it sound like it was the craziest damned question he'd ever heard in his life. "Ma'am, this is a robbery. Just a robbery."

"You got anything valuable?" said Frank.

"No," said the curator.

"Mind if we have a look around?" said Frank.

"Yes," said the curator.

"Well, we're going to anyway," said Frank, pushing past Joel, into the room. Together the brothers made a good show of searching through cabinets and things. Joel pocketed an earring case and Frank took a bottle of oxycodone out of a toiletry bag.

"Probably leave that," said Joel. "They're going to need it." Frank shrugged and put it back.

Now Joel went over to the metal no-crush travel suitcase that was very carefully strapped down on its own bed. "What's in this?"

The curator said, "Just clothes and things."

It was closed with a combination lock.

"What's the combination," said Joel.

"I don't know it," said the curator.

"Yes, you do," said Frank.

"No, I don't," said the curator.

"It doesn't matter," said Joel, reaching for the bolt cutters in his hip pocket. But they were gone. Must have fallen out when he jumped onto the train.

"Shit," he said. He sighed deeply and went out into the hallway. He came back with his gun.

"Are you going to shoot the lock off?" said the curator.

"No," said Joel. "I'm going to shoot you if you don't tell me what the combination is."

He pointed the gun at her. She tugged her knees closer to her chest.

"I really don't know what it is. Please don't shoot me."

Joel sighed again. He knew that she did know. But she seemed to know also that he wasn't going to shoot her. And shooting locks off doesn't work.

He turned to Frank—almost called him by his first name; caught himself in time—and said, "Would you try and hammer that thing off? My arms are a little screwed up."

"Hammer the lock off? What with? All I got's a screwdriver."

"Your gun."

"That lock's metal, it'll fuck it up, break the grip. I'm not fucking up my Redhawk on that thing, it was a present."

"Then go get one of those assholes' Glocks and use that."

"Oh yeah, okay, good idea." Frank reappeared after fifteen seconds with the Glocks, one in each hand.

"Never understood people who prefer semiautos to revolvers," he said, and walked past Joel to the locked suitcase. "Okeydokey."

He smashed the lock with the pistol butt. Once, twice, three times, four times. The Glock's grip shattered.

"See?" said Frank. He tossed the broken Glock to Joel and started in hammering with the second one. Joel opened a window and tossed the Glock out of it.

There was a snap.

"Bingo," said Frank. He pulled off the shattered lock and dropped it on the floor. He handed the second Glock to Joel. Joel tossed that one out the window too. No sense keeping it around. Someone might get hurt.

Frank opened the case.

"What have we here?"

"Just some drawings," said the curator. "My mother made them. They have sentimental value. Please don't take them."

Inside the case was a plastic box sealed with zip ties, wrapped in plastic, and bedded down in foam rubber.

Don't ham it up too much, thought Joel.

"You wanna take this?" asked Frank.

"Yeah," said Joel. "Let's take it and get going."

He turned to the curator. "Sorry about this, ma'am."

She was crying. She just shook her head.

Joel walked out of the room. Frank followed, tipping his hat to the curator as he did.

"You want me to shut the door?" he asked. She just stared at him. For a second he stared back. Joel tugged his shoulder. "I'll leave it open then," he said, and he followed Joel back toward the observation car.

25

"You weren't here so I didn't rob the other roomettes," said Frank, as they stepped over the guy Frank had pistol butted. "You want to go back and do them now?"

"No, fuck it," said Joel, checking his watch. "Let's go."

They had two possible rendezvous scheduled with Wharton, where the train would have to slow down on its own and they could jump off. If they missed those, Caleb would have to slow the train down from the engineer's cab, and then Amtrak mission control, or whatever, would know something had happened and the cops would know where to look for them.

They'd already missed the first rendezvous and Joel didn't want to miss the second. He wanted this over and done with. His watch said they were about three minutes away.

He unlocked the door back into the observation car. Back to the caboose.

"By the way," said Frank, pulling a piece of glass out of Joel's shoulder. "Where the fuck did you come from?"

"The roof," said Joel.

"The roof?"

"Yeah, you know." Joel pointed upward. "The roof."

"How the fuck did you get onto the roof?"

"I jumped," said Joel.

"Off what?"

"The Sangre de Cristo Mountains. What else could I possibly have jumped off?"

They stepped into the observation car where the cowed passengers were sitting just where they'd been left.

Neither they nor the two Fotheringays said anything as Joel and Frank wended their way through the lounge chairs and coffee tables to the door at the train's very end. The black landscape outside was invisible. Joel hit the light switch by the door. The lights went out and the landscape went from black to dim.

Joel pressed the "Emergency Exit Only—Alarm Will Sound" latch on the door, hoping that Caleb had remembered to turn the alarm off. Not that it really mattered at this point.

The door slid open. No alarm. The brothers stepped out onto the narrow caboose platform. Joel checked his watch again. Less than a minute. Frank lit a cigarette.

Joel looked at him—"Seriously?"—and then tapped his watch.

"What," said Frank. "You think I can't jump with a cigarette in my mouth?"

The brothers' walkie-talkies crackled on. It was Caleb: "We're there, boys. I'm getting off."

"Us too," answered Joel into the handset. Then, to Frank, "You first."

Frank nodded, sidled to the starboard side of the platform, swung his leg over the railing, leaned out as far as he could, and jumped.

With the Klimt container hugged tightly to his chest, Joel followed.

Frank splashed into the Purgatory River. Joel splashed down fifteen feet ahead of him.

Somewhere behind them, Caleb was already swimming for shore.

A minute later, the three brothers were squeezing water out of their clothes and loping south toward the spot where Bob was meeting them with their horses.

"You get the drawings?" asked Caleb. Joel held up the sealed plastic box.

"Good, good," said Caleb, and to Frank, "How 'bout you?"

Frank raised the bag of wallets dangling from his wrist.

"You were going to drop those after we found the drawings."

"In the moment," said Frank, "it just didn't make sense."

Joel was too tired to argue.

They spent about half an hour hiking south and east, back onto the Raton Plateau, in the general direction of Bobblers Knob. Of the three of them, Caleb was the freshest, so he took the lead, breaking a trail with a compass and a little star navigation. He and Frank both commented on how good that coffee had been, the stuff Bob had made right before they got going. Joel assumed they knew they'd been dosed and were joking about it but he wasn't sure. He was still feeling off, and tired, and the pain he hadn't felt right after his jump, et cetera, was starting to push through the adrenaline and drugs. So he'd leave the coffee for later.

Just south of Fisher's Peak, Wharton met them with the horses.

"How you boys doing?" said the Nazi, smiling, as the wet and weary Fotheringay boys walked into the grazing meadow where Wharton was waiting.

"Pretty good, pretty good," said Caleb.

"You get that package?" The Nazi was practically rubbing his hands together. Joel held the sealed box up for Wharton to see. He didn't smile. "Great! Great!" said Wharton. He checked his watch. "Why don't you boys take a load off for a little while, and then we'll lope it back to the trailer. Anybody want some more of my special coffee?"

Joel stared at Wharton, who was looking from Caleb to Frank.

"Special coffee?" said Frank, without any suspicion, just a little regular curiosity.

"Yeah," said Wharton. "I mix in a couple crushed Adderall when I need a boost. Adderall's actually an amphetamine—you know, like meth lite. Or maybe caffeine super-plus. Gets you focused, gives you a little extra energy." Wharton was unscrewing the top of a thermos. "You could probably get the same effect from one of those energy drinks, Monster or Red Bull or whatever, but the Adderall's actually less unhealthy than that fuck ton of chemical caffeine and sugar. That's what my, uh, prescribing pharmacist says, anyway." He had a little conspiratorial wink in his voice. Caleb chuckled.

"Yeah, I'll have another cup. I was wondering about that coffee. Real fucking good."

"Me too," said Frank. "I mean, I'll have a cup."

"I think your brother picked up on it," said Wharton, gesturing to Joel, who was still staring at him, trying to decide what to think about all this. "Freaked him out a little bit. I guess I should have warned you . . . I'm just so used to it, I don't even think about it anymore."

He held a cup out to Joel. Joel waited—waited long enough for it to be awkward—and then took it. Wharton's coffee explanation still didn't explain that gunshot, didn't explain why Wharton wouldn't let him have a look at the alleged rattler's nest. But shit, it was too late now, wasn't it? Might as well make the best of the thing. The payoff for that little box of drawings was going to have the ranch back up and running, full strength, and keep it going till the next bull market for sheep.

He drank his cup of coffee and did what Wharton suggested, took a load off. He sat himself down and waited for a chemical-fueled second wind. His brothers did the same.

The coffee was still hot because the Nazi had just finished brewing it, not five minutes before the boys arrived. It wasn't mixed with Adderall, or meth; there were about a hundred milligram tabs of benzos in it. Klonopin. Like Xanax, except less happy-inducing and more sedative.

Five minutes after the boys arrived, they were stretched out on the ground, sound asleep. The Nazi was relieved. He hadn't been sure how many Klons it would take to put someone rushing on meth to sleep. He didn't want to overdo it, though, and have that nosy fucker Joel smell or taste something wrong and stop them drinking it.

Anyway, they were asleep. They hadn't made a fire or anything, so Wharton navigated by moonlight.

He approached Frank first, knelt by his head, put a hand over his mouth, and slit his throat.

Frank's eyes opened, but he was too confused even to look scared. Before he had any idea what was happening to him he was unconscious from blood loss. The Nazi left him to bleed silently to death and moved on to Caleb.

When he put his hand over Caleb's mouth, though, Caleb's eyes flew open, and the son of a bitch actually bit him, then started fighting. Shouted for his brothers. The Nazi gave up the idea of slitting his throat. He started stabbing, chest and stomach, maybe a dozen times, until he was sure Caleb wasn't getting up—because Joel definitely was.

There was moonlight enough for Joel to see a shadow of what was going on—and for the Nazi to see that Joel was going for his gun. The Nazi went for his gun too. And the Nazi was faster. No benzos in him.

He shot Joel through the head. Joel crumpled.

The Nazi checked the three boys' pulses one by one. They were all dead.

The Nazi picked up the sealed box of Klimts and—what the hell—the wallets, too, and then the boys' wallets, and walked toward the horses, which were tied up at the edge of the field. The Nazi picked out the one that looked least tired, to ride back to the truck, and shot the other three.

When he got back to the truck he shot the horse he'd been riding and the spare horse they'd left in the trailer. He unhooked the truck and set the trailer on fire.

As he drove away, he wondered if he'd just started one of those out-of-control wildfires you see on the evening news. The

Southwest was having an awfully dry autumn. He laughed at the thought. Hell, that was someone else's problem. You couldn't expect him to take care of *everything*. He was only one man.

Soon he was heading east on a small paved highway, right along the Colorado–New Mexico border. Route 456. He put on some music and soon was singing along.

26

The deal with Simon—the negotiation over where she was going to hand over the Klimts—had been embarrassing for Kelly, but not too difficult. Simon had assumed he'd just send his plane for her again and she'd bring the Klimts with her. Which is how she *would* have done it if Levi Quintero hadn't told her otherwise. Instead, she told Simon she wasn't willing to do anything illegal on Qatari soil.

Simon chuckled and said she didn't have to worry about that.

She was adamant. She didn't want to be one of those Westerners in an Arab jail whose face you see on TV twice a month for twenty years. That was the embarrassing part. She thought Simon might be offended and just call the whole thing off. Or might threaten her. He had more than enough to blackmail her with. She couldn't take being blackmailed by the good guys *and* the bad guys; her anxiety was already approaching the Xanax point.

But Simon just laughed and said that she was probably thinking of the Ayatollah's jails or Erdogan's, and neither was an Arab—but that he wouldn't try to talk her out of her parochial Western attitude. How about delivering the Klimts in Paris?

Not in France, she said. He couldn't guarantee she wouldn't have to go through customs with them. How about the United States, she countered. He could fly over in his jet, she'd meet him at the airport. He wouldn't even have to get out of the plane.

He shook his head and said no (Quintero had guaranteed he'd refuse but said she ought to suggest it anyway). It was hard, Simon said, for a Qatari to get a visa to the U.S. right now, and the plane would probably be searched when it landed.

"In a month I'm going to be sailing for the Emirates on a yacht. You have a yacht, don't you?" (She knew he didn't. Quintero said he never traveled by sea. Who did these days?)

"No," said Simon. "I get seasick. Do you have a yacht?"

"No, but I've got an invitation. Final destination Singapore."

Simon put on a mock-sad face and said, "I thought I was your only patron, my dear."

Kelly smiled. "You would be, if you had a yacht."

Simon shrugged. "So you're saying you want me to meet you in Abu Dhabi?"

"No," said Kelly. "I want you to meet me on the yacht. We'll keep the territory neutral, somewhere out in the Gulf. So no one has to worry about getting her hands cut off." She pointed over her shoulder to Matt, who was following them silently, and who still had his new sword.

"Helipad?" Simon asked.

160

"Helipad, motor boat. Whatever. Just so long as we're both free and clear."

"Very well," said Simon, with a touch of polite exasperation. "Send me the transit details and I'll have something worked out. Your patron lets you make stops wherever you like?"

"One stop per blow job," said Kelly.

Simon clicked his tongue. "No, no, my dear, that is too high a price. Find a better captain."

"Oh, no, it's okay," said Kelly. "It's what I pay my escort for." She gestured back at Matt and laughed. Simon laughed, too, and Matt's face got red. He had a sudden impulse to dice both of them.

◈

When they got back on the plane to go home—after making it through the private-jet welcoming committee and drink orders, after they'd retired to the private bedroom—the first thing Kelly said was, "You shouldn't have taken his sword."

"He offered," said Matt.

"You should have refused."

"I did."

"Whatever," said Kelly. "It was rude. You really could've fucked me there."

"Go to hell, Kelly." Matt hung up his jacket and the damn pistol she'd asked him to bring, which had been poking into his side for the last six hours. She handed him her jacket to hang up too. He tossed it on the dresser and walked out of the bedroom into the lounge suite, the couch-and-TV room. He'd left the scimitar on the sofa. He sat down next to it, kicked off his shoes, and turned on the TV.

"You can come to bed if you want," said Kelly, standing in the bedroom doorway. She kicked off her own shoes and kicked them back into the bedroom.

"No thanks," said Matt. He clicked the hostess call button. Kelly was still standing in the bedroom doorway, arms crossed, when the hostess appeared fifteen seconds later.

"What may I do for you, Ms. Somerset? Mr. Fisher?" she asked.

Matt answered, "Have you got some silver polish and, or sandpaper on board? I thought maybe you used it for the dinner service."

"Uh, I believe we might, sir. I will look. Is there anything else?"

"Yes," said Matt, holding up the TV remote. "Could you turn this to any channel that's showing sports."

"Certainly, sir." She stepped into the room, took the remote, and clicked the set to a cricket match.

The same match was still going on when they landed in New York ten hours later. The sword was shining like an Olympic silver medal. Matt and Kelly hadn't said another word to each other.

27

They didn't talk in the cab ride home either. Matt had wrapped the sword in the fancy jacket Kelly had bought him. She didn't say anything about it but she figured he could tell she was simmering with irritation. On the other hand, how else could he have gotten it back to her apartment without anyone seeing it? She just hoped it didn't cut up the lining too bad. You think he'd be grateful, the obnoxious dead-eyed little shit.

Maybe this was a good time to break the news to him about Levi Quintero and the big double cross. Or should she wait till after they got the Klimts?

Yes, better to wait. He was still going to get something out of this, but she wanted him in a better frame of mind before she told him. No sense risking a blowup just because she felt like needling him.

"Stop the car," said Matt. The cab pulled over.

"What?" said Kelly.

"I need to stretch my legs," said Matt.

"Wait, what? What about, you know, we've got to be ready to pick them up."

"I'll be back before then."

"But . . . wait—" Matt was climbing out of the cab. "Pop the trunk," he said to the driver.

"Matt," said Kelly, "wait. I want to find out if it went okay, you know? It's happening tomorrow." She had lowered her voice. There was no one on the street; it was about six a.m. in Queens. But she was being careful.

"If it went okay or not," said Matt, "the only news you're going to get about it is in the news. We agreed no contact until the turnover. So either he'll show up or he won't."

"Fuck you, Matt. You can't just take off, we need to talk about things. A lot is going on. What do you mean 'stretch your legs'? For a morning? For a day? A week?"

"I'll be back in a few days. In plenty of time for your thing."

"For *our* thing, Matt. *Our* thing."

"Yeah, sure," said Matt. "I'll see you." Kelly watched Matt, his suitcase, and his sword walk around the corner.

She got back into the cab, sniffed once, and told the driver to keep going.

◆

As it turned out, Matt's tantrum was probably for the best. She'd have had to explain something to him; Levi Quintero was waiting for her in her apartment when she got back. She hated that.

"Don't keep coming in here uninvited," she said, feeling tougher than usual—toughened by how goddamn irritating everyone in her life was being. "I'm pretty sure you need a warrant?"

"I have one," said Quintero.

"Oh," said Kelly.

"You want to tell me how things went?"

"Things went exactly like you wanted them to. We agreed to a price and to make the handoff on the boat. He's going to come out on either a boat or a helicopter. You can handle that, right?"

"Yes," said Levi. "That was the plan. What was the price?"

"What does it matter?" asked Kelly, hanging up her jacket.

"We keep the money afterward." Kelly turned from her closet to look at him.

"Yeah?"

"'We,' the DEA, I mean."

"Oh," said Kelly. "Right. Seven-point-five."

"I thought you were going to get eight."

"I tried. It wasn't easy getting him up past six."

"Okay, well, that's fine. Who was the man you were traveling with?"

Kelly tried to look casual, still standing at the closet, taking off her shoes.

"You were watching me?"

"As much as we can."

"He's an old friend. He speaks Arabic. He was being my bodyguard."

"He's an ex-soldier and an ex-con. You picked him up from Ray Brook prison a few weeks ago and he's been staying here."

Kelly didn't say anything.

"How involved in this is he?"

"Not at all," said Kelly. "He doesn't even know about the counterfeiting."

"He doesn't wonder about all the printers and stuff?"

"I told him I'm a graphic designer. He took my word for it."

Quintero nodded. She wasn't sure if he believed her. After a moment, he said, "We'll get you the travel details to give to Abbas in the next few days."

"Will I actually get to sail across the Atlantic on a luxury yacht?"

"No," said Levi. "We're renting the yacht in Israel or possibly Cyprus. We'll fly you over. You know how long it takes to actually sail across the Atlantic?"

"No," said Kelly.

"Well, it's a long time, and we've got more important things to do," said Levi. "You got anything else to tell me? Keeping in mind that a lack of candor would void your deal with us."

"Not unless you want to hear about his art collection."

"I don't."

Kelly looked at him and shrugged. "I've been on a plane for ten hours. Mind if I take a shower?" She began to unfasten her belt.

"No," said Levi. "Sorry. I'll be in touch."

"Thanks," said Kelly. "When?"

"When I'm ready," said Levi. "I'll show myself out."

When he'd shut the door she whipped her belt at it. The buckle made a small dent and didn't make her feel any better.

28

Matt had been planning to make a more graceful exit, to say he was going to Georgia again for a couple days. But he'd seen the car rental sign. He had a bag packed already, he had the gun with him, and he was annoyed with Kelly, so he figured, fuck her, and told the cab to pull over.

He rented a Ford compact, loaded his stuff in, and got on the road for North Carolina. About eight hours later, in rural south-central Virginia, he stopped at a motel to sleep and shower and change into something less conspicuous—jeans and flannel. He wondered if he should stop somewhere and buy sneakers, but decided that black leather shoes aren't too conspicuous even when they're expensive.

He still had Darrel Clinton's niece's name written down in his wallet, and his niece's daughter's name, and her school's name and phone number. It took Matt stops at three different gas stations before he found a pay phone. He hadn't lived in the South in a long time. He hoped it was still basically trusting and guileless.

"Hello, Cinnamon Ridge Elementary, this is Karen speaking."

"Hi Karen, this is John Colyer—" Matt had Googled the most common names in north North Carolina and was playing the odds "—and my kid Madison's got a playdate with McKenna Clinton this afternoon. Normally her mom handles this stuff but I'm on dad duty today and I don't know where I'm supposed to be picking Madison up later, and I don't have Rhonda's phone number." Rhonda Clinton was Darrel Clinton's niece, the one he was living with.

"Oh no, dad duty, huh?" Karen laughed. "That's no problem, let me just look that up for you." Matt could hear the sound of keys clicking. "You got a pencil, honey?"

"Yup, go for it."

"Her number—I think it's her home number, but it might be a cell, you know everyone's dumping landlines—her number is xxx-424-9099. Her address is 222 Yadkinville Road, up in Pfafftown." Matt had to stop himself asking if she was yanking his chain. Asking if Dr. Seuss had named everything west of Winston-Salem might get her suspicious.

"Awesome, thanks so much, Karen."

"Anytime."

"Buh-bye."

"Bye."

Matt hung up. He felt bad; he was single-handedly ruining the innocence of this school's privacy policy. In the future, parents who actually did need to call a playdate's parents wouldn't be able to. And Karen would probably develop a guilt complex.

Just a few more things to add to the list of Darrel Clinton's crimes.

Matt picked up a map from the Welcome to North Carolina rest stop on I-77. It confirmed that Pfafftown was a real place, just up the road from Cinnamon Ridge, and that Yadkinville Road was a real road.

It was still earlyish in the morning, a little after nine. He could be driving up Yadkinville by around ten. Rhonda Clinton would presumably be at work; McKenna would be at school. Had Darrel found a job yet? Matt decided to swing by Pfafftown and find out.

◆

Two twenty-two Yadkinville was a two-story wood-sided, powder-blue, tidy-looking gabled house. One of the handrails leading up to a front porch was fresh, unstained wood, and the powder-blue was a fresh paint job. Maybe Rhonda had been putting Darrel to work. Or maybe he'd just been earning his keep by helping out with the chores. Maybe it was this conscientious spirit that had got him a good-behavior early release, not long after the rape.

Matt pulled into the driveway, parked, and walked up to the front door. He had the Sig Sauer in his shoulder holster; he'd put it on under his flannel button-up. And tucked under his arm was his suit jacket, wrapped around his new sword.

He rang the doorbell.

No answer. He rang it again. After waiting a minute and a half, just to be sure he hadn't caught Darrel on the can, he walked back off the porch and around to the back of the house.

There was a detached garage back there that had long ago been turned into a work shed. The garage door was up and a man was standing over a tool bench. His back was to Matt. It looked like Darrel. Matt wasn't certain, but it looked like him. The man hadn't heard Matt's car pull up, and he didn't seem to hear him walking up to the garage. As Matt got closer, he saw the man was wearing earplugs. Why? The man started a band saw. Loud as hell. He was cutting dowels. Behind him, on a table, was a dollhouse. Gift for his niece? What a goddamn sweetheart.

"Darrel!" shouted Matt. The man didn't hear him.

"*Darrel!*" shouted Matt, louder. The man still didn't hear him.

The man flipped the band saw off just as Matt touched his shoulder. The man flinched like he was at a horror movie.

"Jesus Christ," he said. He put his hand on his heart and turned around. He smiled at Matt. "You should *not* sneak *up* on a guy like that." He was wearing safety goggles. It was definitely Darrel Clinton. Definitely the Darrel Clinton Matt was looking for.

"Sorry 'bout that."

Darrel was brushing sawdust off his shirt. "It's okay. Can I help you?"

"You don't recognize me?"

Darrel was pulling out his earplugs. Now he looked at Matt hard, as Matt pulled the gun out of his shirt. Darrel was already going pale before he saw the gun. So he had a better memory than Reuben Harry.

"Back up a few paces and get on your knees," said Matt. Darrel's hand went for a hammer on the workbench. Matt cracked him over the head with the gun and he went down. Darrel was in his late forties. He wasn't really in shape for this. He was on the ground, looked dazed; maybe he'd blacked out for a minute. Didn't really matter. Matt slipped on the silver-polishing gloves he'd gotten from the private-jet hostess and took a roll of twine off a peg board.

Darrel was still only semiconscious. Matt rolled him over and tied his hands, tight. Then he straightened up and took a look around the shed. Now here was a head scratcher. Matt had never decapitated anyone before and he wasn't really sure the best way to do it.

He was pretty sure in Saudi Arabia they did it horizontally, with the decapitee on his knees and with his back straight. In Japan he assumed they'd done it kneeling also, because he was pretty sure that was the hara-kiri stance, and he understood from Simon that the belly stab and the head cut were a package deal. In Europe, he was pretty sure they'd done it on a chopping block . . . or was that just his impression from movies? A guy with a Halloween mask and a big ax standing over a guy with his head and shoulders on a stump or something.

That seemed like the easiest way to do it, for a beginner.

There was no chopping block in the shed. There was a pretty solid-looking, low wooden stool. That would probably work. He dragged it over to Darrel's head, then grabbed Darrel's collar and pulled him up onto his knees.

Darrel was awake. While Matt had pondered the stance question, he'd casually watched Darrel's fingers work at the twine tying his hands behind his back, while he played at being knocked out.

As Matt grabbed his collar, Darrel said, "What the fuck, man! What are you doing? What are you going to do to me?"

"Don't struggle or it's going to be a lot worse. A *lot* worse."

Darrel wasn't struggling. Matt leaned him forward onto the stool so his shoulders were on the seat and his head dangled off the far side.

Darrel was repeating the same thing over and over again, in a voice that was getting more plaintive and more pathetic. "What are you going to do to me, man? Please don't. What are you going to do to me?"

Matt unwrapped the jacket that was sheathing the sword and, not wanting to put the jacket down on anything, not wanting to leave fibers, put it on. The lining was a little cut up but it still fit beautifully. He loosened his shoulders a bit and took a couple practice swings.

Darrel had turned his head to the side and was watching this.

"Oh God, oh God, oh please God, what is that, what are you doing?"

The scimitar was so beautifully balanced . . . a real work of art.

"I'm executing you, Darrel. You know why."

"Oh God, please don't, oh God."

"You'd do the same thing in my place, I reckon," said Matt, taking a final practice swing.

"Yeah, man, maybe. But be the better man, please, don't do this, please."

"Now don't move. If I do this right it's not going to hurt. I'm not trying to make you suffer. Not that you don't deserve it, but I still don't want you to suffer. Look at the ground and don't move."

Darrel looked at the ground. The concrete floor. Matt couldn't see if he'd shut his eyes or not.

"Please. Please."

Matt swung down and Darrel's head came smoothly off. It was as easy as splitting dry wood with a sharp maul. Like a hot knife through butter.

Blood began to pump out of the body, and Matt backed away before any could get on his shoes. He wiped the sword off on the back of Darrel's shirt and turned to leave.

He turned back toward the worktable and grabbed some scrap newspaper, a nail, and a felt-tip pen.

He stepped out of the garage and pulled the sliding door down. Pushing the nail into the door's soft, weathered wood, he tacked up the paper, and wrote on it, in big block letters:

DO NOT GO IN HERE. CALL 911.

He underlined "not" three times. He didn't want Darrel's niece or, God forbid, his grand-niece to see what was in there.

He dropped the pen on the ground and walked back to the front of the house, taking off his gloves and jacket and rewrapping the sword.

He got back into his car, and back onto Yadkinville Road. In an hour he'd be back in Virginia, and eight hours after that in Queens. Aside from Darrel, he hadn't seen or spoken to a single person in North Carolina.

If you didn't count Karen. He hoped she wouldn't find out about this. She seemed like a good egg. And this was a filthy business.

29

Matt spent another night on the road, in a B&B in the Blue Ridge Mountains, in the little sliver of West Virginia that touches Maryland. He wanted to swing through West Virginia for no particular reason—just because he felt like it, because he was in no rush to get back to Kelly, because he liked John Denver, because he missed the South, and because he felt that West Virginia was a paragon of good southern manners, even if it wasn't actually part of the South. He was thinking about that—how it wasn't part of the South—as he sat on the B&B's back porch the next morning, looking out over the mist on the autumn leaves, a big sweeping Appalachian valley, and smoked a corncob pipe he'd bought at the reception desk for a dollar.

West Virginia was not part of the South. In fact, West Virginia had seceded from Virginia because Virginia was seceding from the United States of America and West Virginians didn't want any part of slavery or the Confederacy. They just wanted to be left alone in their mountains, to live their lives and mind their own business. And they'd been rewarded for it with a century and a half of being the butt of every cracker and bumpkin stereotype Hollywood could rustle up. The kind of stuff that Matt, as a Georgia boy, reserved for Mississippians. Oh well. Life isn't fair. Anyway, the jokes didn't seem to have bothered them. Maybe they hadn't heard any of them. It was possible television hadn't made it up here yet. Anyway, it was the only state with a state song any one gave a damn about. "Take Me Home, Country Roads." That probably balmed them a little, if they needed it. Did they play it before high school basketball games the way "The Star-Spangled Banner" was played? He smiled and smoked his pipe. Goddamn but the view was beautiful.

The matron half of the elderly couple that ran the B&B poured him another cup of coffee and another glass of milk, and asked if he wanted another couple pancakes. Matt said no, he really ought to be getting back on the road soon. Which was true. Though as he sipped his coffee he felt like indulging in a day of bone idleness. He was two-thirds done with his revenge program, which was nice. He puffed the corncob and watched heavy blue pipe smoke drift over the porch railing and float off into the morning fog that blanketed the receding blue mountains. He ought to be nicer to Kelly. She'd really been nothing but good to him since she'd picked him up from prison. Itself, no small favor. He shouldn't be so sensitive about stuff. Maybe that's why he felt particularly good this morning—the satisfaction at Darrel Clinton and Reuben Harry both being dead. He felt more like himself. Now he just had to kill Captain Kirby Monroe and he could move on with his life. And do it with a little money in his pocket, thanks to Kelly.

Yet that was why he didn't especially feel like driving straight back to Queens. Today was the day the drawings-to-be-stolen were scheduled to set off on their train journey from LA to the MoMA. Kelly was going to be strung out on stress and anxiety. He had enough of his own to worry about. He'd rather she chewed her nails in private.

Not very gallant of him. He sighed. He really should get back on the road. His pipe had gone out. He banged it clean on the sole of his shoe, stood up, and stamped out the smoldering tobacco leaves and ashes and, with the same foot, swept them off the deck. He watched them blow away, down into the valley, finished his milk, paid for his room, and got back into his car. The first thing he did was check the rear footwell to make sure his sword was still there. He'd gotten his fill of John Denver; he was driving northeast by east out of the mountains, and he put on an alt station, hoping for something from the mid-1990s.

30

"**W**here the fuck have you been?" said Kelly, as he let himself into her apartment.

She didn't sound mad, though, she sounded excited. Matt had won the battle against his conscience, taken the long way back, and spent the day in Gettysburg, walking the battlefield and thinking about the war fought for other men's freedom. Matt didn't know much about his family tree; he wondered which side his ancestors had fought on. About one in ten of the southerners who fought in the Civil War fought for the Union. In elementary school, there'd been a serious debate over his English teacher teaching the kids the verse from "Marching Through Georgia" about the pro-Union Georgians who'd wept to see the Stars and Stripes for the first time in four long years. That the march through Georgia remained controversial was an understatement. On the other hand, you couldn't walk ten feet in Georgia without seeing the Stars and Stripes flying in someone's yard or pasted to someone's rear windshield. It was a curious contradiction. Not something Matt normally would have given much thought to. But he'd spent the whole day feeling bizarrely emotional. He couldn't figure it out. He'd tried to force himself back in line, shouting at himself, in his head, the way he shouted at his squad when he was a sergeant. Telling himself he was acting like he had a bad case of PMS. When he'd been sitting in the dark theater at the Gettysburg museum, and they'd played Jeff Daniels reciting the Gettysburg Address, he'd wept. Full on, water pouring down his face crying. He'd had to hide his face in his hands as people walked past him, when the lights came up and they filed out of the theater, while he was still trying to pull himself together.

He'd succeeded before too long. Finding a radio station playing angry 1990s rap had helped. He was pretty much himself again by the time he'd returned the car and walked back to Kelly's apartment.

He was glad, because right after she greeted him by saying "where the fuck have you been?" she ran over and hugged him, and the feel of her warm arms around his neck almost got him tearing up again.

She kissed his cheek and said, "Have you seen the news?"

"What news," said Matt. "It's like four in the morning."

"On Twitter!" said Kelly, holding up her phone. "People who had tickets to get on the Southwest Chief in Colorado are tweeting like crazy!" She began to read: "'Southwest Chief Amtrak train is stopped in Trinidad Station in south Colorado, and no one's saying why' . . . 'They won't let us on the train . . . cops everywhere.' Look at this picture!"

She held her phone up for him again. The screen showed a sea of red and blue lights bathing a long, shiny Amtrak train. She went back to reading: "'Ambulance here but no one's been put in it or treated or anything . . . cops say no one's dead and it wasn't a mechanical issue, but won't tell us anything else . . . won't say if we'll be able to get on at all . . . want to talk to everyone with a ticket and won't let us leave the station! Won't let anyone off the train!'"

She hugged him again, and kissed him again, this time on both cheeks. "They did it! Your . . . people, whoever, did it!"

She danced over to her couch and plopped down onto it. "I can't believe it! I mean, I actually can't believe it. I didn't *really* believe it would *really* happen. Jesus lord in heaven. My heart is pounding out of my chest. I feel like I'm floating, like I'm floating along with the clouds. My whole body feels tingly. *Wheeee-ewwwww.*" She sighed deeply.

Matt laughed. She was happy to see him smile. "Turn on the fan," she said, reaching awkwardly overhead and sliding open a window with the palms of her hands. "I bought a pack of Wides, as a treat. Could you get them? They're by my computer." She was gazing excitedly at her phone, fingering the screen, scrolling up and down, rereading her favorite tweets. Matt turned on the fan and carried over the Camel Wides, opened the pack, put two in his mouth, lit them. He stuck one between Kelly's lips—she didn't look away from her phone, but smiled and said "thanks," with the filter clutched in her teeth. Matt lay down on the sofa next to her, put his head on her lap, and smoked, listening to her read and reread Twitter updates. She stroked his hair, and—over his feet, propped up on the arm of the couch—he watched the sun rise.

31

The handover of the Klimt drawings had been planned in advance by Kelly, who wanted to make sure she never had any direct contact with the hard-core criminals. Matt would hand over the money in a parking garage in Queens, the Nazi would count it and then give Matt the combination to a locker in Penn Station, where Kelly would be waiting. Once Kelly certified the Klimts were there and in order, Matt and the Nazi would go their separate ways, and Matt and Kelly would rendezvous back at her apartment.

Matt was already waiting on the top floor of the parking garage—looking out at a sliver of the East River ten or fifteen miles away—when the Nazi arrived in the orange Bronco. It pulled into an empty spot and Matt walked over to it, unslung the gym bag on his shoulder, and climbed in.

"Howdy," said the Nazi.

"Hey," said Matt. "Seems from the news everything went well."

"Yes, it did," said the Nazi.

"You get the sense anyone's on to you?"

"Nope," said the Nazi. "I'm very good at this."

"Well, I mean," said Matt, lighting a cigarette. "We did meet in prison."

"Eh. No one's perfect. I wasn't in a good place at the time. Mentally. I was stressing about the Broncos." He cranked down the window slightly to let Matt's smoke out. "My record'd still be clean if they'd signed Peyton a few years earlier."

"Yeah," said Matt. "Anyways." He unzipped the gym bag and showed the Nazi the money. Hot off of Kelly's presses. She'd emphasized to Matt, as they'd packed it into bundles of ten thousand, that Simon really ought to just be buying her fake hundreds, 'cause they were works of artistic genius. Each one a work of art. Her best work ever. They almost made her sad she was getting out of the business. She saw no need for humbleness about her counterfeits.

"Two million in hundreds. The bundles are a hundred bills each."

"You won't be insulted if I count them, will you?" asked the Nazi, reaching into the bag and pulling a bundle out.

"No," said Matt.

"I'm not going to find dye packs in here, am I?"

"No."

"That was a joke, Matt," said the Nazi. "Lighten up."

He began to count—every bill in every packet. It took about fifteen minutes.

"Okay," he said. "Locker number ninety-two. Thirty-four left, thirty-two right, twenty-four left."

Matt dialed Kelly and repeated the numbers.

She headed down into the lower levels of the rat-maze train station under Madison Square Garden—Penn Station—the ghost of the beautiful Penn Station that was torn down in 1963, the thought of which made Kelly sad every time she came here. She remembered studying it in her art history class. Somewhere in the PATH Train section, she walked down a line of lockers to number ninety-two and opened it. It was one of the floor-level lockers for big bags. Inside was a plastic rolling suitcase. She rolled it out, unzipped it, and looked inside. There was a plastic box, sealed in saran wrap. She slit the saran with her thumb nail and opened the box. Inside were six heavy plastic envelopes.

She looked around. There were people walking back and forth, a few other people opening lockers. A few feet to her right a lady was locking up a large hikers' backpack. A few yards to her left a guy was leaning back against the wall of lockers, texting someone. No one seemed to be paying her any attention. Kelly slipped out one of the envelopes.

The plastic was heavy but transparent. Staring back at Kelly, with her hair stacked neatly on her head and a heavy jeweled choker around her neck, was the face of Adele Bloch-Bauer. The woman in gold. Kelly sucked in a sharp breath of air. The long, free, easy pen strokes. The single stroke that was her collarbone. The slight hint of a Mona Lisa smile. The jumble of thready hair above the face, cocked to the right and leaning on a graceful hand. Just beautiful. This was not the time to look at her, though.

Kelly moved on to the next envelope, and the next, and the next. They were all there, all beautiful, all just as they were supposed to be. All matching the insurance photos—right down to the almost slimy-feeling heavy plastic envelopes. She put them back into their box, clicked it shut, zipped up the bag, and got off her knees.

The man to her left wasn't leaning on the locker anymore. He was looking at her with his phone held out in front of him. He clicked the screen of his phone, then walked past her and into a flow of people heading for an escalator.

Had he taken her picture?

She watched him walk away. Jeans and a heavy, pale green jacket. He was wearing heavy boots. Doc Martens. She'd noticed them when he'd been leaning on the locker. Red shoe laces in them, sort of unusual. He was only about twenty, maybe even a little younger. Short buzzed hair.

He'd gone the way she'd been planning to go, but there were a million exits and she decided she'd use a different one. She walked off in the opposite direction, rolling the Klimt case behind her.

Back at street level, she first walked toward the cab line, then thought better of it and called an Uber. She slid the case onto the back seat and climbed in beside it. Across the street, a young guy in a green jacket and a baseball cap and sunglasses climbed into the passenger seat of an old gray Mercedes. She wasn't sure if it was the same guy. She couldn't see his feet. She wondered if she was being crazy.

Her Uber pulled out into traffic. So did the Mercedes. The Mercedes followed her onto Sixth Avenue, and then onto 36th Street.

She texted Matt: *Got the stuff but I think someone's following me.*

In the parking garage, still in the orange Bronco, Matt's phone buzzed. The Nazi glanced over at it.

"Are we good?" Matt still had the bag of money on his lap. He'd rezipped it after the Nazi was done counting.

"You have someone following my partner?" said Matt, once he'd read the text.

He and the Nazi locked eyes. The Nazi seemed to be thinking something over.

"Yes," he said, and shrugged. "I like to know who I'm working with. Don't like an uneven partnership."

"Call him off," said Matt.

Their eyes were still locked.

"No," said the Nazi.

Matt pulled the Sig Sauer out of his flannel overshirt. He rested it on the bag of money, pointed at the Nazi's stomach.

"Call him off," said Matt.

The Nazi looked down at the gun and then back up at Matt's eyes. He took a moment to think it over.

"Fine," said the Nazi.

"Keep your hands on the wheel for right now, okay?" said Matt. "Which pocket's your phone in?"

"Right front." Matt reached over the gear shift and slid it out, then handed it to its owner. The Nazi dialed.

"Hey," he said into the phone. "Turn around and go home. Don't be subtle about it." He waited for an answer.

"No," he said into the phone. "Now." He waited for another answer, then hung up.

"Okay," said the Nazi. "Called off."

Matt answered Kelly's text: *Yes you're being followed. Still there or gone?*

Kelly was watching the Mercedes in the Uber's rearview mirror. As she crossed Third Avenue, the Mercedes turned left and headed uptown. Guess she was just being paranoid. Her phone buzzed; she read Matt's text and answered it. *Gone.*

Matt put away his phone, and then his gun. "Thanks," he said to the Nazi. "I appreciate it." He handed over the bag of money.

"Likewise," said the Nazi.

"I'll see you around," said Matt, and climbed out of the Bronco. Instead of walking back to Kelly's, he walked to the subway and rode around for a while, just to make sure he wasn't being followed either.

32

"These are nice," said Levi Quintero, looking over the six Klimts—six drawings of Adele Bloch-Bauer—laid out on Kelly's dining table, each one sitting on top of its plastic envelope. Kelly had boxes of cotton gloves she used for handling her counterfeit bills during production. She'd insisted that Quintero put a pair on. She was wearing a pair too. Matt had gloved only his left hand, so he could use his right to smoke. Kelly had banished him and his cigarette to the fire escape and he was watching her talk to Quintero through the window, like a kid looking through the glass at an aquarium.

Kelly didn't know what to do about Matt. She was utterly confused. When she'd told him, about an hour earlier, about the DEA, and the cocaine and the arms sales and Hezbollah, and the fact that they weren't getting any real money out of this after all, and that she had lied to him, but that she'd been in a jam, and hadn't had any choice—and then promised to make it up to him—he hadn't seemed mad at all. Or confused. Or surprised. He'd just shrugged and said he'd gotten plenty out of it, and didn't regret being involved. He mentioned that stupid fucking sword. Kelly repeated her promise to make it up to him. He'd shrugged again and lit a cigarette and she'd asked him not to do it around the de-enveloped Klimts.

"Yes," said Kelly, to Quintero. "They are nice."

"I mean, I don't know much about art," said Quintero, "having a real job and all. But I've got to say, there is something about these."

"Yes," said Kelly, without any irony in her voice. "There really is, isn't there?"

"I don't like that you lied to me, Kelly, about them being stolen already. You know that makes the DEA accessories to the theft, in a manner of speaking. I can void your whole deal over this."

"But you're not going to, right? I mean, you still want to get Abbas."

"Yes, we do. You cunt." The choice of words caught Kelly off guard. Quintero hadn't raised his voice or anything, but she could feel how angry he was. It was almost like he was radiating heat, like a piece of metal that had just been pulled out of a blast furnace. But fuck him. *He* was using *her*, why shouldn't she have used him right back? Anyway, if she hadn't lied, the DEA would be at a dead end with Abbas. He ought to thank her. The, ugh . . . dick. She'd need to think of something nastier to call him.

"If I hadn't lied, I wouldn't have had anything to sell Abbas, and you DEA shitheads would still be sitting around with your thumbs up your asses trying to figure out some way to arrest him. You ought to thank me."

"Three people are dead," said Quintero, who was still looking at the Klimts.

"I wasn't involved with any of the planning. The news said they were the robbers."

"That doesn't make them any less dead, Ms. Haggerty. And there's a fourth person missing, a New Mexican. Disappeared same time, same place—more or less—as the great train robbery."

"I thought they said he was the one who killed the other three."

"That isn't clear yet." Quintero was bending down to look more closely at one of the studies for *Adele II.*

"Anyway," said Kelly. "If you still want me to do this, I want my immunity deal to spell out that I won't face any charges resulting from the train robbery or anything connected to it."

"What makes you think," said Quintero, "that I won't just go ahead with this deal without you? I've got the drawings. The plans are already in motion."

"I think you won't 'cause you're worried Abbas'll get cold feet and not go through with it. I think if you thought you could go ahead without me you would've arrested me already."

Quintero took off his cotton gloves and dropped them into a trash can.

"Yes, Ms. Haggerty. That's all correct. Because the ethics of the situation makes it pretty clear that it makes more sense to stop Hezbollah's coke-for-guns program than it does to try to lock you up for stealing six paintings and getting a few people killed. But that doesn't stop you being a cunt."

Matt, who was still outside on the fire escape, tapped on the glass. Kelly and Levi both looked at him. His voice was muted by the closed window.

"Mr. Quintero," said Matt. "You call her that again and you're going to fucking regret it."

"You wanna bet?" said Quintero.

"Yes," said Matt. Quintero turned back to Kelly.

"Anyways," he said. "Let's talk about what's going to happen in the Persian Gulf."

"And I want Matt included in the deal or it's a no-go."

"Absolutely not. He's taking his chances."

"Then you might as well just arrest me now." Kelly knew she wasn't actually going to go to jail to get Matt immunity. But it didn't hurt to ask, right?

Quintero pressed his thumb into his forehead. He was . . . incandescently mad, but still he hadn't raised his voice.

"You know I can only get you protection from federal charges, right? If New Mexico or Colorado want to make something of this, you're on your own."

"I understand. But I'm pretty sure these are all federal crimes."

"Yes," said Quintero.

"Anyway," said Kelly, after waiting a beat for Quintero to go on, which he didn't, "Abbas is going to expect to see Matt with me. I already told him Matt was coming along—as my security, my aide-de-camp. It'll make him suspicious if Matt's not there, and if you don't include Matt in the deal, how's he going to come along? I mean, what reason would he have?"

Quintero took a deep breath and let it out slowly.

"I am agreeing to this," said Quintero, "only because I happen to know that Sergeant Matthew Kubelsky has been royally fucked by the American legal system once already and I'm an inherently justice-seeking kind of a guy. But I do want to be clear about this: I still think you're a cunt."

"All right," said Matt, throwing away his cigarette, sliding open the window, and climbing back into the apartment. "That's it."

"Come and get it," said Quintero, rolling up his sleeves.

"Please don't, Matt," said Kelly, getting between them. "Please."

The two men stared each other down.

"Please," said Kelly again, looking at Matt.

"Fine," he said, finally. "But only if you put the freaking art away and let me smoke inside. It's chilly out there."

Quintero laughed.

33

When Quintero had told Kelly they were going to rent a yacht in Israel or Cyprus, Kelly assumed she was in for a long cruise on a luxurious yacht. If they were going 10 or 12 knots, which seemed to be the superyacht average cruising speed, it would take about two weeks for them to make the trip. Two glorious weeks on a superyacht, circumnavigating (almost) the Arabian Peninsula. She bought new bikinis and sunglasses and big floppy hats to celebrate. She also figured the trip would take her through the Suez Canal—unless they wanted to go all the way around Africa—and that was awfully exciting to the engineer in her.

It turned out what Quintero had meant was that the yacht would be rented in Israel or Cyprus and then sailed to the American naval base at Bahrain—home of the Fifth Fleet—and Kelly and Matt and their DEA escort would join it there. The DEA escort had been one of the guys Kelly had caught rifling through her stuff on that first night Quintero had ambushed her at her apartment. She didn't like him and made a point of not talking to him. Unfortunately, he'd served in Iraq at the same time and in roughly the same place as Matt, and they quickly became bosom buddies. That annoyed the hell out of Kelly, who felt that—after all, wasn't she getting Matt off scot-free for the train robbery?—he ought to join her in giving the DEA the silent treatment. But she didn't say anything, because from the time the DEA guy met them at her apartment till the time Quintero met them at NSA Bahrain, she and Matt were never alone.

After a very brief hello, the only words she spoke on the entire trip were to ask the DEA guy why they were advertising an NSA franchise in Bahrain. He said NSA stood for "Naval Support Activity" and laughed at her, in a very patronizing way. She asked him what the fuck "naval support activity" meant, and he said "naval base," and she said that was fucking stupid, that a base was a place and an activity obviously wasn't. He said maybe if she'd served her country instead of being a fucking criminal she'd understand the lingo better. Matt told him to cool it. Kelly answered that maybe if the American military spent less time coming up with bureaucratic nonsense lingo and more time killing bad guys it would have won a war in the last seventy years. Matt told Kelly to cool it. But you could've cut the bad will with a dull knife by the time they landed at Manama, the capital of Bahrain. Matt tried to lighten the mood by humming a little of the Muppets' "Manama-na, do-do-do-do-do" song, but then Kelly told him that was offensive and, after that, no one said anything to anyone until Quintero met them at the gates of NSA Bahrain in a big black SUV.

They didn't go into the base. Quintero had just been through a final coordination meeting with the local Navy and State Department potentates and everything had already been loaded onto the yacht—including the Klimts, which Quintero had taken custody of after the meeting in Kelly's apartment. Quintero had made the yacht his base of operations. When Kelly saw it, she understood why. It was unbelievably lavish and about two hundred feet long. Quintero was set up in the giant dining room, where a table was covered with papers and laptops, and a small portable safe in which Kelly assumed the Klimts were locked. He'd left the master bedroom for her, however, which struck her as chivalrous, and set aside the bedroom next to it for Matt, which struck her as both chivalrous and charmingly old-fashioned, given that he knew she and Matt had been more or less living together for months.

After dropping their travel bags in Kelly's room, she and Matt were summoned to the dining-planning room to meet the rest of the team. Mostly they were the cadre who'd searched Kelly's apartment, plus some "assault team" guys who were going to make the arrest after the money was transferred. The assaulters all had thick special forces beards, and two of the five seemed to recognize Matt, or at least know who he was—pointedly calling him Sergeant Kubelsky, shaking his hand and saluting him when Quintero dismissed Matt and Kelly back to their rooms for the night, with bagged lunches for dinner. They were going to spend the evening in the Manama harbor, sail at night, and be in position a little after dawn. The rendezvous would take place twelve nautical miles (just under fourteen normal miles) directly north of Qatar's Halul Island, just outside Qatar's territorial waters, and outside the tanker channels that crisscrossed the Persian Gulf like uncooked spaghetti spilled on a glass stovetop.

Abbas would arrive by helicopter at noon. Quintero would play the role of Kelly's wealthy host and then excuse himself so the art sale could be conducted privately, in the dining room, which was already being cleared of its DEA control-room stuff. Abbas would look at the drawings, give his final imprimatur, and then transfer the money to Kelly's account, which would actually be a DEA account. Once the money arrived, he would be arrested in accordance with Articles 15 and 19 of the United Nations Convention on the High Seas, a treaty signed and ratified by the United States and most of the other UN member states. The relevant articles state that "the act of receiving or possessing illegally obtained public or private property, for private ends, by the crew or passengers of a private vessel or private aircraft, outside the jurisdiction of any State, shall constitute an act of piracy."

Quintero read this out to the whole team, including Matt and Kelly, during a final evening briefing in Manama's harbor.

"On the high seas, or in any other place outside the jurisdiction of any State, every State may arrest the persons and seize the property concerned with committing an act of piracy. The courts of the State that carried out the seizure may decide upon the penalties to be imposed, subject to the rights of third parties acting in good faith."

Quintero put down the paper he was reading from and picked up another.

"Code of Laws of the United States, Title Eighteen, Crimes and Criminal Procedures, Part One, Chapter Eighty-One, Section Sixteen-Fifty-One: Piracy Under Law of Nations. 'Whoever, on the high seas, commits the crime of piracy as defined by the law of nations, and is afterward brought into or found in the United States, shall be imprisoned for life.'"

Quintero looked around the room, which had taken on a solemn, somber feel. He smiled at everyone. That broke the tension.

"Of course, it used to be we could just hang 'em from a yardarm. But, anyway, we can take him in and charge him with this," he brandished the paper, "and then, all in good time, with the trafficking and the terrorism. We'll see if he wants to treat with us after that. We're going to be getting a good thing done here. Keep that in mind."

He put the paper down and took a deep breath before slowly making eye contact with everyone in the room, one at a time. The solemnity was back.

"Everyone get a good night's sleep."

34

Matt slept in Kelly's room, and slept pretty well. The sound of the ocean washing along the sides of the ship, once they were under way, was remarkably calming, and he loved the smell of salt air. The two or three times he woke up during the night, he saw Kelly standing on the balcony—the master bedroom took up most of the rear half of the second-highest deck of the ship, underneath the bridge, or the wheelhouse, or whatever it was called on a yacht. The rear of the bedroom opened onto a balcony, where Kelly seemed to stand all night, chain smoking.

The first time Matt woke up and saw her out there, he called her back to bed. She waved him off. The second time he went out to see if she was all right and she said she was fine but that her stupid new cigarette lighter was out of fluid and could he bring her the mini lighter-fluid can she had stashed in her makeup bag. The third time he saw her out there he rolled over and went back to sleep.

In the morning the scene was set. Kelly got into costume, which was a loose-knit robe-shawl thing over a turquoise bikini. Matt put on his fancy suit. Quintero appeared in a fancy suit of his own—white linen, right (he said) for the climate. Some of the DEA people were dressed in ship steward uniforms. The others, and the assault team guys with the big beards, were hidden belowdecks, waiting on word that the money had been transferred and that Abbas had officially become a purchaser of stolen goods (on the high seas).

Kelly was spread out on a lounge chair, getting sun and trying to look rich and luxurious (and calm), with Matt and Quintero nearby talking about baseball, when the low buzz of a helicopter began to drift over the boat. The buzz was replaced by a loud *chop chop chop* sound, and after about ten minutes of delicate, awkward maneuvering a sleek, news and traffic–sized Airbus helicopter landed on the helipad, which was on the yacht's long, pointy nose (or bow section, or whatever it was called on a yacht).

Quintero and Kelly greeted Abbas. Matt stood in the background, looking like a security man, and couldn't hear the greetings over the sound of the rotor blades slowing to a stop. But when Abbas saw him he smiled and walked over to shake his hand.

"How's the sword?"

"Wonderful," said Matt. "It's the best gift I've ever been given."

"Good, good," said Abbas, smiling and clapping Matt on the elbow.

"I'll let you . . . do whatever it is you're doing and excuse myself," said Quintero, waving a goodbye to Abbas and walking off, as if he were anxious to get back to his various rich man's activities. The gesture seemed familiar to Abbas, who bowed in answer to it. Now Abbas's Canadian-accented assistant was climbing out of the helicopter, carrying a large metal briefcase and holding up the hem of his long, traditional robes that were a dramatic contrast to Abbas's neat and trendy bright-blue suit.

"Let's go inside," said Kelly, waving Simon into the big dining room as the Canadian bowed his head to Kelly and Matt in turn. Matt stuck out his hand to shake and the Canadian gave him a little wink. "The curling team's really coming together."

"Am I still invited to the trials?" asked Matt.

"Most certainly," said Abbas's assistant. They followed Abbas and Kelly inside, Matt standing aside to let the Canadian go first, the Canadian patting him on the shoulder in thanks. Matt hoped they weren't going to try to arrest the assistant along with his employer. He seemed like a good guy.

In the dining room, the six Klimt drawings were carefully laid out on a white tablecloth. Kelly made a sweeping *voilà* gesture and Abbas made a *wow* sound.

He went from one to another, bending down, squinting at details, shaking his head and saying things like "my god" and "exquisite. Simply exquisite!" When he straightened up from the last drawing, which showed Adele Bloch-Bauer leaning back against a wall, surrounded by geometric wallpaper, Abbas turned to Kelly and said, "I congratulate you. These are simply wonderful." Kelly bowed in appreciation of the compliment and said nothing.

Abbas pointed to his assistant and then to the table. The assistant laid out the metal case and removed a laptop from it. One side of the case was cut foam to hold the laptop, the other to hold the drawings. That's what it looked like to Matt, anyway.

Kelly lit a cigarette.

"My dear," said Abbas, "have you the number of the account you'd like the money deposited in?"

Kelly nodded and handed him a slip of paper. "Right here. Suisse."

Abbas smiled. "Naturally." He handed the slip to his assistant, who started arranging the wire transfer.

"Seven million, five hundred thousand dollars?" he said to Abbas.

"Unless she's lowered her price," said Abbas, playfully, looking at Kelly. Kelly shook her head.

"'Fraid not, Simon. This is already the friends and family rate, remember?"

"Mhmm," said Abbas. "Oh well. Seven-point-five it is."

His assistant typed several strings of numbers—he was standing over the laptop; no one had offered him a chair. Matt would have, but he didn't want to stop the flow of the transaction. The assistant hit a return key.

"The money is on its way," he said to the room.

"Thank you," said Abbas.

Kelly reached into her pocket and fished out her cell phone. "My banker said he'd call when it came through." Abbas nodded.

For about forty-five seconds they stood in silence, all looking at one another. Kelly threw a cigarette butt out a window onto the main deck's teak decking and stuck a fresh one into her mouth, holding the Zippo with a steady hand, when her phone rang. She lit the cigarette, dropped the lighter on the table, and answered the phone. Matt watched a little damp spot begin to appear under the Zippo. She'd overfilled it and lighter fluid was leaking. Typical of Zippos. She'd been nervous last night when she'd asked him to get her the refill can. Matt regretted not having offered to do the refill himself. Not that it really mattered.

He was looking absentmindedly at the puddle around the Zippo when his attention was suddenly yanked to Kelly's phone call.

She'd answered it "Kelly Somerset" and said "yes," and then "yes," and then "perfect, yes, Zurich." That was what grabbed Matt's attention. He had to force himself not to twist his head toward her. "Zurich" was the code word she and Quintero had agreed on to indicate that Abbas had a weapon drawn and that the arrest team should come in "hot." Matt was confused. Had she misspoken? Or did Simon have his hand on a gun? Matt couldn't see his right hand; it was hanging around his waist. Holster in his waistband? Was Kelly just jumpy? God fucking damn it, he thought, keeping his face blank. He knew what was about to happen. He'd been through it before and he hated it.

At the far end of the dining room a beautiful wooden door was slammed open. A flash-bang grenade was tossed through it. Matt closed his eyes and covered his ears. The flash of a flash-bang grenade is as bright as the sun at noon on a perfectly clear day, multiplied by ten thousand. The bang is louder than a howitzer being fired a foot from your head. Those are actually the correct figures, not hyperbole. Matt had learned them in basic training. The flash-bang's bang is so loud that the sound waves compress and heat the air as they pass through it. Between the bang and the flash, anyone in the vicinity who hasn't got his eyes and ears protected can expect five or ten seconds of blindness and several minutes of intense dizziness, as his inner ear and equilibrium are knocked for a loop.

Between the heat of the flash and the heat of the bang, flash-bangs occasionally set fires. It's rare, but it happens. Quintero's guys had damped the carpet in the dining room as a precaution in case it came to this.

But it seemed that wasn't enough. Even with his eyes and ears covered, the grenade had still dimmed Matt's vision and thrown off his balance. He couldn't see what was going on. He heard the sound of tasers going off. The table was on fire. The tablecloth was burning. The Klimts were burning with it. Kelly was squinting at them, half-blind, like Matt, stumbling dizzily, trying to keep her balance. The cigarette that had been dangling from her lips was missing. Matt hoped she hadn't sucked it into her mouth when the blast hit her, hadn't swallowed it. The room was filled with smoke. He grabbed her and pulled her out a sliding door onto the deck, where they both gasped for air.

As Matt's vision cleared, he could see Abbas and his assistant facedown on the ground, being handcuffed with plastic zip ties. Kelly was coughing and her eyes were watering. Or maybe she was crying. Matt was coughing too. She leaned over the side of the boat and vomited. A second later, Matt did too.

35

Kelly didn't see Abbas again. He was taken somewhere belowdecks for an initial interrogation. So was his assistant, even though Matt had put in a good word for him with Quintero. The helicopter, which was now DEA property, was lashed to the deck, and the yacht was headed back to Manama.

Abbas had not had a gun but his assistant had, buried under his robes. Quintero had started out furious that the drawings had burned up—he thought Kelly had overreacted. She shouldn't have said "Zurich" when a simple "Geneva" would have sufficed. But when he saw how Kelly looked, almost comatose with grief, he toned it down. He said he understood how she felt. It was a damn shame. The DEA would probably have to pay off the insurance company unless they tried to cover up the provenance, which Quintero was disinclined to do. But the important thing, the *really important* thing, he said to Kelly, was that they'd gotten Salman

Abbas and that he was sure to cut a deal with them to avoid life in a supermax, and that a lot of terrorists and drug dealers were going to get ID'd and arrested, and a lot of drug and gun money was going to get seized.

When Quintero saw that this wasn't cheering Kelly up any, he squeezed her shoulder and told her it wasn't her fault, that they were only studies for paintings, not the paintings themselves. That these things happen. That the Nazis had intentionally burned dozens of Klimts, according to his operation-prep research on Wikipedia.

That didn't really help either, so he squeezed her shoulder again, told her the counterfeiting charges, etc., would be dropped as agreed, and left her alone with Matt. They were in the master bedroom. Matt suggested maybe Kelly would like to get some air. Kelly said she just needed some time alone. Matt offered to leave but Kelly opted instead to disappear for a while into the en suite bathroom. Before long he heard the shower running. He thought for a moment about the fact that he'd missed his chance to shower on a plane, and now he'd probably never get to shower on a boat either. Then he decided to go look for something to eat.

◆

Matt brought some cellophane-wrapped sandwiches back to the room for Kelly and found her sleeping (it was about five in the evening, and twilight). He tossed the sandwiches onto the bed for her in case she woke up, then went out on deck to enjoy the last of his luxury cruise. The lights of Bahrain were already on the horizon. He wasn't sure how to feel about the whole thing.

He didn't really care about the drawings. He was sorry, he supposed, that they'd been burnt, but it wasn't something he could get worked up over. He didn't like that Kelly had lied to him but it had actually unburdened his conscience somewhat. He hadn't been sure he could spend money obtained through theft. He wasn't sure he *couldn't*—but he had a strong suspicion. He was surprised that not having to make the decision was a relief, but it was. He didn't think of himself as a criminal, and he preferred it that way. Were Brutus and Cassius criminals? Was the Grim Reaper? Matt was a grim reaper.

Kelly's lie had let him get his reaping done. That was enough to get out of it. Only one more stop when they got home and he'd be done. He'd head back south, and probably get a security contractor job. Blackwater—or whatever it was called now—was based somewhere south of DC; he didn't remember where exactly. He'd probably drop them a line. Or maybe he'd look into Brink's. Or the Georgia state police . . . did they take rehabilitated convicts? He'd have to check.

He lay back on the deck chair Kelly had used to sun herself that morning. The fresh air was finally starting to get the acrid flash-bang smell out of his head.

He wondered if the DEA chaperone was going to fly back with them. He was a nice enough guy. Maybe he could put Matt on to some work. Shit, maybe the DEA was hiring.

36

The DEA chaperone did fly back with them and Matt did ask him about work. The DEA guy gave him some names and some numbers he could call. Kelly and the DEA guy didn't speak at all, except when he told her (at baggage claim at JFK airport) that all the pardon stuff would be signed by a judge and delivered to her lawyer in a few days. No more than a week. He asked if Matt's papers should go to the same lawyer and she said "yes" and then, grudgingly, "thank you."

They parted in the taxi line. The DEA guy was off to LaGuardia for the DC shuttle, and Matt and Kelly were going back to Kelly's apartment. Even once the chaperone was gone Kelly was unusually quiet. Maybe she didn't want to talk around the cabdriver. Once they were back in her apartment, she told him, matter-of-factly, that everything was going to be all right now. She had some plans, stuff in the works, involving him. Nothing felonious; he shouldn't worry. And he shouldn't worry about money just because the Klimt thing fell through. But she wanted to make sure they didn't get screwed on the pardon deals first. She'd tell him what she had in mind as soon as her lawyer gave her the word.

He said he didn't want to be involved in counterfeiting or anything like that, and that she shouldn't either, now that she was going to be free and clear, have a blank slate to start over with.

She agreed with him. Said it had nothing to do with counterfeiting. Then she said that she hated "commercial" air travel, that the Airbus airline had been disgusting, and she was going to shower. Then maybe they could order Chinese or something. Her treat.

He said that sounded good but not tonight. Tomorrow night. He had an errand he had to run and he didn't want to put it off any longer than he already had. Said he'd be back in the morning. She didn't ask him to explain.

She went to shower and he went to the nearest subway station. He rode the 7 train to the last stop and rented a car near the Long Island end of the Whitestone Bridge. Then he headed north, toward Connecticut. Greenwich, Connecticut, and the home of army inquisitor Captain Kirby Monroe. It was late evening and rush hour was over. He'd be there in about half an hour.

He'd decided to leave his fancy suit on. This seemed like a formal occasion.

And anyway, the suit seemed to go well with his sword.

◆

Kelly, meanwhile, was glad to have Matt out of her hair for a spell. She needed time to think about what she was going to do with him. First, though, she needed to de-stress. She took a long, hot shower—didn't want to get out of the shower—decided to turn it into a long, hot bath, and might have stayed in it till the water got cold if she hadn't heard a bang out in her apartment.

Her first thought was that one of the folding tables holding up her precious printers had collapsed. Cursing gravity, and plastic furniture, she climbed out of the tub and wrapped herself in a towel. She opened the bathroom door, stepped out of the steamy mist into her cold apartment, and stopped dead.

A man she didn't recognize was standing in the center of the room. Behind him, on either side, were two men—boys—in their late teens or early twenties. She recognized the one on the left as the kid who'd followed her out of Penn Station. They both had close-shave buzz cuts and were wearing boots with red laces in them.

The man in the center stepped forward and stuck his hand out to Kelly. "Sorry to intrude, ma'am. I'm Bob Wharton. I don't know if Matt Kubelsky mentioned me?" He paused. Kelly shook her head "no," and Wharton continued, "Well, anyway, I think we have some things to talk about. Take a seat." He dragged her desk chair into the center of the room.

"Mind if I get dressed first?"

"I said take a seat," said Wharton. Kelly sat down.

"A good friend of mine is in jail. In Switzerland."

"Oh. That's nice. Switzerland's beautiful this time of year."

"Do you know why he's in jail?"

Kelly was trying to keep the nerves out of her voice. Succeeding pretty well. The last couple of months had been good practice.

"Jaywalking?"

Wharton slapped her across the face, very hard. A blood vessel burst in her left eye and the white started to turn red.

"He tried to deposit two million dollars for me. As a favor. Except the two million dollars wasn't two million dollars, it was twenty thousand pieces of paper with Ben Franklin's face on them. You follow me?"

Kelly shook her head no and rubbed her face where Wharton had slapped it.

"I thought maybe Matty Kubelsky had pulled a fast one on me. I was hoping I might find him here, or maybe you could tell me where he was. But now that I look at your setup . . ." The Nazi gestured to Kelly's printers. "I think maybe you know more about this than Kubelsky does."

Kelly was running her tongue along her teeth to see if the slap had loosened any of them. She was trying not to make eye contact.

"Anyway," said the Nazi. "Someone owes me two million dollars, plus bail and lawyers' fees for the Swiss. You and I are going to talk about a payment plan."

◆

Matt was sitting in the toll booth traffic jam on the north side of the Whitestone Bridge when his phone rang. It was Kelly. He answered it.

"Matt, this is Bob Wharton."

A chill rode up Matt's back.

"Where's Kelly?"

"I'm owed about two million dollars, Matt. Plus fees and expenses. Your girlfriend here—Kelly?—is being sort of tight-lipped about how she intends to pay. So let's make things simple. You can have her back when I get my money. I don't think I need to specify that it needs to be real money this time. We'll call it two million, five hundred thousand and we're all square. And that way no one, and no one's girlfriend, needs to be hurt in any way that won't heal up."

"Fine," said Matt. "Fine. That's fair. Two million, five hundred K and you can keep her safe till then. But put her on now so I know she's okay."

"Well," said the Nazi, "I wouldn't say she's okay, exactly. She's hurt. But like I said before, nothing that won't heal. Not yet, anyway. But sure, you can talk to her—I do want to move this along."

◆

Kelly was bent over a kitchen stool. The Nazi had torn off her towel and rolled it up and lashed her across the back a few times when he'd been asking her how she was going to pay him and she'd said she didn't know, she didn't know, she'd come up with something but she didn't know. Her back was a little torn up, red and puffy and bleeding in places. She'd had no idea rolled cotton could do that.

The Nazi poked her in the shoulder and said stand up. She straightened, fighting back tears and scowling before she turned to look at him. He handed her the phone—her phone—which he'd used to call Matt.

"Poor guy wants to know if you're okay," said the Nazi with a smile. "You can speak freely."

"Hello," said Kelly, choking up slightly and clearing her throat. "Hello, Matt?"

Matt spoke very fast.

"Kelly, listen very carefully. Tell them you need to go to the bathroom. Lock the door and break the glass of the ceiling lamp. I hid a gun in it, taped to the ceiling above the bulb. If anyone gets through the door, kill him. I'll be back there in twenty minutes. If you understand, tell me you'll be fine."

"I'll be fine," said Kelly. "Please get them the money fast. I'll find a way to pay you back."

"Good, I'm on my way. I love you. Now give the phone back to Wharton."

"Thanks, me too," said Kelly. She handed the Nazi her phone.

"Bob," said Matt, "I'm going to begin calling in favors. I think I can get the money together by the end of the day tomorrow or maybe the day after. Don't hurt her any more or I'll kill you. You understand me?"

"Tomorrow or the day after should be fine, Matt. You know how to get in touch with me."

The Nazi hung up and tossed Kelly's phone onto her kitchen counter. Kelly was naked and defiantly not covering herself.

"Okay, we should get moving," he said, looking her up and down. "We've got a bit of a drive ahead of us."

"Mind if I get dressed?"

"If you like," said the Nazi, walking over to her refrigerator and opening it. "You have three minutes."

Kelly went to her bureau and pulled out a shirt and slacks, socks and underwear, and began to carry them toward the bathroom.

"Dress out here," said the Nazi.

"I have to pee too. You want me to do that out here?" She bundled the clothes under her arm and pulled on her panties.

"Fine, go. Two and a half minutes left."

Kelly pulled on a sports bra—wincing at the welts on her back—and was pulling on her pants as she stepped into the bathroom and shut the door behind her. She dead-bolted it, then pulled on her T-shirt, grabbed a towel, and climbed onto the sink, knocking over a dozen makeup odds and ends as she did. She held the towel over the half-dome ceiling lamp and punched it as hard as she could.

It didn't break. She pulled the towel back. The glass wasn't even cracked. She'd never thought about it before, but her bathroom ceiling lamp looked exactly like a breast, with a center screw for a nipple. She grabbed a can of hair spray from the sink, where she'd knocked it, put the towel over her head, and swung the can at the lamp.

It shattered and glass tinkled to the floor. She wished she'd brought shoes with her. She threw the towel over the shards and looked up at the bare bulb, which was still on. A shiny silver revolver was taped behind it.

Bob Wharton's voice called from outside the door: "If you're trying to get out a window, I'm going to cut off one of your fingers."

Kelly smiled ironically. She wished there was a window in here. Wherever she lived next—if she lived—there would be windows in the bathroom.

She watched the bathroom doorknob turn. The dead bolt kept the door closed.

Wharton's voice was calm. "If you make me break this door down, I'll cut off a whole hand."

There was a gap between the bathtub—which was still full—and the exterior wall. Kelly climbed down off the sink and slid herself into the gap, crouching as low as she could, wondering if a full bathtub would stop a bullet. She rested the butt of the revolver on the edge of the tub and pulled back the hammer with her thumb. She'd never fired a gun before. But she'd heard that it wasn't very complicated.

She aimed at the door.

Half a minute later, a body heaved against it, trying to force it open.

The dead bolt held.

Another, maybe, fifteen seconds passed. Another crash of a body into the door.

The dead bolt held. There was indistinct cussing from the other side.

Another half minute, and then a third crash.

The dead bolt held but she could see it was bent inward now. She was pretty sure the next one would do it.

A fourth crash. The door flew open. Kelly pulled the trigger.

The man—the boy—who'd followed her out of Penn Station staggered and fell forward into the bathroom. There was a large hole in his back, where Kelly's bullet had exited his stomach.

She checked that the hammer was back again, then leveled her aim at the open doorway.

No one came through it. But something white and orange did. It flew through the open door and landed on top of the dead man's body. It was a pillow off her bed, on fire. The room started to fill with smoke. She tried to scoop water from the bathtub onto the burning pillow. It wasn't working. There was a thick fog in front of her eyes. She turned the shower on and pointed it at the fire, coughing and hacking, trying to see. Through the smoke, a hand grabbed her and yanked her out of the bathroom.

She was coughing too hard to scream.

37

Matt was in his rental car a block away from Kelly's building when he saw Wharton and some skinhead carry Kelly—half-mummified with duct tape binding her legs and hands and covering her mouth—out into the street. They threw her into the trunk of the orange Bronco and drove off. Did anyone else see them do it? Was anyone going to call the cops? The street seemed empty, and it was dark. A cab was driving by but the driver was on the wrong side to have seen anything. Probably wouldn't have wanted to get involved if he had.

Should Matt call the cops?

They'd kill her if he did, he was sure of that.

So instead he slowed down and followed the Bronco, trying to drive casually and look nondescript. Luckily all rental cars look nondescript.

The Bronco headed north, over Randalls Island and into the Bronx. Then across northern Manhattan, across the George Washington Bridge, and into New Jersey. Then northwest across a corner of Jersey and into lower upstate New York. The city had turned into slums and then crowded commuter suburbs. Then it started to get rural. And then Matt's phone rang.

He slid it out of his pocket and answered it.

"Matty boy," said the Nazi. "If you don't stop following me, I'm going to shoot your girl. I think we're far enough out in the sticks for that now, don't you?"

"If you kill her, you're out two million bucks, aren't you?"

"I didn't say I'd kill her. I said I'd shoot her."

Matt saw a flash of light inside the Bronco. It was accompanied by a loud *bang* through the phone. Matt instinctively pulled it away from his ear—but not far enough that he didn't hear Kelly's gagged, agonized scream.

"That was her thigh, I think, mostly—and now I've got goddamn blood all over the back of my truck. Now think carefully, Matty, 'cause the next bullet's going through her knee. Turn on your high beams, and leave them on, and pull over so I can see you've pulled over. Get out and stand in the beams so I can see you, walk a hundred feet in front of your car, and stay there till my truck's out of sight. Then I'd suggest you get going calling in those favors. I'm not taking your girl here to a doctor or anything, so I suggest you hurry."

The line went dead. Matt put his phone back in his pocket, turned on his high beams, and pulled to the side of the road.

Ahead of him, he could see the Bronco had rolled to a stop. Matt climbed out of the car and started walking forward, lit up by his headlights. After he'd taken fifty or so paces the Bronco shifted back into gear and started driving away. Half a minute later its taillights disappeared over a hill, and Matt began to walk back to his car.

He pulled out his phone and dialed a number from memory. He hoped he had it right. He hadn't been expecting to call it, ever.

"Yeah, who's this?"

Matt exhaled, silently, in relief. He recognized the voice.

"Adam? It's Matt Kubelsky."

"Matt. Good to hear from you. Grapevine says you got out. Pretty recent, as I understand it. Glad you decided to stay in touch."

"Yeah, about staying in touch, that's why I'm calling. You're still an Eighty-Eight, right?"

"What the fuck kind of question is that? What'd I be talking to you for if I wasn't still an Eighty-Eight? It's not a fucking country club, you know, where you re-up every year." Under different circumstances Matt would have laughed. Adam—Adam Gideon Frankincense Jepson—had the most peculiar accent in the world. Half-Appalachia, half-Boston; he'd ended up in Charlestown after being orphaned. Matt didn't know the details of Adam's parents' death. There were rumors of a connection to sexual deviancy. It was a topic other prisoners, non-Eighty-Eights, liked to joke about. A particularly disgusting joke, directed at Adam while he and Matt and the jokester were working in the prison kitchen, had provoked Matt to hit the offender in the face with a whole frozen chicken, soon to be defrosted for the Christmas feast. Matt hit him with the chicken from about fifteen feet away. Perfect fastball, a strike to the face. Knocked a lot of teeth out. Adam had never repaid the favor. Matt had never asked him to.

"Adam, I need a favor."

"Okay," said Adam. "You going to tell me what it is?"

"I need somewhere to lay low for a couple days. Have we got anything up around northern New Jersey, northeast Pennsylvania, south-central New York? I was doing a little private work, unsanctioned, wanted to keep it quiet from the big guys, you know? I know they don't cotton to unsupervised troublemaking."

"You can fucking say that again, and neither do I. But yeah, you dumb fuck, I guess when I was your age I needed a crash site every now and then too. We got something just north of Neversink. You know where that is? 'Bout thirty miles west of Poughkeepsie, in the Catskills. On the edge of the Big Indian Wilderness."

"Big Indian Wilderness?"

"Yeah, that's its real name. We didn't make that shit up, that's what it's called. There's a lodge and a shooting range and some Quonset huts but not much else. It belonged to a guy who trained guard dogs—real *mean* guard dogs. He was an early Eighty-Eight, not a founder but an early one, and he willed it to us. I don't think there're any dogs anymore, but there's still dog pens and an obstacle course or some shit like that. I haven't been up there in a while. These days it's mostly like a fucking summer camp. Guys bring their kids up there so they can learn to hunt and fish, and about the races and the brotherhood of Aryans. Meet other kids, get into the life. It's convenient 'cause there's a lot of Jews in the Catskills, so the kids can get a look at 'em, and since it's on the wilderness there's lots of room to kick around in, no one worrying about tags, that kinda thing. From Neversink, you head north to this tiny town called Clareyville. The road's called Clareyville Road, over the Neversink River and then onto Frost Valley Road, and then follow that for like five, six miles, till you see an old wooden sign that says "Hunters Dog Farm" and a metal one that says "Private Property" and another one that says "Warning—Live Fire Area." Head up the drive about a mile or a touch more and you'll come to it. Probably no one there this time of year, or maybe some old-timers hunting, or some kids getting drunk. The camp kids, the young ones, usually get brought up in the summer so it might be empty. There's a diesel generator if no one's there and you need it. If you run it and leave it empty, though, I swear I'll find you and beat you in the face with a frozen chicken."

Adam laughed.

"You're a lifesaver, Adam. Any other spots we've got in the area?"

"Why?" said Adam. "But no. That's it till the Ohio Valley."

"Thanks, Adam. You're a lifesaver. I'll talk to you sometime. And if you keep this whole thing to yourself, I'd appreciate it."

"Yeah, whatever. Fuck you for telling me twice, but fine, I'll take it to the grave. That it?"

"That's it."

Matt heard the line go dead.

So he was pretty sure now he knew where Wharton was taking Kelly. He couldn't be certain. If he was wrong . . . what would he do? Rob a bank? Guess he'd have to. How else was he going to raise two million—two and a half million—dollars? The only things he owned that were worth anything were sitting in his rental car—the Sig Sauer the Nazi had sold him, which was worth about eight hundred, maybe a thousand dollars, and the execution sword, which Matt figured might be worth . . . anywhere from a thousand to a hundred thousand dollars? It didn't really matter. It could be worth a million and he'd still be a million four hundred and ninety-nine thousand dollars short.

Kelly was worth robbing a bank for. But he was pretty sure it wouldn't come to that. Pretty sure. Wharton had taken all the right roads to be heading to the Catskills from Queens. It sounded like the right sort of place.

Matt was already back in his car, wondering if he should drive with his lights off and catch up or try to steal Kelly back at this Dog Farm place. Too risky to do it on the road. She was already in pretty bad shape and Wharton might actually kill her. He'd shot her.

Fuck—he'd shot her. She was there, in his stupid damned orange truck, scared out of her mind, wrapped in tape, bleeding, in pain.

That made Matt certain of one thing. Win or lose, Wharton was going to find out what it's like meeting a grim reaper.

38

After she'd been shot, Kelly had screamed through her gag, then started to hyperventilate. She nearly fainted—felt woozy, lightheaded, like she was floating. Someone—either Wharton or his surviving skinhead assistant—pushed a pair of clumsy fingers into the flesh of her neck, searched around for a pulse, and when he found one said, "Yep, she's alive. Just quiet. I don't know if she's awake."

Kelly wasn't sure whose voice it was but decided pretending to be unconscious or asleep was probably a good idea. She wouldn't miss anything, keeping her eyes closed. The only thing she could see from the Bronco's trunk was an occasional treetop lit up by the lights of a passing car.

Would Matt come for her?

Yes. Yes he would. She would have doubted it, after all the trouble she caused him, the lies, the, uh, possibility that he felt used by her. But on the phone he'd said he loved her. After all these years he still loved her.

Why hadn't she said it back?

In the moment—the instant—she had to respond, she hadn't wanted to lie to him, so she'd said "me too," which could be defended, as an answer to "I love you," as meaning "I love me too."

God. Why was she like this? Her nonanswer hadn't *really* been any less dishonest and the half-assedness of it might be enough for him to give up on her. He certainly didn't owe her anything. Why was she like this? Stupid, stupid, stupid cunt. Quintero was right about her. Stupid goddamned idiot fucking no good bitch of a cunt. Whipped and shot. I hate myself, I hate myself, I hate myself.

She suppressed a sniffle that might give her away, tip off the Nazis that she was conscious.

Was Matt coming for her? She hoped so. She hoped so. The Nazi's half of the phone call made it sound like he was.

But just in case, she got back to work trying to cut through the duct tape binding her hands with the fingernail on her thumb. She'd gotten a manicure in preparation for the yacht meeting and her nails were still hard and sharp, and her fingers were flexible enough to get her right thumb up inside the tape loops around her wrists. She'd scraped off most of the sticky stuff on the tape's innermost layer. Now she was trying to slice her nail through the little threads inside the tape's plastic-y silver part. When they'd been tying her up (so to speak) she'd closed her eyes and tried to count the number of loops they'd taped around her hands. She thought it was four. It could have been five. She'd been in a lot of pain.

But if she could get her hands free, she could pull the latch on the inside of the tailgate and roll out onto the street. It would hurt.

Possibly less than being whipped and shot. If she could roll out onto the street, a passing car might see her and call 911. If not, maybe the fall would scrape off enough tape and leave enough flesh and bone for her to crawl into the forest and hide.

This was not, she admitted to herself, a great plan.

But it was better than doing nothing.

Come on, Matt, come on, Matt, come on, Matt. Save me so I can tell you I love you.

39

It took Matt two hours to get to Hunters Dog Farm. He'd had to get gas, and he borrowed a map to figure out where exactly he was going. The delay meant he wasn't worried anymore about catching up to the Nazis by accident, before he wanted to. He found the wood sign and the metal ones just as Adam had described them. He drove a few hundred yards past them, then pulled off into the underbrush on the opposite side of the road. Pulled off far enough for his car to be hidden. Not that there was too much chance of anyone seeing it even if he hadn't. He hadn't seen a car in a half hour and, anyway, it was just about midnight and the moonlight was enough to see by only if you took some time in the dark to adjust.

Matt's gun was in his costume-shop shoulder holster. He wasn't sure what to do about his sword. He couldn't carry it and still move fast, keep his balance, and keep quiet. If he stuck it in his belt it would probably just slice through the leather and fall out. Probably at the worst and noisiest time.

What he settled on was taking off his jacket and making a crimp in it, left to right, about where his shoulder blades would be. He pushed the sword through it like you'd push a needle through a fold of cloth to keep from losing it. The cross guard on the sword's hilt kept it from sliding all the way through, kept it in place. It looked a little silly, but it would work as well as any makeshift sheath he could have hoped for. (Shame you can't just buy sword holsters, Matt reflected.) He slipped his jacket on, feeling the coldness of the metal blade through the cloth, crossing his back from his right shoulder to his left hip.

He hoped he'd get a chance to use it. Mostly because it would be a lot quieter than a gun. But also because, in the moment, an executioner's sword felt *right*.

He was a black-suited grim reaper stalking through the late autumn forest, trying not to crunch the leaves too loudly. There had never been any leaves on the ground in Iraq. There had been in Afghanistan, and plenty in boot camp. And of course in Georgia, growing up, playing cowboys and Indians. Stalking through the woods is like riding a bike. Seems impossible, then difficult, then a muscle memory you never forget.

Matt crossed over the road—Frost Valley Road—and into the forest on the far side. He moved back toward where he'd seen the sign but then stopped and turned.

Coming from somewhere far off to his right, bouncing around the bare trees, Matt heard the clattering of a diesel generator.

40

K elly was lying in the dark when she heard the generator begin to rumble. She'd been carried into some kind of wood cabin or something and unceremoniously dumped on a table on her torn-up back. She thought she might pass out from the pain and almost hoped she would. The bullet tear through her left thigh had been stuck together by dried blood. Being dropped onto the table had reopened it.

But she *was* through the first three layers of duct tape, and she continued to work away at it with utterly worn-out thumb and worn-down thumbnail. She wasn't sure now what she'd do if she got her hands free. Obviously, she'd lost her chance at flagging down a stranger's car. But she felt certain that free hands would be better than bound ones—and, more important, she had to do something to keep busy and keep from becoming hopeless. So she kept at it. Scrape, scrape, scrape, scrape.

After about ten seconds of generator rumble the lights came on. Kelly tilted her head to the left and right, tried to get a look at the room. It looked like a rec room in a Vermont hunting lodge, except dirtier and with a swastika flag on the wall next to the dart board. Opposite the swastika someone had hacked the numbers 1488 into the wooden wall and that stupid lightning bolt "SS" logo on either side of it.

Besides that, there were some stuffed fish and animal heads and, past her feet, something so absurd and bizarre she might have laughed under different circumstances. There was a big bar mirror with a shelf running along the bottom and some bottles of booze. In the center was a design in black electrical tape—a familiar, abstract design that she recognized but couldn't place right away and then realized: it was a Hitler mustache and Hitler hair. Did people stand in front of the mirror and imagine themselves with a Hitler mustache? Nazis were the biggest goddamn . . . dorks. Jesus.

She laid her head back down on the table, which, in the light, she realized was a pool table. She rubbed her hair back and forth on the felt a few times. The softness, which she could just barely feel through the dizzy haze of pain and blood loss, was comforting, for some reason . . . made her think of a flannel blanket on a cold night. She was cold. Very cold. She kept scraping at the duct tape. She looked at the bare wooden ceiling and concentrated on machete-ing her nail through the tape. Here she was in a Nazi rec room where guys could drink and shoot pool and pretend to be Hitler. Maybe she was dreaming.

If not, she hoped at least that her blood ruined their pool table. Who'd have the last laugh then, Nazis?

Behind her head a door opened and someone walked into the room. Someone walked toward the pool table, then around it to her bloody thigh. It was the elder Nazi, Bob Wharton. He didn't say anything. She watched as he peeled back the tape around the bullet hole—bullet slice, really—he'd made in the outside of her thigh. She screamed behind her duct-tape gag, and then started to hyperventilate again. Wharton opened a tube of antibiotic ointment and squeezed a line of it onto the gash, the way you'd squeeze toothpaste onto a toothbrush. Then he opened a tampon and pushed it lengthwise into the cut, on top of the ointment, and then duct taped it in place.

Then he walked out of the room again. Hadn't looked her in the face or said a single word. Hadn't seemed to notice when she'd screamed. He'd dressed a bullet wound on her leg as if it were none of her business.

She closed her eyes, tried to ignore the pain, and hoped the ointment had been the kind with a topical anesthetic in it. She wished she had some for her back. She continued to work her nail through the tape on her wrists and hoped Matt was coming for her.

How could he know where she was?

He was a soldier. A noncommissioned officer and a gentleman. He'd figure it out. He'd figure it out. He was coming.

But, just in case, she kept her thumbnail working.

41

Bent over in a semicrouch, Matt moved toward the sound of the generator. He was going uphill and as fast as he could without making too much noise. He could have gone more slowly and been silent, but the noise of the generator was giving him some cover. He really had no idea what to expect. Assuming Wharton was even here, Matt didn't know if he'd be by himself, or if he'd be with the guy who'd helped him carry Kelly to the car, or if Wharton had a larger posse that Matt hadn't seen. Plus, Matt knew from prison (and television) that neo-Nazis love to play at being soldiers. There might be militia-types, wearing army-navy store surplus and guarding or patrolling. Adam said they weren't *training* guard dogs here anymore, but there might still be guard dogs *guarding*. Big German shepherds, who answered German commands.

Based on what Adam had said, there might be a dozen families camped around a fire, singing "Lieb Vaterland" like the German officers in Rick's Café Américain in *Casablanca*. The scene where Victor Laszlo gets the band to play "La Marseillaise." They'd showed *Casablanca* a lot in prison; it was one of twenty or so DVDs that had been donated over the years. As a tattooed member of the 1488s, Matt—like Captain Renault—was obliged to seem pro-Nazi. But that scene always made him choke up, even though he didn't particularly like the French. He always wanted to get to his feet and sing along—*"Allons enfants de la Patrie, something-something-something arrivé!"*

Better yet, he would have liked to get up and lead the prison in "The Star-Spangled Banner," spit that back at the '88s singing along with the movie Nazis. But not everyone gets to be Victor Laszlo. Most people don't even get to be Captain Renault.

Matt came to the top of the hill he'd been climbing. He was on a ridge looking down (only about ten feet down) at a cleared patch of land the size of a football field. And it looked just like Adam had described. A few Quonset huts, a lodge building, some fenced-in pens that had probably been for dogs, and some sort of dog obstacle course. There were lights on inside the lodge. Off to one side, there was the clattering generator and, in between the two, Matt assumed, a heavy-duty electrical cable.

More important—much more important—Matt could see the front of the lodge, orthogonal to the side with the generator. There was a small screened-in porch. Through the screen—it was indistinct but Matt was sure anyway—he could see a boxy orange shape. Wharton's Bronco. That boxy orange shape was the best news Matt had gotten in a long, long time. He felt like a thousand-ton weight had been lifted off his chest. If it hadn't been there . . . God alone knew what would've happened next.

Still in a crouch, Matt began to move to his left, along the spine of the ridge, until he had a clear view of the dirt patch in front of the lodge—the parking lot at the end of the dirt driveway. And there it was, no longer just a boxy shape: the orange Bronco, plain as day, lit up by a naked lightbulb that hung inside the porch and cast square-grid shadows through the insect screens.

Sitting next to the orange Bronco was a white panel van.

That was less-good news. That was a big complication.

Matt was ready to kill Wharton and his partner-in-kidnapping. But what was he going to do with the people who belonged to that van? And how many of them were there? One he could maybe knock out, or scare off into the woods. Maybe hog-tie him and throw him in one of the dog pens. But if there were two, three, five, ten? How many people fit in a van?

He couldn't just kill them. They hadn't done anything.

Though of course they knew . . . they had to know that Kelly was being held there against her will. Did that make them complicit? Yes. That's what complicit means. But was that enough to justify killing them?

No. He wished it were, but no. There was a clear line in Matt's mind that separated killing and murder: murder being killing that isn't just. And he couldn't start murdering people. It wasn't in his nature. He wouldn't be able to live with himself. Even to save Kelly. Even if the van people knew she was there, and hadn't called the police, and were willing to just let Wharton do what he wanted with her. For that, he'd happily kick their teeth in, but he wouldn't kill them. Cowardice isn't a capital crime.

Anyway, he didn't actually *know* that whoever belonged to that van *hadn't* called the police. Maybe the police were on their way right now.

No, he couldn't kill them. He'd just have to come up with some way of . . . dealing with them. He'd think of something. Right now, though, he had to get down to those two cars. Or trucks. Whatever they were. A Jeep knockoff and a van. No matter what he did next, what he had to do first was get the air out of those tires. He couldn't risk anyone escaping before he had control of the situation. Couldn't risk someone driving off with Kelly and disappearing—this time, maybe, for good.

He reached over his shoulder and pulled the sword out of his coat.

42

"So, now," said Wharton, walking up a hallway from the rec room to the living room, throwing out the plastic wrapping of the tampon he'd just taped to Kelly's leg, "who the fuck are you people?"

"We're Fourteen Eighty-Eights," said a punk in his early twenties. "Punk" in the sense that he was wearing tight jeans and a sleeveless tee and had a spiked mohawk.

"Yeah, I figured," said Wharton. "I need a little more detail. Before I decide what to do with you."

"We're a band," said the same punk. "We're playing the brotherhood gathering in Maine. Maybe you heard about it? The Head Bangor?"

Wharton shook his head. "No," he said. "Aryan Brotherhood?"

"Just white nation brothers in general. Metal heads. You know. Metal heads. The headliners are some of the Austrian and German bands that can't play their shit in Europe 'cause it's illegal."

Wharton nodded. "Okay, that's fine. I'm still waiting for one of you to tell me why you're here."

"We're from Spokane," said another punk. Another mohawk. No spikes, shaved close to his head and dyed green. "We've been touring."

"God," said Wharton cutting him off. "This place *reeks*." The young Nazi who'd helped Wharton kidnap Kelly was kicking through the band's stuff. Four sleeping bags for the four-man band and a dozen piles of food wrappers and dirty laundry.

"Let's take this outside," said Wharton, walking toward the front door.

"You going to make them clean their shit up?" asked his co-kidnapper.

"We'll get to that," said Wharton, waving the band out of the lodge's living room and onto the screened-in porch.

Wharton and the five twenty-something Nazis stepped outside. The smell of body odor was diminished but still unpleasant. Wharton waved his hand in front of his nose and lit a cigarette to help drown it out.

"Sit down," he said to the four bandmates, sitting down himself in a lawn chair. All the porch furniture was lawn furniture. Three of the bandmates sat on a nylon couch and the fourth on a wood and wicker stool that he slid over to one of the porch's insect-screen walls. He leaned back on the screen and absentmindedly started rubbing his head on it, scratching an itch on the nape of his neck.

"Continue," said Wharton.

"We were touring," repeated the punk with the green mohawk. "We played in Idaho, Montana, South Dakota, Indiana. Small clubs. Ohio. We had one booked near Pittsburgh and then one in Scranton."

"Fuckers canceled us," said a third punk. Three out of four. The third and fourth were dressed the same as the first two but skinheaded.

"'Cause you're Eighty-Eights?" said Wharton.

"Nah," said the first punk. "We don't advertise it. No they canceled 'cause we wanted to be paid. One guy owns both clubs, said he wanted us to do it for *exposure*." The punk gestured quotation marks around the word "exposure." "We told him we didn't do that anymore. So he canceled us."

"We didn't have anywhere to go," said the second punk. Green mohawk. "But Nicky's dad"—he gestured to the fourth punk, the one who hadn't spoken yet—"took him to this place when he was a kid, and he remembered it, so we figured we'd come up here and crash a few days till we head to Maine. We were going to leave day after tomorrow."

Wharton nodded. He was looking out at his Bronco and the band's van. In fact, he was looking right at Matt but didn't know it; Matt was crouched between the two trucks and hidden by the darkness.

But Matt could see Wharton. And could hear him.

"Well," said Wharton, "I'm not going to force any of my brothers out into the night. So you have two options. You can either clean your shit up and leave, and say you were never here, or you can clean your shit up and stay and not bother me." Wharton looked at his wristwatch. "I have to call goddamned *Switzerland*.

I'll be in the back, in the office. Tony," he said to his kidnapping assistant, "check how much diesel's in the generator and, if it's less than half, fill it up."

Tony the Nazi nodded. "Yeah, sure."

Wharton took a step back toward the living room.

"Mister," said the fourth band member, Nicky. "That girl you guys carried in. You mind if we fuck her?"

Wharton was already opening the lodge's front door and stepping inside. He looked at the four punks over his shoulder.

"If you can do it without cutting off the duct tape be my guest."

Wharton let the door swing closed behind him.

Still crouched and hidden in the darkness, Matt heard the question, the answer, and the negotiations over the order in which they were going to rape Kelly. They were playing rock-paper-scissors-shoot, and Matt was boiling over with disgust and anger and righteous fury. He felt . . . hot. Explosive. He felt like a piece of tinfoil in a microwave.

But, he told himself, he didn't have to worry anymore about leaving any of them alive.

Tony the Nazi opened a screen door on the porch and stepped out into the mosquito-filled night. He began to walk around the lodge toward the generator.

Very slowly, keeping to the dark, Matt followed him.

43

Kelly's flogged back had mellowed to the low boil of a bad sunburn. And, bound behind, her hands and arms were numb up to the shoulder. The only part of them she could feel was her thumb, because her thumbnail had been worn down to the quick and a good deal of skin had gone with it. She wondered how much longer till she scraped it down to the bone. But she was down to the last layer of tape, and now she was shuffling her body around, trying to get some blood flow back into her arms, getting ready for one last burst of energy, to tear the last layer apart and get her hands free.

Every movement made her wince. The tampon seemed to have stopped the bleeding, and the sharp pain in her thigh had changed to a dull throbbing except when she moved. But the moving was working. She rolled her shoulder a few times, and started to get that pins and needles feeling, which, at least, was *feeling*. She took a deep breath, gritted her teeth, and yanked her arms apart.

The last layer of duct tape snapped and the door to the rec room opened. She couldn't see it because her feet were pointed away from the door, but she heard someone walk in. Kelly kept her hands together so Wharton wouldn't know she'd gotten them free. But the face that came into view, directly above her head and upside down, didn't belong to Wharton. It belonged to a kid—fifteen years younger than her? College age? Shaved head. Skinhead. Must have been one of the people she'd heard Wharton yelling at as they'd carried her into the building.

This kid had a sickly sweet smile on his face.

"Hey there, Ms. Hostage." He walked around her so instead of being upside down his face was at a right angle.

"Sorry I can't take the tape off your mouth. I'm sure your mouth is beautiful, like the rest of you." He bent down and kissed the duct-tape gag. Then he slid his left hand onto Kelly's left breast, down her torso, and into her pants.

At the same time, Kelly slid her right hand toward the pool table's side pocket. Inside, she found the billiard ball she'd been hoping for. She wrapped her hand around it. The kid still had his lips on her gag. As he slid his fingers into her panties she slammed the solid ivory ball into the side of his head.

He stumbled backward, lolling back and forth, trying to touch his hand to his temple, but suddenly unable to coordinate his limbs with his eyes. He made a grab for the pool table to steady himself but his knees buckled and he fell to the floor.

Kelly's legs were still wrapped in duct tape from her knees to her ankles. But she used her empty left hand to pull herself to the edge of the table, to roll herself off the table, onto the stupefied skinhead, and she hit him again, in the head, with her green striped billiard ball. She hit him again. And again. And then the lights went out.

44

Tony the Nazi was pulling the dipstick out of the generator's fuel tank when Matt's hand closed over his mouth and his sword pushed through his lower torso. After a few short convulsions, Tony's body went limp and Matt let it drop to the ground. Matt began to slip off his jacket, to wrap it around the hilt of the scimitar so he could chop the electrical cable that connected the generator to the lodge without getting electrocuted. He was vaguely disappointed when he realized that, of course, he could just flip the cutoff switch, which he did.

The generator grumbled to a halt and the lights inside the lodge went out.

Matt could hear voices inside; they sounded either confused or annoyed, he wasn't sure. He walked casually back around to the porch, walked through it and into the living room, which was now utterly black. It didn't even have the modest moonlight Matt had had outdoors.

"Tony, right?" said one of the band punks. "What happened? Out of gas?"

Matt took two steps toward the voice and swung the scimitar at it, diagonally downward, with both hands. He felt the blade cut deep into something, presumably the aspiring rapist's shoulder, down toward his spine. There was no scream, just agonized gurgling and the sound of a body dropping to the floor.

Matt yanked the sword back out of the body; it made a sucking sound as it came.

Someone standing a few feet to Matt's right said, "What the fuck?" Matt turned to the new voice as the sword pulled free of the first body and, in a single smooth motion, swung at it, horizontally. It sliced into something, stomach high. The second voice screamed. Matt stabbed toward it a second time, sunk the shaft into something soft and spongy. Somewhere else in the room there was the sound of someone scrabbling around the floor like a rat. Matt pulled his sword out of the second body and it pludded to the ground like a sack of potatoes.

There was a bright flash and a concussive bang as a bullet was fired in Matt's general direction. Matt took a few calm, silent steps to his left and began to circle toward where he'd seen the muzzle flash.

The muzzle flashed again. Another bullet, another enormously loud bang filling the room. Three more shots in quick succession—none of them coming anywhere near Matt as he creeped circuitously toward their source. Even with his ears ringing he could hear the shooter breathing hard, panting in terror. As he walked over what he figured was either a sleeping bag or a shag carpet, there was one more muzzle flash, one more random shot into the room, and Matt swung down at it. There was another scream. Matt figured he'd probably chopped the punk Nazi's arm off. He swung again toward the source of the scream and figured that this time he'd probably got the punk's face. The screaming stopped and Matt stood still, unsure if there was anyone else in the room. He knew there were at least two more Nazis in the building—and Kelly. Somewhere.

He waited about thirty seconds. When he didn't hear anything, he pulled a cigarette lighter out of his pocket and flicked it on. It cast just enough light for Matt to see the three dead bodies around him, and that in the right rear corner of the room there was a hallway. Matt walked toward it.

By the light of his lighter, he could see the hallway stretch the length of the building, all the way to a back door. There were three closed doors in the hallway's left wall.

Standing next to the first—off to the side, so he wouldn't get shot when he opened it—Matt blew out his lighter, turned the doorknob, and pushed. He waited to see if someone would fire a shot into the hallway and, when no one did, he flicked the lighter on again and looked inside. It was a bathroom. Judging from the smell, it was a composting bathroom—a hole above an indoor cesspit. It reminded him of the army. He closed the door again.

He moved to the second door and did the same thing. When no one took a shot at the sound of the opening door, Matt struck his lighter and peeked inside. It looked like an office. A desk with a phone on it, an ink blotter, and a twenty-year-old PC. A couple of file cabinets off to one side. Probably the center of Dog Farm operations, back in the day. There was an open window at the back of the room and leaves of an open newspaper were being blown off the desk and onto the floor. Matt closed the second door and moved on to the third—where he heard what sounded like bodies rolling around on the floor. He threw the door open, ready to stab into the back of a rapist caught in the act.

Instead, he saw Kelly sitting on the floor. A split-second later, a green billiard ball was flying toward his face. He ducked and the ball flew over his head and out into the hallway. He saw Kelly scramble out of a pile of duct tape, still hobbled by it, and over to a rack of pool cues.

He put up his hand to signal her to be quiet. She grabbed a pool cue and swung it at his head. It hit him in the throat. He dropped the lighter. The room went black. She hit him with the cue again, this time in the gut.

"*For fuck's sake,*" he hissed—a loud whisper. "*Kelly, it's me, it's Matt.*"

"*It doesn't sound like Matt,*" she hissed back.

"*That's because you hit me in the fucking throat!*"

"*Turn the light back on.*"

"*I can't, the generator's off.*"

"*I mean, the cigarette lighter.*"

"*I dropped it, hold on.*" Matt crouched and began to feel around for his lighter.

"*Say something only Matt would know,*" whispered Kelly.

"*You have awful,* awful *morning breath. It's disgusting.*"

"*What? No I don't.*"

"*If you're going to eat garlic-heavy Chinese takeout every night, you* have *to brush before bed.*"

Matt flicked the lighter on and stood up.

"*You know I spent ten years in the army with no running water and my breath never smelled as bad as yours does in the morning.*"

"*I've been shot, you know.*"

"*Yeah, I heard it over the phone. Are you okay?*"

"*No, I'm not okay, I have a bullet hole in my leg. And I think I just killed someone.*"

Matt looked down at the body amidst the pile of torn-off duct tape. The face was staved in.

"*Yeah, look at that. How'd you do that?*"

Kelly was bent over at the waist, trying to pull the last few loops of tape off her ankles without moving her hip too much. Matt was at the body, looking for a pulse. It was definitely dead.

"*I used a pool ball,*" whispered Kelly.

"*The one you threw at my head?*"

"*Yes,*" whispered Kelly.

"*Almost cracked open my skull. You should be less trigger happy.*"

"*Well, that's a fucking laugh coming from you.*"

"*Fuck you, Kelly. This is one hundred percent your fault.*"

"*You're the one who hired the Nazis!*" whispered Kelly, loudly.

"*Anyway,*" whispered Matt, loudly, "*was there anyone here besides your corpse, the three guys in the living room, and the two guys who kidnapped you?*"

"*I don't know. I don't think so. I couldn't really see when they carried me in. I could only see the ceiling. But I think there were just the guys in the living room and the two who brought me. Plus there was another one at my apartment. The one who followed me from Penn Station. I think I killed him too.*" It was hard to tell, because she was whispering, but Matt thought he heard her voice crack. In the silence, he was certain he heard a sniffle. She cleared her throat.

"*You did the right thing,*" said Matt. "*You did what you had to do. Anyone would've done the same thing in your place. Anyway, you're right, I was the one who hired Wharton. I'm going to go take care of that now.*"

Matt pulled the pistol out of his shoulder holster.

"*Do you know where he is?*" whispered Matt.

"*No,*" said Kelly. "*He just dumped me in here and left.*"

Matt stuck the pistol out for Kelly to take.

"*I'm going to close the door behind me. When I come back, I'll knock 'shave and a haircut,' so you'll know it's me. If anyone else comes through that door, shoot him.*"

After a moment's hesitation, Kelly took the gun.

"*What's 'shave and a haircut'?*" she asked.

"*Shave and a haircut, two bits?*"

"*I have no idea what you're talking about.*"

"*For fuck's sake, Kelly. Forget it. I'll knock three times, okay? If anyone comes in here without knocking three times, open fire.*"

"*Okay.*"

"*That gun doesn't have a safety, so all you have to do is pull the trigger.*"

"*Okay.*"

"*Please don't shoot me,*" whispered Matt.

"*I'll try,*" whispered Kelly.

"*Good luck,*" whispered Matt. "*And sorry I can't leave you the lighter.*"

"*It's okay,*" whispered Kelly. "*And you too.*" She reached out her left hand and touched Matt's cheek. "*Matt, I love you.*"

"I know. You told me before, on the phone. But thanks." He took her hand off his cheek, kissed it, and walked out of the room.

❖

Matt went to the back door, the door at the end of the hallway, and found it padlocked. He'd heard Wharton say he was going to the office to call Switzerland. The office window was open. Wharton had gone out of it, clearly. Matt was willing to bet he was headed for his stupid orange Bronco.

But just in case he was waiting for Matt to follow him out the window, Matt would go out through the porch. He wanted, anyway, to go through the living room again and pick up the gun that had been shooting at him. Wharton, Matt knew, had a gun, and Matt didn't want to be the guy who brings a sword to a gunfight. He'd seen *Indiana Jones*.

Back in the living room, after pausing to listen to the blackness and see if there was anyone *alive* in the living room, Matt flicked the lighter on and surveyed the gore. Two guys were sliced up pretty thoroughly. The third was missing a hand and a head. None of the three was Wharton. The detached hand was holding a revolver. Six shots. Matt was pretty sure all six had been fired at him. He checked to make sure he hadn't counted wrong, and he hadn't. The gun was empty. Nothing left but brass.

Matt made a quick search through the headless body's pockets, hoping he kept a few spare shells with him. All Matt found was a wallet, some nicotine gum, and the keys to the van, which were useless because Matt had slashed its tires. Driving on rims on a dirt road he wouldn't get a hundred yards.

At the same time, he heard the engine of the Bronco turn over. Matt stepped over the headless corpse and out onto the porch. He saw the Bronco make a tight U-turn and tear up the dirt driveway, back toward Frost Valley Road. Even in the dim red taillight, Matt could see the grooves it was cutting in the dirt.

Matt hesitated for a moment—wondering if he should go back and search the other band punks, or maybe their van, for another gun or some bullets. But there wasn't time. Right now he knew where Wharton was and he couldn't risk losing him.

Matt sprinted off the porch and after the Bronco.

45

Wharton hadn't noticed his tires had been slashed but it didn't take him long to figure it out. It felt like he was driving on sand. The steering wheel was almost useless. After ten seconds it was completely useless. Wharton tried the brakes but they were useless, too, and the Bronco went off the road and into a ditch. Wharton shifted into reverse and tried to back it out. The wheel rims spun.

Through his back window, lit red by his taillights, he could see Matt Kubelsky running toward him. And the fucking madman had a sword. A *sword*. A fucking *sword*. *Bob, how the hell did you get mixed up with this fucking lunatic?*

Wharton pulled out his gun, pushed open the car door, and climbed out. He fired two shots at the insane swordsman. Kubelsky ducked and swerved into the forest at the side of the road. Wharton ran around the Bronco and into the forest on the opposite side.

He was in decent shape. He was running through the forest but he could barely see where he was going. There was light from his headlights pouring through the trees, casting crazy shadows. It had kind of a dazzling effect on him; it was disorienting. And it wasn't lighting up the ground at all.

Behind him, he heard running, leaves crunching. He looked over his shoulder and tried to spot Kubelsky. Couldn't be more than thirty yards behind him. A thought popped into Wharton's head—that he'd almost forgotten what it felt like to be scared.

He caught his foot on a root and fell, rolled down a small bank, splashed into a tiny creek. He needed to get to the main road. Once he got to the road he could flag down a car, shoot the driver, drive back to civilization. Call in some backup.

He climbed out of the stream and took a second to get his bearings. His headlights had been pointing approximately toward the road. He'd been following the driveway, and that's where the driveway pointed. So he followed the direction of the shadows.

After maybe ten feet he stopped again.

He couldn't hear Kubelsky behind him anymore.

◆

Matt heard the Nazi trip and fall and splash into something. He was only a little ways ahead. Matt froze, listened, and squinted. He could just make out Wharton's shape, climbing out of a ditch and stumbling off into the woods again. Wharton stopped and looked over his shoulder. For the second time in the last hour he looked straight at Matt but didn't see him. He looked frightened. He turned and ran off again into the woods.

Matt ran after him.

◆

Wharton knew he was being chased again. He didn't dare look back. He knew he'd trip and that would be the end of it. He had to get to the road. And he thought maybe he was getting close . . . after going downhill for a while, he was going uphill again, and he was sure the road had been built on a berm.

Okay, yes, it was getting steep now . . . and he saw something ahead of him. Ahead and above him. Lights of a car driving south. He was almost there. He began to climb up an embankment. He could still hear Kubelsky crashing through the woods behind him . . . Very close now. He could almost reach the road's guardrail.

He felt something cut into the backs of his ankles. His Achilles tendons tore. He crumpled backward, fell back down the embankment. Reached for his gun . . . realized it wasn't there . . . he'd dropped it. Had he dropped it in the creek? Fuck. Fuck. It's all over now. That's all she wrote.

Matt Kubelsky was standing over him, catching his breath.

Wharton took a few deep breaths too. He was sprawled on the ground like a rag doll. The deep breaths were painful. He must have broken a rib. He slipped a hand into his pocket and pulled out his pack of cigarettes. He stuck one into his mouth. Matt reached down and lit it for him. Wharton held up the pack and Matt slipped a cigarette out of it.

"Thanks," he said. For about a minute they smoked in silence. Not looking at each other. No need to make this awkward.

After a while, Wharton said, "So. I guess you're going to kill me."

Matt exhaled a puff of smoke and nodded. "Uh-huh. I don't see that I have much choice."

Wharton shook his head. "No. I guess you don't." He took a drag on his cigarette.

"I'd rather you do it with a gun," he said. "Bullet to the head. Instead of the sword."

"Sorry," said Matt. "I'd like to oblige you but I haven't got a gun."

Wharton snorted a short laugh. "You haven't got a gun? Why the fuck was I running away from you?"

"What'd you think I was carrying the sword for?" said Matt, tapping some ash off the tip of his Marlboro.

"Melodrama?" said the Nazi. Now Matt laughed. A short, sharp laugh.

"Yeah, geez, I bet I looked like a fucking nightmare."

"Yes, you did," said Wharton, smiling, shaking his head.

"Like a grim reaper."

"More or less," said Wharton.

Matt exhaled another puff. "What about your gun?"

"Lost it," said Wharton. Matt shrugged.

They both went silent again and smoked their cigarettes.

"Sorry I shot your girlfriend," said Wharton.

"She's going to be okay," said Matt. "Sorry we paid you in counterfeit money."

Wharton shrugged, then winced. Definitely a broken rib. "Eh, it's my own fault. We counterfeited a lot back in the nineties. I should have been able to tell."

"Don't beat yourself up, even the DEA says they're very good fakes."

"The DEA's involved in this?"

"Yeah," said Matt.

There was another short silence.

"Okay," said Matt. "I got to get back to Kelly. You ready? Any last words?"

"Nope," said Wharton.

Matt raised the sword, then lowered it again.

"Oh, wait. I've wanted to tell you for the longest time. I'm Jewish."

Wharton laughed. "Are you really?"

Matt smiled. "Yup."

Wharton laughed harder. "And you had to have a fucking swastika tattooed on your neck for what, four years?"

Matt was laughing too. "Almost five. I can't tell you how much I fucking hate all of you."

Wharton had his hand pressed to his ribs; he was laughing so hard that tears started to run down his cheeks.

"I fucking bet you did," he said. "Jesus Christ."

He started to cough, but he kept laughing, and so did Matt.

"I've wanted to kill you since *literally* the first day we met."

"It's nice when things work out in the end, isn't it?" said Wharton, wiping the corner of his eye.

"Yeah, it is," said Matt.

The two men were smiling at each other, like a couple of best friends who'd just survived a plane crash.

"That's just fucking *rich*," said Wharton.

"Yes, it is," said Matt. He raised the sword again.

"Do you believe in hell?" said Wharton.

"Nope," said Matt.

"I'll be waiting there for you." Wharton flicked away his cigarette and Matt sliced off his head.

On the road above them another car drove past. Matt walked back into the forest, back toward the lodge, using the beams of the Bronco's headlights to guide him.

46

On his way back into the lodge, Matt stopped at the generator, turned it back on, and then wiped off the cutoff switch. He was planning on calling the cops. But he didn't want any of his fingerprints found.

He walked back around, through the porch, through the living room, avoiding looking at the blood spatters he'd caused, now that the lights were on, and down the hall to the pool room where Kelly was waiting. With a gun.

"Kelly, it's okay, it's me," was what he was going to say. All he actually said was "Kell—", and a bullet shot through the door. It hit him in the left shoulder. He fell backward and slid down the wall.

"Jesus! Fucking! Christ!" he yelled.

"Matt?" The door flew open and Kelly limped through it as fast as she could. "Oh my god, Matt. What the fuck! Are you okay?"

"No, I'm not okay! *You just fucking shot me!*"

"You said to shoot anyone who didn't knock three times!"

"Didn't you recognize my voice?"

"I was trying to recognize your knocks, you asshole! Are you okay?"

"*Yes*, yes, fuck you, yes, I'm okay. It's just my . . . deltoid, or whatever. Only grazed me. It'll be fine."

Matt had an awful impulse to flick Kelly on the leg, where she'd been shot. He resisted it. She helped pull him to his feet.

"Let's get out of here, Matt. I don't want to be here anymore."

"I'm with you," said Matt. "We just need to wipe off anything you've touched. My DNA isn't on file, I don't think, and I doubt yours is either, but let's clean up as much of your blood as we can too. And whatever I'm dripping out right now."

"Okay," she said. "Aren't we going to tell the police about this? I mean, someone's going to find it eventually. If we don't report it, it'll make us look . . . very guilty. Won't it?"

"I'm going to call the police, but it's still better that they not know we were here. I was thinking about it walking back here. I'm going to phone in an anonymous tip."

"Walking back? From where?"

"Bob Wharton's body."

"You killed him?"

Matt nodded. Kelly nodded in answer.

"There's a bathroom over there," said Matt, pointing, wincing. "See if there's cleaning stuff in it. Check for bleach. And try not to look in the living room."

"What are you going to do?"

"I'm going to start wiping off doorknobs. Think about what you might have touched."

"Just the pool cue. And the pool ball."

"Where's the ball?"

"I don't know. I threw it at you."

Matt laughed, then groaned. "I'll look for it."

Kelly smiled a cocked smile at him and walked away, toward the bathroom.

"Trigger-happy bitch," said Matt.

"Employer of Nazis!" said Kelly.

"Mediocre counterfeiter!" shouted Matt.

Kelly screamed. Matt stumbled down the hallway toward her. She was standing at the end of the hall, looking at the mess in the living room.

Matt put his hand on her arm. She turned around, slowly, and then buried her face in his shoulder and began to sob.

He held her close, and then tried to move her head to his other shoulder.

"Sorry," he said. "It's going to be okay. It's just . . . that's the shoulder you shot me in."

He felt her chest heave as she laughed, in spite of herself.

"It's going to be okay," said Matt. "I won't say you get used to this kind of thing because this isn't ever going to happen to you again. But it'll be okay. None of it's your fault."

Kelly's voice was muffled by Matt's shoulder. "All of it's my fault."

"No, no," said Matt. "It really isn't."

It mostly was, but it's not like Matt was going to say that to her.

◆

They spent about half an hour cleaning anything either one of them had touched and any bloodstains they thought might be theirs. Kelly found the tube of antiseptic ointment, and Matt spread it on her back. Matt found the bloody billiard ball, and Kelly found some bleach. Matt used it to soak the pool table's felt and to douse the duct tape Kelly had torn off. He dropped the duct tape into the composting toilet cesspit and then poured the rest of the bleach in after it. He suggested Kelly close her eyes and that he would lead her through the living room. She said she would be fine and she was. Matt had left the sword out on the porch, bundled up in his jacket. Kelly asked if he shouldn't clean that off too. Matt said he would later.

They left by the dirt driveway. Kelly was limping pretty badly. Matt said he'd have been able to carry her if she hadn't shot him in the shoulder. Instead, they sort of leaned on each other and walked slowly. It took forty-five minutes to get back to Matt's rental car. Kelly had suggested they just take the band's van. Matt said he didn't want to lose his rental deposit and, anyway, he'd slashed the van's tires.

Along the way they passed the orange Bronco. The headlights were starting to dim as the battery ran down. Matt and Kelly had both forgotten about it. Matt gave it a quick wipe down—anything he might have touched on previous visits—and used one of the floor mats to dab Kelly's blood out of the trunk. He rolled up the mat and stuck it under his arm with his sword bundle and they kept going.

Back on the main road, near the spot Matt had hidden the rental car, he clicked the key fob's unlock button and the car revealed itself by flashing its fog lights.

"You want to drive?" said Matt.

"Are you kidding me? There's a bullet hole in my leg," said Kelly.

"It's an automatic, you only need your right leg. That's the one that's fine, right?"

"Neither of them's *fine*, Matt."

"Fine," said Matt. "I'll drive. It's not like anyone shot *me* in a limb that's important for driving, right?"

"You're such a whiny, bratty crybaby," said Kelly.

"It's funny," said Matt. "That's just what the judge said when he sentenced me to twenty-five years in prison."

"Oh boo-hoo," said Kelly, limping toward the passenger door. "Call me when you get whipped and kidnapped and taken as a hostage to a Nazi compound in the forest. Where are we, by the way?"

"The Catskills."

"A Nazi compound in the mountains." She climbed into the car and shut the door behind her. Matt lit a cigarette and climbed into the driver's seat.

"Can I have one of those?" said Kelly.

"No," said Matt. "Cigarettes are for drivers."

Kelly reached over and plucked the cigarette out of Matt's mouth. Matt lit himself a new one.

He turned on the car and backed out of the forest and onto the road. Turning his head to look over his shoulder made him wince, so Kelly gave directions. Once they were back on pavement and heading south, back toward Queens, Kelly asked if Matt wanted to listen to the radio. Matt said there was Weezer in the CD player. Kelly said she didn't want to listen to Weezer. Matt told her if she didn't want to listen to Weezer she was welcome to get out of the car and walk home.

47

It felt like an eternity but the whole excursion to the Catskills had taken only about three, three and a half hours. They were in Queens by around four in the morning. When they got back to Kelly's apartment they found a dead body in it. The one Kelly had shot. It had slipped her mind.

Kelly wondered if they should just call the police, say he was a burglar and she'd shot him lawfully. Matt pointed out that she didn't have a pistol license and the gun was owned illegally. Kelly suggested she could say she'd overpowered him, or that Matt had, and he'd been shot with his *own* gun. Matt agreed that was a good idea. But after looking around for a while, they realized that the Nazis must have pocketed the bathroom-lamp gun when they'd taken her. In fact, Matt realized, it might have been the revolver that punk bastard had shot at him. Anyway, they couldn't have a shot body and no gun—the police would find that fishy. Kelly suggested the Sig Sauer that she'd shot Matt with—which was now in his pocket, seeing as how he couldn't wear the shoulder holster anymore. But he told her it was the wrong caliber.

It wasn't a problem, said Matt. He'd get rid of the body.

"Maybe sleep for a while first?" said Kelly. "You must be wrecked. We both are."

Matt shook his head. "No, I'll do it now. I have to go out anyway. I still have that errand to run."

Kelly stared at him. "You must be joking."

Matt shook his head.

"Fine," said Kelly. "You take the body. I'll clean up the apartment." Her bathroom door was smashed, her bathroom floor was covered in glass and blood. The roll of duct tape the Nazis had used to bind her was sitting on the bureau, like a thick silver bracelet. With the back of her hand she slid it off the bureau into a trash can.

"Have you got any sheets you're not too attached to? A tablecloth would be better."

"Yeah," said Kelly. "I've got a tablecloth."

Matt wrapped the body, then went down to the street and stole a big plastic, rolling recycling bin from in front of an apartment building two blocks away. He folded the body at the waist, put it in the recycling bin, told Kelly he'd be back in a couple hours, put the rolling bin in the trunk of the rental car, and drove to the Whitestone Bridge. Twenty-five minutes later he was in Connecticut. It wasn't quite five o'clock in the morning.

Kirby Monroe. Captain Kirby Monroe. The source of all the evil in the world, as far as Matt was concerned. The source of all the evil in Matt's life, certainly. His discharge. His imprisonment. The things that had happened in prison. Most important, by far, the death of his lieutenant. Just twenty-four years old and already a fine man. A very fine man. A man Matt had seen risk his life to save the lives of people he'd never met, people who would never know his name, who he'd never see or hear about again. The smartest guy Matt had ever met. Smarter even than Kelly. He spoke and read Latin and Greek. Ancient Greek. He liked to quote the opening lines of the *Iliad*. "Mainen-ey-*yey*-da-thay-*ah*, pay-*lay*-ee-a-*dyo*-ach-ee-*lay*-oos," he'd say, all the goddamned time, whenever things got especially shitty, when there was something especially unpleasant to do. Sing, goddess, of the wrath of Peleus' son Achilles (that brought down on the Greeks unnumbered sorrows; that sent the souls of many brave men to Hades, and left their bodies to be eaten by dogs and vultures).

Matt's lieutenant could have gone into politics, but he swore up and down that he never would, that he'd rather be dead in a ditch, and Matt believed he meant it, which made him admire the lieutenant even more. The man could have been president. He had a big life ahead of him. All it took to kill him, to push him over the edge—the edge he'd been clinging to through years of having to shoot at the corpses of dead dogs because there might be bombs in them, of seeing children blown up or thrown in front of trucks, of seeing men who were like his brothers, men he was responsible for, killed in front of him, die in agony—he had *just* been hanging on, and all it took to push him off was Captain Kirby Monroe deciding that justice would best be served by losing a bloodstained bread knife. By leaving out some exonerating evidence. Captain Kirby believed that, morally, the lieutenant was guilty because he'd provoked the guy who stabbed him. So Captain Kirby took justice into his own hands. Vigilante justice. Probably thought of himself as a Batman of war-crimes prosecution. Probably saw himself as a modern-day judge at Nuremberg.

Matt wondered if Kirby had felt guilt, or even sadness, when he heard that a twenty-four-year-old lieutenant had hanged himself alone in a jail cell ten thousand miles from his home, from his parents, from his bedroom. From his cat. He was the only man Matt ever knew who preferred cats to dogs. It was absurd but the lieutenant was one of a kind. Matt wondered if, when he'd heard about the suicide, Captain Kirby felt that justice had been done. That good had won and bad had lost.

Captain Kirby Monroe's house was in a nice, quiet part of Greenwich. Though, Matt guessed, every part of Greenwich is a nice, quiet part of Greenwich. It's one of the richest towns in America. So Matt had learned during his research session at that public library in Pennsylvania. (It felt like a lifetime ago.) Captain Kirby's house had a backyard that bordered the golf course at a supremely fancy country club. Matt assumed Kirby had inherited the house from rich parents. Perhaps the Monroes were a New England institution and the house had been built in the 1800s. Maybe Monroes and Kubelskys had fought in the Civil War together.

Or maybe Captain Kirby Monroe had bought the house himself. Technically, these days, he was Lieutenant Colonel Kirby Monroe—freshly promoted and, according to his youngish wife's Facebook page, "back home FINALLY!!!" But to Matt, Kirby would always be that same steely eyed, idealistic captain whose hands were stained in blood up to his elbows.

Matt parked his car in the Round Tree Country Club's employee parking lot. The lot was mostly empty; it was five to five in the morning. Matt had hoped to get there sooner. Ideally, while it was still empty and a little further from dawn. But he'd had to make a short stop at a nearby lake, Putnam Lake, where he'd gathered stones to put in the clothes of the corpse he had in his trunk. The Nazi Kelly had shot the night before (was it really just . . . eight—nine?—hours ago?). He weighed the corpse down and dumped it into the lake. He watched it sink. He'd cut open its chest and stomach cavities—working from Kelly's bullet hole—and it sank fast. He left its wheelie recycling bin by the lake's campsite dumpster. (Matt noted it as the only dumpster he'd ever seen without a hint of rust. No rust in Greenwich, apparently.) Then he drove to the country club. Still a little before five, and still a few hours before the sun came up. He had plenty of time.

His sword, still wrapped in his jacket, was tucked under his arm. He walked out onto the golf course, staying as close as he could to the tree line, just in case there was an early-bird grounds-keeper around. He followed it until he reached the stone wall that he was pretty sure separated the golf course from Captain Kirby's backyard. The wall was about a foot taller than Matt was. He pulled himself to the top. Not easily. He would have found it less difficult if Kelly hadn't shot him. She'd only nicked him, really, but still . . .

Holding himself up on his elbows, Matt checked for a few land-marks. On Google Maps, he'd seen Captain Kirby's swimming pool and an octagonal pool house. The pool house turned out to be a gazebo but it was the right shape and in the right place. This was the Monroe residence. Matt had wanted to be sure, and he was. He recognized the back garden from Mrs. Captain Kirby's Facebook photos. There was a hideous metal lawn ornament, some sort of abstract scrap-metal sculpture that looked like a nightmare ballerina. It was no Chihuly, that was for sure. Anyway, he was in the right place.

There was a single light on in the house. Maybe an all-night bathroom light? A guard against stubbed toes? There were no other signs of life. Matt decided he still had time.

He dropped the wrapped-up sword into Kirby's yard, swung his legs over the wall, and dropped down next to it. In the dim predawn light he could see how perfectly mowed the grass was, in stripes, like a major league outfield. He'd noticed that on Google Maps too.

There were roses, or something, planted around the gazebo.

Matt walked over to them, got down on his knees, and, with his bare hands, gently began to scoop soil away from their roots.

48

Matt scraped some dirt out of his fingernails and dialed his phone. After a moment, a prerecorded voice answered, "Department of Defense, Office of Inspector General hotline.

"To ensure your anonymity this is an automated system. If this is an emergency, please hang up and call 911, or if currently stationed overseas or at a state or federal military installation in the United States, Puerto Rico, or Guam, for emergency assistance please contact the Military Police.

"Please select the category of your whistleblower report from the following options. If you do not feel that any of the options is correct for your report, it may be that the crime or activity you are choosing to report does not fall within the investigatorial authority of the Office of the Inspector General of the Department of Defense. Please visit our website at dee-oh-dee-eye-el-dot-mil to confirm the types of crimes and activities the Office of the Inspector General is authorized to investigate, or to file an anonymous complaint online.

"To report a violation connected to threats to homeland security, press one.

"Trafficking in persons, press two.

"Leaks of classified information, press three.

"Bribery and acceptance of gratuities, press four.

"Counterfeit or substandard parts, press five.

"Improper military mental health evaluations, press six.

"Sexual assault, press seven.

"Other health and safety issues, press eight."

Matt pressed eight. The recorded voice was cut off, and after about five seconds of silence it resumed.

"At the tone indicating the end of this message, please state the full details of the crime or activity you wish to report. There is no time limit, and the recording will continue until you hang up or otherwise terminate the phone call. At the end of your report, please hang up, or if you would like to request that your report be voice-modulated before an inspector listens to it, please press zero. Be aware that every report filed through this hotline *will* be listened to and fully evaluated by one of our inspectors. Please do not include any personal or identifying information, unless you wish to do so. Please begin your report at the tone."

"Umm," Matt said. "I, uh, I'm not one hundred percent sure that this is the right menu option . . . But uh, I got back from Iraq not that long ago? And there was an officer who was on the same C-130 home as me—um, that is, the same flight home with me—and during the stop at Ramstein, at the, uh, refueling stop in Germany, I think maybe he had a few drinks at the officers' club or something, I don't know. I think he was slightly tipsy, or maybe he was just excited to be going home, I don't know, but he was talking about how, 'why were we fighting ISIS fascists in Iraq and Syria if we were just going to ignore domestic fascists and neo-Nazis in America.' And he showed me this sword he had. He said he'd gotten it in Saudi Arabia, it was used for beheading criminals. And he was hoping to put it to work back in the United States, said that his 'deployment was over but his mission wasn't' and he still had 'people to deal with' and kind of winked. He didn't actually wink, you know, but he made this kind of eyebrow movement . . . expression. Anyways, I don't know if he was being serious or not, but anyways I'm pretty sure the sword is illegal for him to have anyway, and I worry he might have some kind of PTSD or hero complex or something and might be a danger to himself or his family or other people. His name was Kirby Monroe, Colonel Kirby Monroe. Or Lieutenant Colonel Kirby Monroe, I guess. Anyway, just thought I should tell someone. Thanks."

Matt pressed zero and hung up his cell phone. He didn't know how long it would take them to listen to the message, but he knew they'd listen to it. He didn't know how long it would take them to investigate, but he was pretty sure they'd investigate. He didn't know how long it would take for someone to visit the Hunters Dog Farm and find all those dead Nazis, but if no one had in a week—that is, if he hadn't seen it on the news in a week—he'd make an anonymous call to the Neversink police department and report it himself.

He didn't know how long it would take someone to find the body he'd dumped in Putnam Lake but he was sure someone would—either it would start to float or a fisherman would see it in the shallow water near the boat ramp. With its patina of swastikas and 1488 tattoos, it wouldn't take long to identify. Matt didn't know how long it would take the Defense Department investigators to make the connection—but he was certain they'd make it. If they didn't, he could always call them again.

Once they made the connection, he didn't think it would take them too long to find the sword buried in Captain Kirby's backyard. It wouldn't take long for them to test the blood on it and find DNA matches with the bodies at the Dog Farm and the body in Putnam Lake.

Between the sword, the bodies, Kirby's well-known lust for justice . . . motive, opportunity, and evidence, Matt felt a murder conviction was likely. He looked forward to following the trial in the news. Maybe he could send some clippings to the lieutenant's parents.

To call the whistleblower hotline, Matt had pulled into a rest stop on I-95, in New Rochelle, about halfway between Greenwich and Queens. Now he pulled back onto the highway and headed back toward the Whitestone Bridge, feeling more at peace than he could ever remember having felt before.

49

As terrible as she felt, Kelly didn't want to rest until she'd cleaned and straightened her apartment. She worked at it until everything was back in order except her door frame, which had been smashed when Bob Wharton's skinheads kicked it open, and the lamp in her bathroom, which she'd smashed to get at Matt's gun.

Her next step was cleaning the bullet hole on her leg. The duct tape, tampon, and antiseptic ointment had done a surprisingly good job of getting the bleeding stopped and the two sides of the gash were already sticking together—not seamlessly but it didn't look like she'd lost any flesh, just some skin. Matt had told her to go to an ER if she was worried about it, but what worried her was being asked why she had a bullet hole in her thigh, so she decided she would at least give it a few days to heal on its own before involving a doctor. Ditto her back, which the bullet wound had almost made her forget about.

She showered, then rebandaged everything and got into bed. Then she got out of bed again and took a codeine from a bottle she'd seen tucked among Matt's things, an old hospital prescription he hadn't finished.

When he got home she was sound asleep. They both slept through the day. Matt was still asleep when Kelly woke up at about nine in the evening (it was dark again; she had missed an entire day's daylight). Kelly went to the bodega on the corner and bought some comfort snack food and some mouthwash. Back at her apartment, she checked her email and found a message from her lawyer saying that the DEA paperwork protecting her from prosecution had arrived and was all in order. So was the paperwork for Matt and would she be paying for his having reviewed it or would Matt pay himself?

Kelly wrote back that she'd pay for it, to please send her a bill along with a copy of both agreements. The lawyer's email specified that they didn't have to be signed or notarized or anything, that they were simply a judge's orders that went into effect by default. But she wanted copies on file anyway.

Knowing she wouldn't hear back from the lawyer until morning, she closed her email, plugged in her earbuds, and watched three episodes of *Frasier*, eating an entire bag of chocolate chips and drinking a blueberry slushy. Then she went back to sleep.

She slept through to the next morning. When she woke up Matt was in bed next to her, with his hands behind his head, staring contentedly at the ceiling, looking like he was deep in a daydream and miles away.

After a while he felt her looking at him. He rolled his head toward her and smiled.

"How you feeling?" he asked her.

She smiled. "Pretty good." She squeezed his hand. "Except for my body, which feels terrible."

Matt laughed. "Yeah. Mine too."

She started to sit up. Matt pulled her back down. "Don't go. Stay here awhile," he said, pulling her into a clinch.

"No, no," she said, slithering out of it. "I need to brush my teeth."

Matt snorted.

"And I need to check my email," said Kelly. "And could you do me a favor and run down to the corner and buy me a pack of cigarettes? I'm out."

"You can smoke mine," said Matt.

"Do you have menthols?" asked Kelly.

"No, of course not," said Matt.

"I've got a craving for menthols. Could you get me some? And maybe some chocolate milk. I feel like chocolate milk."

"Have we got regular milk?" asked Matt, reluctantly climbing out of bed.

"I don't know. Check."

"I'll get some regular milk too," he said. "What brand of menthols?"

"Whatever," said Kelly. "Let me give you some money."

"It's okay," said Matt, pulling on jeans and a T-shirt, slipping into his regular, nonfancy shoes.

"No, really," said Kelly.

"No, really," said Matt, and walked out of the apartment.

From the hallway, he said, "But call your super about the door." Kelly listened to his footsteps disappearing down the stairs.

Then she started pulling stuff out of her closet.

50

When Matt got back to Kelly's apartment he found her dining table covered in a white lace tablecloth. Kelly was standing behind it. She spread her hands as if to say *voilà* and took a little bow. Matt walked over to her, confused.

"What's up?" he said.

"I present to you," said Kelly, gesturing to the tabletop before her, "six drawings in ink and pencil of Adele Bloch-Bauer by Gustav Klimt. Value: approximately twelve million dollars."

Matt was still confused.

"I don't understand," he said. "I saw them burn up. Are these copies? Counterfeits?"

"No, idiot. *Those* were copies. The ones that burned. They were counterfeit Klimts. The word's forgery, actually, but yeah. Quintero's a good man but not an art connoisseur. And—it's probably pretty obvious—faking black-and-white ink-and-pencil drawings is a lot easier than faking multicolored, security-feature, micro-printed, watermarked, cloth-paper money. The whole process took me all of one night. You slept through it." She smiled and added, "You snore *very* loudly."

"I know," he said. He was grinning but still trying to wrap his head around it. Her Zippo leaking lighter fluid . . . her calling for the flash-bang grenade . . . the lit cigarette that had been missing from her mouth . . . the drawings being reduced to ash while everyone focused on arresting the armed terrorists.

"Holy shit, Kelly," said Matt, with genuine, intense admiration. "Holy shit."

He looked the drawings over. Kelly watched him, smiling like a Cheshire cat.

"You're a marvel," he said, after a full minute's reflection. Kelly had opened the plastic bag Matt had brought back from the bodega and was drinking chocolate milk straight from the bottle, like a Viking with a horn of mead.

"And, of course," she said, "though they're ten percent yours, per our agreement, I was thinking we'd just split them fifty-fifty." She smiled even wider.

So did Matt. Though his smile was more of a grin.

"Thank you, Kelly. I appreciate that." He took a deep, satisfied breath. "I think we should give them back."

Kelly kept smiling and pointed a finger at him.

"Shut the fuck up."

Matt kept smiling too. "I mean, if it's fifty-fifty . . . I do own three of them, right?"

Kelly threw her chocolate milk at him.

ACKNOWLEDGMENTS

I'd like to thank all the Mysterious Press people who worked on this book—in particular, publisher Charles Perry and managing editor Will Luckman, who turned a pretty rough manuscript into a real-life book, and Otto Penzler, the headman at the Mysterious Press. Otto bought the book and edited it, and, while whipping it into shape, managed to eradicate innumerable egregious typos without blowing a gasket, which is certainly more than I could have done in his place. (Though I maintain that there's nothing wrong with having multiple semi-colons in a single sentence.) Otto's career as an editor and publisher is sufficiently storied that anything I might add would be little noted nor long remembered—I will nevertheless say that he's everything he's cracked up to be. He's a hell of a good editor and it was a thrill for me getting to work with him.

I'd like also to thank my family—my parents and brother in particular, who've spent hours and hours reading the roughest of rough drafts and helping me smooth them out. Ditto my proofreading friends, who've given my work so much of their time over the years—Anthony, Allison, Sarah, Kate, Beth, and Christin. Thanks for not blocking my number after the twentieth time I texted, "hey, could you look at something for me?"

Thanks to my friend John, at whose home I happened to be staying when I first heard from Otto about publishing *Fake Money, Blue Smoke*. John helped me celebrate in style by helping me sneak into an abandoned James Bond movie set—which is how every book deal should be celebrated.

And finally, thanks to my utterly indefatigable agent Warren, who got this whole thing started. Not just this book, but my career. Thanks a million.